# HIS BELOVED

THE MATE SERIES

BOOK ONE

ANNA SANTOS

**Cover Design:** Moonchild Ljilja

**Editor:** May Freighter

**Proofreader:** Stacy Kennedy

*This is a work of fiction. Names, characters, places, brands, media, and incidents are either the product of the author's imagination or are used fictitiously. Any resemblance to similarly named places or to persons living or deceased is unintentional.*

ISBN: 1976025095

ISBN-13: 978-1976025099

# DEDICATION

*To my husband for taking care of me when I forgot to eat, drink, and sleep because I was too busy finishing writing or editing this story.*

*To my fans for all the support they gave me to finish and publish this book. Especially to Stacy, Jasmine, and Rae.*

# BOOK DESCRIPTION

**His Beloved—Book 1 of The Mate Series**

Absurdly rich and gorgeous Daniel Wolfe is used to get what he wants. And he wants Jade. The powerful vampire male picks her from the crowd of screaming females willing to do anything to please him. He's convinced that she's the One, His Beloved. But he wasn't prepared for a feisty girl who loathes vampires and doesn't want to be his for all Eternity.

Jade will sacrifice anything—even her freedom—to protect her orphaned little brother. But when she's forced to join a reality show that may keep her away from him, she has to survive hell and temptation to get the money she needs to pay for her brother's treatment.

In a world that reveres vampires and reality shows rule the entertainment channels, Jade needs to endure Daniel's seductive games for a week before she can be released from her contract and go back to take care of her brother.

However, not everything is what it seems and despite her secret past and her hate for vampires, Jade may be facing a worse danger than being bitten: falling in love.

*I am all in a sea of wonders.*

*I doubt; I fear; I think strange things which I dare not confess to my own soul.*

—BRAM STOKER, IN *DRACULA*

# CURRENTLY AVAILABLE

*His Beloved–Book 1*

**Coming Soon:**

*His Mate—Book 2*

Be notified!

For an updated list of books, and to have access to my upcoming releases, check my **website**:

http://www.annasantosauthor.com

**Or Facebook:**

https://www.facebook.com/AnnaSantosAuthor

You can also sign up for **my Newsletter** to get a notification the day a new book comes out and find more about my other books and giveaways.

# CHAPTER ONE: THE SELECTION

**THE LAST THING JADE** wanted to do was follow her best friend, Jenna, into that fancy nightclub. It was the type of place where people would do anything to get chosen by a vampire—even beg. Most of them either wanted to be turned or become a vampire's personal pet for a week. She sure didn't want to be one—a vampire, or a pet. Her favorite color was pink for God's sake! She also didn't like reality shows and thought *Who Wants to Be a Vampire?* was the most pathetic of them all.

"I can't believe I let you talk me into this," she complained, raising her voice so Jenna heard her against the loud boom of music and chatter.

"That's what friends are for," Jenna replied. "My purpose is to talk you into doing something you would never do."

Jade rolled her eyes, drinking her non-alcoholic beverage through a straw.

"Just relax! You are here to keep me company. Nothing bad will happen. These are friendly vampires."

"Right!" Jade rolled her eyes. "I can't believe there are so many people paying for this!"

"It's a really famous reality show. You have no idea how many people want to be a vampire."

"I have no idea why." Jade shrugged. "Vampires are dead, they can't come out into the sun, and they have to drink blood to continue living. They are evil creatures that think they're better than the rest of us. They use these girls and boys for sex and blood, only to discard them and choose someone new the next week."

Jenna kept smiling. Jade knew that this wasn't the first time her best friend had listened to that speech. Jenna was one of the few people who knew why Jade didn't like vampires.

Jade arched an eyebrow. "What else did I forget? Who in their right mind wants to be a vampire?"

Jenna puckered her lips. "Jade, a lot of people would disagree with you."

"Why? Because they are immortal? Maybe they can live for a long time, but they can be killed."

"Keep it down," Jenna mumbled as she looked around to see if anyone was eavesdropping. Leaning closer, she whispered in Jade's ear, "The last thing I want is for my best friend to be kicked out of the club for talking about killing vampires."

Jade lowered her voice. "In my opinion, having to drink blood is pretty much a deal-breaker. Besides, they don't actually choose anyone to spend their eternity with," she said while air-quoting 'eternity'. "How many humans have been turned or chosen to be their beloveds since the show began?"

Jenna shrugged. "I just want to meet Seth."

Jade kept rambling. "I just think it's scary how many humans treat them as if they are gods. It's like they're willing to be used just so they can appear on TV."

Jenna was going to say something, but she was interrupted when some girls started to scream louder than the music. She looked around frantically, with her hands against her chest.

"They have arrived," Jenna said, breathless.

"I'll be fine. Go look for the vampire of your dreams, even if I think you deserve a lot better than a bloodsucking, arrogant, rotting corpse."

Jenna giggled, putting her hand on Jade's shoulder. "I'll come find you in a bit. I just need to see Seth and the other vampires. Who knows, they might pick me!"

With a shrug, Jade scanned the club for a safe place to stay out of sight while Jenna went to flirt and try to find a sexy vampire willing to adopt her. She chose the darkest corner, away from the crowd of dancing bodies and humans desperate for attention. The creepiest of the supporters had a picture of one of the vampires—Seth—on their chest like some kind of treasure. Of course, he was gorgeous and famous. They would only pick the dazzling undead to be the main attraction in the show. There was no point in choosing ugly, old-looking vampires. It wouldn't sell and people wouldn't line up, desperate to be chosen.

The show had seven vampires, each one known for being a singer, an actor, or a famous socialite. Seth was the most famous of them all because he had once been the lead singer in some boy band. She couldn't recall the name of the band because it had been a while since he was famous for singing. Now he was well-known for doing low budget movies and for being a hot vamp. He was going by the name of 'Seth' for the last few decades, with his perfect curly hair and deep blue eyes.

Since Jade wasn't remotely interested in being turned or becoming a vampire's pet, she didn't need to worry about looking pretty when she got dressed to go to the club. She was content in her pink tank top and a blue pair of skinny jeans. Actually, the last thing she wanted was to catch the attention of one of those men. After the selection, she could go back home and resume her quiet existence.

All the screaming and colorful lights were giving her a headache. Meanwhile, Jenna was nowhere to be found. She was probably making out with one of those creepy, cold bloodsuckers. The thought made her cringe. The whole idea of exchanging saliva with a being that drank blood wasn't at all appealing.

Someone behind her cleared their throat. "Excuse me."

She jumped, startled, and held her hands to her chest while her heart raced and almost burst. She thought she was all alone and safe from danger. How could someone suddenly be present when there was a wall behind her?

"Could you move? You are in my way," the man said.

Jade turned around and saw an open door behind her and a man standing there.

She swore that the door wasn't there before. Her vision narrowed to the guy in front of her. Her face was just in front of his chest; it was a rather sculpted and interesting chest. He was wearing a black cotton sweater that molded his ripped torso perfectly. He had nice abs and smelled good. *Probably because of some ridiculously expensive men's cologne.*

"So," the guy sighed with impatience, "are you moving?"

Jade blushed. Finding her voice, she said,

"Sorry." Looking up, she lost her voice again when she saw his stern face. His heavenly, gorgeous, and breathtaking face. He had a stunning pair of piercing blue eyes. Then she noticed his shiny, raven hair was styled messily, which made him even sexier.

Her mouth went dry and her palms began to sweat as she stepped away to let him pass. He didn't even give her a second glance or thank her. Rude.

"Annoying human groupies," he growled. His teeth clenched as he moved forward, leaving a scent of woody, herbal, and fruity notes caressing the air she breathed.

Her fascination quickly dissipated. He was a vampire. There it was: the arrogance and the rudeness. He could be attractive, but he was an asshole. He was probably running late for his leggy, blonde nighttime snack. She fought the urge to throw up in her mouth.

Jade didn't have time for additional assumptions because a cute little teenage girl with golden locks exited from the same door in the wall. She was pretty, but her choice of clothing was really odd. She looked like a cartoon girl from Japanese manga, wearing a short all black Victorian-style baby doll dress with a magician's hat on her head and black lace gloves on her hands. With a sweet, happy smile on her face, she winked at Jade with a giggle.

In a swift movement, the door closed and all that was left was the wall. It was a secret passage of some sort.

Jade sighed deeply. She had no peace there; she

couldn't even be safe in some faraway place without a vampire showing up and creeping her out. She leaned back and took out her phone, distracting herself. Despite her efforts to keep a low profile, a few different guys tried to make conversation, asking her to dance or offering her drinks. She refused everyone. She was more interested in finding out when Jenna would show up so they could leave. Perusing the crowd, Jade searched for her best friend, but she knew that she needed to wait for the selection for Jenna to want to leave.

"Hi," said a vaguely familiar male voice.

"I'm not interested," she replied, loud enough for him to hear without taking her eyes from the game she was playing on her phone.

"I need you to move, so I can go inside," he said.

Jade lifted her eyes from the screen. It was the rude vampire. Again.

For a few seconds, she had a hard time taking her eyes away from his. She had seen him around, not very far from the place where he had crawled out. He had been talking with people in the VIP area, but he didn't seem to want to be there. It was something they had in common, at least, but it didn't make him any less of a jerk. The proof was in the way he was staring at her as if she were an inconvenience.

"I'm not even near the door," she muttered, looking sideways toward the couple obstructing his secret door.

Moving forward to reach the wall, he explained, "The panel to open the door is behind you."

Jade recoiled, panicking from the closeness.

"Personal space," she complained, trying to evade the touch of his arm. The last thing she wanted was to be touched by a bloodsucking monster.

Leaning closer, he whispered in her ear, "Why do you smell so good?"

His question sent unwelcome, frightened shivers down her spine. Listening to those words from a vampire wasn't on her bucket list. She could feel his presence, but she was sure that there was no panel behind her because she didn't hear the door opening.

"What's your name?" he asked, backing away.

"Again," she said, gaining the courage to face him. "I'm not interested. Now would you please step aside, so I can leave?"

He narrowed his eyes and clenched his teeth.

Jade gulped back her fear, unsure if he was going to do something rash. Vampires could be unpredictable, and she had just wounded his enormous ego. She was sure of it.

Seconds later, he touched his ear and gave her a sexy demonic smirk. "We'll talk later, Jade. Don't go too far."

The blood ran from her face at the sound of her name. He swiped his phone and the door opened. The people around them moved, so he could enter, and Jade ran to look for Jenna.

HALF AN HOUR LATER, she was still uncomfortable

with the thought of a vampire knowing her name—and worse—that he had possibly shown an interest in her. Meanwhile, Jenna was nowhere to be found, and the crowd of people inside the club was making Jade feel claustrophobic.

The loud squeal of a microphone shut everyone up for a moment. It was time for the show. Young women and men would be chosen and taken by their new vampire masters. The host, a vampire man, would go up to the stage area and read names aloud or point to people in the crowd. The hysterical chosen ones would jump and scream, thrilled about being a vampire snack and excited to have a chance to convince a vampire to turn them. Nothing new about that.

It was a clever idea. She had to give them credit—to the vampires, not the humans. They didn't need to hunt for food. Food walked straight through their front door and begged them to be eaten. They even profited from the cover charge people paid to get in and from the live broadcast show that ran every Sunday night. The reality show also earned a crazy amount of money from sponsorships, and it was apparently one of the most viewed programs in the world.

Jade always felt sick thinking about it. At least deaths by vampire attacks were diminishing and the vampire population was under control as it was rare for them to actually turn someone. They just used the show as bait to convince people to donate their bodies and blood willingly and with a smile on their lips—all for a vague promise of immortality.

As expected, after a lot of talking and drama with vampires saying goodbye to their older pets, the host began to pair the new girls and boys. He would call their names while the vampires were also on the stage, waiting. It was usually the same vampires every week and every week they left with someone new.

When the chosen girls were brought to the stage, they hugged each other like best friends and screamed and jumped like they had just won the Miss Universe title.

Jade decided the night had been a complete waste of her time. She had better things to do than to watch something she didn't even watch on TV. How did Jenna convince her to come here? Right, she had promised to take Stevie to school for a whole month. At least it was almost over, and she could finally go home.

"And now, the sponsor of this party will pick one of you to spend an entire week with him and maybe turn you into his beloved. You heard me right! His beloved! Our famous bachelor is looking for a companion for eternity! You can be the lucky one," the show host said happily, pointing a finger toward the crowd while the girls released shrieks of excitement.

*More propaganda and more empty promises with some new vampire to add to the team.* Jade stared at the stage, impatient, becoming deaf to the screams and shouts.

"Did you hear that?" Jenna mysteriously appeared next to Jade. She gripped Jade's arm tight and jumped in her tiny red dress. Her blonde hair bounced up and down along with her boobs.

Jenna was blonde and pretty. Maybe she would get picked and stop getting Jade into trouble and forcing her to attend parties like this one. But then,

Jade would miss her.

"We can still be picked!" Jenna said with enthusiasm.

Jade narrowed her eyes at her. "I'm not blonde, and I don't want to be picked. I'm here against my will."

"Oh, stop being such an old lady and have some fun!"

Jade was going to answer her, but something caught her attention from the corner of her eye. On the stage, a tall, black-haired vampire stepped forward and with his penetrating blue eyes stared coldly at the crowd. Jade's heart almost stopped in her chest when she recognized him. He was the one who had tried to flirt with her earlier. He also scared her senseless when he said her name. If he was the sponsor of the party that meant he owned the nightclub and was also the reason why he had a secret doorway in the wall.

Something inside her stomach clenched at the idea that he was going to be part of the freak show.

Jade didn't realize she had been staring with her eyes fixed on him until Jenna spoke in her ear. "He's hot, isn't he? This is so exciting!"

"I really want to go back home," she mumbled, noticing how his arrival was making everybody go quiet.

Meanwhile, on the stage, the vampire scanned the crowd once, twice. Many girls were holding their breath while Jade was trying to free her arm from Jenna's tight grip. Jenna was hurting her.

"This is stupid! I'm leaving," Jade muttered and pushed Jenna away.

She was about to exit when she heard a creepy and authoritative voice say, "You!"

The vampire had picked his new prey. She couldn't care less about who the poor bastard was. She just sighed, bit her nail, and stared at Jenna.

"Can we go now?"

Jenna had turned quiet and serious as if in shock. When Jade looked at the silent crowd, a bunch of eyes stared back at them. It wasn't just in her head. They were definitely staring at them.

"Me?" Jenna asked.

Jade was going to lose her best friend to a vampire! What horror would she experience in his company?

"No!" The vampire's answer sounded like thunder hitting the ground. "You," he said with a powerful roar that made Jenna stare at Jade.

Jade stared at the stage. Is he choosing me? No way. He had to be kidding. *Is this a sick joke?*

"Come again?" Jade asked, swallowing hard. The ground disappeared beneath her feet.

"And there you have it, folks. The girl has been chosen," the host said, sharing the good news with everyone else. The crowd cheered around them and the music started playing again. Jade stopped breathing for a moment and looked at the vampire, terrified.

"Go get her!" the vampire ordered. The camera spotlights followed the two big and muscular men in expensive, gray, Italian suits. They were probably his bodyguards.

"But I'm not even a cute blonde!" Jade cried, not

believing what was happening to her. She didn't have time to think about it because the two men held her by her arms and took her to their master.

## CHAPTER TWO: THE CONTRACT

**THERE WERE NO CAMERAS** or spotlights where Jade was taken. Jenna had followed behind the two brawny bodyguards. They only let Jade go when they put her in front of the vampire who had chosen her as if she were a pair of shoes rather than a living, breathing person.

Jade glared at him, and he stared back at her coldly.

He grabbed her face and studied her. "She will do."

"She will most definitely not do," Jade disagreed as she took his creepy, cold hand off her face and stepped back. "She is a person and she doesn't want anything to do with you." She crossed her arms, defying him with a fierce pair of hazelnut-colored eyes. "I'm not leaving with you!"

The vampire smirked at her. He wasn't intimidated. And why should he be? He could smash her into a wall with a flick of his wrist.

"You really need to learn how to deal with rejection," Jade said. "I'm not leaving here with you. You must be out of your mind."

The vampire narrowed his eyes, losing his smile. "Did you sign the papers when you came here today?"

Jade frowned. She stared at him blankly, trying to recall what he was talking about.

"Yes," she answered, pursing her lips. But did she read it? She remembered complaining about signing the suspicious piece of paper to get in, but Jenna had urged her to hurry. Without signing, she couldn't get in. Well, it seemed that not reading it had been a big mistake!

"Did you use a fake ID to get in?" the vampire asked again.

"No!" she shouted, outraged by his question.

"Then," he said, leaning his face over hers. His enticing scent hit her, and she swallowed. She had to admit it, he smelled good. Damn good, actually. He looked good, too. Very healthy for someone who was dead. Okay, fine. He was gorgeous, but his arrogance was exasperating. "You are mine for at least a week." He smirked as if he enjoyed rubbing it in her face.

She started to dislike his pretentious smirks very much.

"You humans should read contracts before signing them," he said.

Jade clenched her hands into fists and gritted her teeth. If she could kill with her eyes, he would've burst into flames. Just her damn luck to be chosen by an insufferable and conceited bloodsucker who thought he knew it all.

"Let's go. I have somewhere else to be and my time is short." He motioned for her to follow him like an obedient, little pet.

He moved forward with his small army of bodyguards behind him. Jade didn't move an inch.

The vampire stopped, noticing she wasn't following him. He looked sideways and breathed deeply as if he actually needed oxygen. He was probably losing his patience. She couldn't care less.

"Do I need to drag you?" he asked with a menacing tone.

"I want to read the contract," she said.

Jenna touched her arm, most likely afraid of what could happen. Everybody knew that defying a vampire was risky.

"You should just go. I can explain to your brother what happened and take care of him. It's just for a week anyhow," Jenna whispered in her ear.

"Not before I read the contract," Jade replied.

"You can read it in the limo," the vampire said, coming back to get her.

"Goodie, goodie!" a girl cheerfully squealed in excitement next to Jade, catching her attention because she didn't hear the stranger's arrival. "I'll have a new friend to play with."

Jade recognized her as the girl who dressed like an anime character. She still thought the girl was peculiar but nice. She seemed genuinely happy that she had a new toy, which was a little odd. Jade sucked in deep breaths to disperse her terror. She was already beginning to regret that fateful moment when she had agreed to go out with Jenna.

"You will like us. We are nice," the girl said with a smile.

Somehow, Jade seriously doubted that. She wanted to run away and get the hell out of this place.

"Complete name?" the vampire next to her asked. He was too damn close.

She didn't want to touch him, afraid of the coldness and paleness of his skin. Even if he smelled like vanilla with spices, it wouldn't be enough reason to be next to a vampire. She shivered from the closeness as she stepped away from him. He noticed, and his eyes became darker.

If she didn't know any better, Jade would think that he was offended.

"Name?" he barked.

"Are you going to pretend now that you don't know my name?" Jade narrowed her eyes. "You twisted and sick—"

Jenna covered Jade's mouth, so the rest of her insults were muffled.

"Her name is Jade Sullivan," Jenna said. "She didn't lie about it if that's what you're thinking."

The vampire looked at his men. "Go get a copy of the contract to show Miss Sullivan."

Jade glanced at Jenna and then at the serious vampire, feeling really scared for the first time. "I have a job to go to, bills to pay, and classes to attend. Pick someone else—one of those extra-large boob chicks with nothing better to do."

"Pick me instead," Jenna said. "It's my fault. She didn't even want to be here."

"I'm not into blondes," he said, and Jade rolled her eyes.

Is he teasing me or just being an idiot? Not that there was much difference.

"Well, I'm not into vampires," Jade sneered at him, folding her arms.

"You will be. Come. Now," he ordered, reaching to grab her arm.

She stepped back, alarmed. "Don't touch me!"

Jenna put herself between them. "Let me talk to her."

He eventually nodded.

Jenna turned around. "I'll try to fix this, but just go with him."

"But, Jenna..."

"There's no point in being stubborn. He won't choose anyone else." Frowning, Jenna glanced over her shoulder at the vampire. "Are you going to pick someone else?"

He answered with a round and certain 'no', and Jade gasped impatiently. She felt like growling and telling him to go to hell and rot there for all eternity.

Her best friend put her hands on her shoulders, calming her a little. "I'll call my parents and tell them what happened. They will take care of Stevie while you...are on a vacation. I'm sure nothing bad will happen."

"And my job?"

"I'll call your boss."

"I don't like him one bit," Jade muttered, glaring at the vampire.

"He clearly likes you," Jenna said, gripping Jade's shoulders harder. "Some girls would kill to be in your shoes, you know."

"Yeah? So where are they when I need them?"

Jenna snickered, amused by her sarcasm. "Come on, he looks harmless enough."

The vampire smiled as if to prove Jenna's point.

Jade rolled her eyes and shook her head, not believing for a second that he was cuddly and fun to be around. She knew better.

Suddenly, he turned around, touching his ear. "We will be leaving the nightclub soon, Jack. No, I don't want any cameras outside or inside the limos. Wait for me at the exit. I'm leaving with the girl… I couldn't care less about what you think."

"Here is the contract," a man announced, arriving next to them, breathless and waving a sheet.

"Good." The vampire stepped closer to Jade. "Say goodbye to your friend and happy reading," he urged, giving her the paper she desperately wanted to read. "Now," he added, gripping her arm and giving her the chills. Panic took over her stomach and her breathing grew erratic. "Come!"

As Jade followed him unwillingly, she felt as if everything in her perfect world was crumbling. Her future looked bleak. Who knew what scary and weird things he wanted to do to her?

JADE FROWNED AT HIM while she sat in the corner of the limo's back seat, uncomfortable in his presence. He had demanded that they be left alone. The rest of the weird entourage was following them in another car. For the time being, it was just her, the vampire, and the driver. But she was betting that the driver wouldn't do a thing if that sick being decided to pounce on her throat...or worse.

She loathed vampires. From experience, she knew that they were full of themselves and had no respect for life whatsoever. Being in a closed space with one made her anxious. She was trying to conceal her fear but was failing miserably since he kept staring at her as if she were a rare animal on display.

"So, have you read the contract?" he asked after making sure his clothes were not wrinkled and his hair was in place. He was cocky and knew he was hot, and she would be attracted to him if she were into that kind of guy.

She let him wait awhile for her response. "I did."

The vampire raised a brow; he didn't like the delay. The glint in his eyes proved he was daring her to be rude to him.

"Are you going to stay grumpy for the rest of the night?" he asked.

Jade avoided his piercing blue eyes. "It's nowhere written that I have to be nice to you."

He smirked as he whispered, "This is going to be fun."

Jade squinted at him. *What is that supposed to mean?* She wasn't sure if she wanted an answer, so she didn't ask. She simply muttered, "I don't have to pretend to like you, either."

"You will," he teased as he got closer, making her recoil in her seat. "Relax and look at me."

"What part of 'I'm not interested in you' didn't you understand?"

The vampire rested his arm along the back of the seat. "I'm intrigued. Do you just not like me or is it vampires in general?"

"Vampires in general, and now you."

He frowned as he studied her attentively. He scooted closer, and she felt his breath against her ear as his cologne hit her nostrils. Her vision blurred. He smelled amazing, and it was making her want to close her eyes and lean into him.

His voice came out husky and enthralling. "Can't you feel it, Jade?"

"What?" she mumbled. She was fighting the urge to bite her lower lip as she shivered. His voice was soft and sexy when he wasn't bossing her around.

"The pull," he whispered, caressing her skin with his warm breath. She gulped and her heart raced ahead. "It's insane how good you smell..."

Jade held her breath. She realized that he was sniffing her as if she was food. Blood ran cold in her veins. She tried to get away from him, but she was already on the edge of her seat.

His sultry words coaxed her ear. "Relax, I'm not going to bite you unless you ask me to. I have a strict diet, and I've already fed today."

"I don't give a damn about your diet and there is no way I would want you to bite me, you freak!" she snapped.

With a sly grin, he warned, "Careful, Jade, I might want to make you regret those words."

The hair on the back of her neck stood up. "Just get away from me." Jade turned her head to face him and her gaze plunged right inside his blue irises.

He grinned at her, which made him seem devilishly handsome. Okay, there was definitely something wrong with her. She shouldn't be falling for his looks!

"WHY ARE YOU AFRAID OF ME?" he asked, trying to understand the reason for her panic. Her pulse was racing, her heart was pounding fast, and she was scared, but she was still trying to look brave. "Tell me."

He played with a lock of her silky hair, noticing how soft and long it was. She had an adorable mouth and a perky nose. She was extremely appealing to the eye and had an attitude—something he always found alluring in a woman.

Grinning to clear the air, he asked, "Did some big and mean vampire do something bad to you or your family?"

Her watering eyes and sad face caught him off-guard. He had struck a nerve, and it angered him. Not at her, but that someone could have hurt her.

Listening to the sudden throbbing of her heart warned him that the darkness had spread to his eyes. He was using his supernatural sight to look for any sign of puncture marks or other lesions left behind. The fact that she didn't look like someone who had been hurt by a vampire before, or bitten for that matter, soothed his nerves. Even if that made him less tense, it didn't reassure him. She might have been attacked when she was younger. It could have been a terrifying experience. The desire to protect her grew stronger. He wanted to hold and comfort her.

"Stop staring at me," she demanded.

He leaned back in his seat, taking control of his feral senses and arguing with his heart for being so impetuous around her. Eluding Jade's eyes, he pinched the bridge of his nose and closed his eyes with a sigh.

It was going to be a long ride home.

# CHAPTER THREE: I DON'T FIND YOU SEXY AT ALL

**BOTHERED BY THE SILENCE**, Jade asked, "Aren't you going to ask me what happened?"

His reactions intrigued her, so she dared to look at him more attentively, noticing his pale, flawless skin. Despite his light complexion, he didn't look or smell like a corpse. He appeared to be about mid-twenties, but it didn't mean he was that young.

"Do you assume that all vampires are bad?" he asked.

His question brought her back to reality. "I think all vampires are arrogant and self-absorbed. You all think you can have whatever and whomever you want. Clearly, you aren't an exception."

Mr. Undead smirked as if she had said something amusing. She was sure she hadn't. "I've been having a terrible month. And I thought I would have another terrible night before I found you, but you aren't making things easier," he said.

"I don't understand."

"The irony is that you hate my guts for something that someone else did to you."

Jade moved uncomfortably in her seat. "Actually, I hate your guts because I didn't want to come with you in the first place. You just needed to choose someone else—one of those annoying groupies."

"And clearly you are one," he said with a smug

grin.

She shook her head.

Frowning, he asked, “You don’t even know who I am, do you?”

“Why, should I?” His furrowed eyebrows and pursed lips indicated that he doubted Jade’s words. “I have better things to do than watching a vampire channel or read gossip magazines.”

He laid his arm across the back of the seat. “I’ve always enjoyed challenges.”

“I’m not a challenge. I’m a person, jerk!”

The vampire eased his body against the seat and crossed his legs. “You really need to stop with the hostility. I’m not going to hurt you, and I’m perfectly aware that you are a person. The challenge is for you to also see that.”

Jade examined him, unsure of how to react to his words. She looked out the window. They were driving fast. “Where are we going?”

“To my house,” he replied.

She blinked several times. “Not to the reality show’s mansion?”

“No, we aren’t going to join the others. I have no intention of leaving the comfort of my home.”

“I don’t really want to be here,” she whispered. “My brother needs me and...”

“Save it, Jade. I’m not going to be moved by your sappy story. We all have our sad stories. I’m not going to tell you mine, so I don’t need to know yours.”

His words came out cold, and Jade lost all the empathy that she could have developed for him. He was a jerk. There was no doubt about it. He was heartless and an idiot. The little display of humanity he had performed before had her fooled for a moment, but that moment was gone.

"Oh, don't look so mad," he whispered, drawing a smile on his face and making Jade narrow her eyes at him. "If you wish, you can tell me all about your past in front of the cameras. There aren't any cameras here right now, so you don't need to appeal to the rest of the nation's heartstrings. All you need to do is act nice and adorable until the end of the week, and you will be home in no time."

"I would rather go home right now. I have no urge to share my story with the world," Jade declared, crossing her arms over her chest.

The vampire stared at her cleavage.

"Hey, freak, stop staring at my breasts!"

"Don't flatter yourself. I've seen better. I was thinking that we'll need to get you a new wardrobe since you don't seem to have anything good enough."

His arrogance hit a nerve, and she snapped, "I wasn't planning on being kidnapped by a vampire!"

He didn't flinch at her accusation. "Not kidnapped, chosen."

"It looks like kidnapping to me! I didn't want to come, and you forced me."

"The contract you signed forced you."

"Tomato, *tomahto*!"

The vampire let out a sizzling laughter that Jade found puzzling. When he stopped, he leaned closer to her face. “You look hot when you stare at me like that.”

“Like what?”

“Flustered.”

“Jerk!”

He edged closer with an amused expression. “Would it all be better if I kissed you?”

“Of course not!”

“Are you sure? You look like you are in need of a kiss, maybe more than one. What do you say? Let’s just get this sexual tension between us over with and get along.”

“If you even try, I’ll smack you.”

He smirked again; his eyes flickered with darkness. Jade gulped and moved back in an attempt to escape his unsettling gaze. “You are really fun to tease, Jade.”

“I’m not finding this situation funny. I want to go home. I have someone who needs me to be there.”

His expression suddenly became annoyed. “You said you were single in your contract application.”

“You didn’t even look at it,” she muttered.

“Maybe I did, even before picking you.”

Jade tensed. “What are you saying?”

“Maybe I wanted to pick you all along.”

“Maybe you’re mad.”

"I could be, but now you have to spend an entire week with me in my house, and you will eventually like me—possibly even more than like me."

"You aren't just mad, you're deranged!"

The vampire drew back and fixed his hair. Then, with a cocky grin, he said, "You liked me when you first saw me."

"What?"

"I could see it in your eyes."

"You were a total jerk!"

With a shrug, he said, "Yes, well, normally I am."

Jade stared deep into his eyes, confused by his words. Okay, that was odd. *Is he admitting to being a jerk?*

"Has the cat got your tongue?" After a moment, he added, "Do you like what you see?"

Jade sighed and rolled her eyes. "Are you always this annoying?"

He shrugged after a pondering moment. "Well, yes, I guess. I don't really think that I need to please people. A bit like yourself."

"What do you mean by that?"

"You are not nice."

"I'm extremely nice!" She was offended by his statement. "You know nothing about me."

"Well, you know nothing about me either, and you're assuming that I'm evil and arrogant. Besides, you aren't being nice to me." Jade growled, but he continued, "You should be nicer to me. After all, I'm a vampire, you are just a human and…you're going to be spending a lot of time alone with me."

"Is that a threat?"

"No, of course not. I don't hurt women or humans in general."

Jade arched an eyebrow. "Why should I believe you? You just said that… Never mind. I don't have to talk to you either."

"Why don't you like me?"

She shifted uncomfortably on the seat. Jade didn't expect his question. She sighed. "You are a vampire. I don't like vampires."

"You don't need to like vampires. You just need to like me," he whispered, scooping her face between his hands. He made her look into his eyes as his breath caressed her skin. "Because you see, Jade, you are mine now and there is no way to escape me for the next week."

She drew back in panic, afraid of his words.

His voice came out husky, contradicting what Jade assumed to be a threat. "We are just skipping some steps, love. And, in my defense, I've tried to talk to you in the nightclub."

Jade felt flustered once again because he was too close to her. "I wasn't there to…"

"To what? Mingle with vampires?" He dared to finish her sentence.

"To mingle with people in general," she corrected him.

He arched a brow. "Why not?"

Jade folded her arms and bit her lower lip with no intention of sharing her inner thoughts or secrets with him. It was a rather personal answer to that question. “It’s complicated.”

“You’re too young to see life as complicated,” he said.

She gazed at him, understanding that his words meant that he was a lot older than he appeared to be. “Not everybody lives an easy life.”

The vampire sneered. “Do you think my life is easy? You have no idea, sweetheart.”

He reclined in his seat.

“I’m not your sweetheart,” Jade mumbled as the vampire began to close his eyes.

His eyes flung wide open at her comment and his lips twisted into a curl.

“You can keep the pet names for someone who gives a damn,” she added.

“Then what should I call you?” he asked.

“I have a name. Why not use it?”

“Yes, you have a name. It’s a beautiful one, too. It suits you perfectly. A beautiful name for a gorgeous girl.”

Despite the corny pickup line, Jade felt her cheeks burning.

Clearing his throat, the vampire changed the subject. “What happened to your parents? Why do you need to look after your brother?”

“They died some time ago in a car accident,” she said, giving the standard and harmless explanation without going into details.

“Were they nice?”

Jade frowned at his words before answering with a shaky voice. “They were the best parents.”

After an awkward moment of silence, the vampire said, “It will be okay, Jade. I’ve found you. Nothing will ever hurt you again.”

Her eyes lingered on his. “You are seriously mistaken about me if you think that your money can change my mind about you.”

He moved swiftly to her side, hovering above her face. His voice came out sexy, weakening her defenses. “Not money, Jade. Love.” He claimed her lips with his.

# CHAPTER FOUR: WELCOME TO YOUR NEW LIFE

**AT FIRST, SHE WASN'T SURE** if his lips were really on hers or not. Then, when he pressed harder, she tried to deflect him. It was pointless. He gripped her waist, pulling her closer and leaning forward to chase down her mouth. Their lips touched again as his hand propped up her head and caressed her hair. She panicked for a while, thinking he was going to force his tongue inside her mouth, but he just waited for her to move her lips against his.

The vampire opened his eyes, and she closed hers, surrendering. She felt his smile against her lips. Her body turned boneless when he pressed harder. She relaxed into his embrace and the gentleness of his kiss as her lips replied to his.

Moments later, Jade moaned against his mouth. Heat spread down her body and attraction broke down her last defenses. His mouth was soft like that of any human. She was pressed against his ripped chest, and she perceived warmth coming from him. *Vampires are supposed to be cold, aren't they?*

His kisses kept sending shivers down her spine, numbing her limbs and causing her heart to race inside her ribcage. She could barely hear herself think while her heartbeat pounded in her head. It had been years since she was kissed by a man. She had forgotten how good it was. But his kisses were more than good; they were addictive and overwhelming.

The vampire continued to move his mouth against hers. He softly nibbled and sucked on her lower lip until his tongue caressed her lips. Trailing kisses down her face, he prolonged his touch, pressing his lower lip against hers and nudging it downward. His tongue entered her mouth when she finally gave him permission to explore.

Their tongues touched and played. Her hands pulled him closer as she kneeled, so she could take control of their kiss. It was confusing how amazing he tasted and how good he felt against her body. It was insane what was going on, but she couldn't stop kissing him. Her whole body craved his touch. Her hands tugged on his soft hair and their mouths together felt perfect. She was losing herself in his arms and didn't give a damn about that. Feeling lost never felt so good!

They clung to each other as if their lives depended on it. Jade's legs were wrapped around his waist. Her fingers were buried in his hair, forcing his mouth against hers. He had his hands on her back, pressing her against his chest. Neither realized that the limo had stopped.

The driver lowered the privacy screen and cleared his throat to make it known they had arrived.

It was the vampire who first evaded her mouth and tried to control her movements.

"We've arrived, honey," he whispered, opening his eyes to meet hers.

Gasping and with her cheeks burning, she cleared her throat. "Where?"

"Home."

Jade adjusted her eyes to the light, understanding that she was all over him. She blushed harder when she realized that she had lost her mind and had let him kiss her.

"Look at me." He imprisoned her face between his fingers. "There will be cameras outside. Fix your hair and clean up your lipstick," he said softly.

She nodded. His arms released her, and she moved back into her seat as her body complained about the lack of contact.

"Did you drug me or something?" she asked, feeling out of place. Feeling tired and dizzy, she realized her hair was a mess and the vampire's lips were smeared with her lipstick. She had responded to his kiss. Not only that, she had almost ripped off his clothes. It was insane!

He smirked at her words. Then, he cleaned his lips with a white handkerchief and helped her remove the smeared lipstick off her face.

"No, I don't need to drug you for you to kiss me like that. Now fix your hair. There are a lot of leeches with their cameras outside, and I don't want them to photograph you like this."

The vampire got out, leaving Jade to stare blankly at his back with wide eyes. Flashes from cameras hit him, and he just smiled as if he was born to be under their lenses and adored like a god.

Inside the limo, Jade combed her hair with her fingers and listened to him replying to their questions about her. He was being charming, but the photographers seemed eager to photograph her.

The reporters were curious as to why she was taking so long.

"Come now. I won't let them touch you," he whispered, turning to Jade and offering his hand. "Just try to smile a bit to erase that conflicted look on your face and all will be well."

Jade obeyed, offering him her hand and stepping out of the limo, only to be hit by the bright lights and the constant flood of questions. It was terrifying. The only thing that was making her feel safe was the vampire's arm around her waist and his other hand gripping hers.

JADE HAD NEVER BEEN in a home like the one the vampire owned. It was gigantic and absurdly beautiful. The floors were made of white and black marble, and the walls were stark white and lavishly beautifully decorated with fancy paintings and golden columns. She took a deep breath when the photographers and cameras were left outside. Then, with mouth agape, she stared at the decor of the mansion.

The entrance had a circular foyer with a view of an upper landing and arched stairs descending into the center of the foyer. The foyer wall was white marble with a dark tiled floor. There was a crystal chandelier hanging down from the arched ceiling over the hallway, which led up to a landing overlooking the kitchen. There were other rooms downstairs, but she didn't have time to see them since he led her upstairs, turned left, and went down a corridor without ever removing his arm from around her waist. He didn't rush, though. He let her stare at everything, probably hoping to impress her with his money.

He pressed her closer to his side and spoke into her ear. "Do you like your new place?"

Sucking in a breath, she spared him a look. "This is not my new place. It's yours."

"If you are going to be mine, then this is going to be yours."

"I think you have mistaken me for someone who gives a damn about the money you've got," Jade stated with a serious face that she hoped would contradict the previous fire that had consumed her.

"Good. I don't want someone who cares about my money."

Jade squinted, not enticed by his words. He spun her around, and she found herself pinned to the wall next to a door. She gulped when she noticed his black eyes.

"I don't want you being so close to me." She tried to push him back with her hands but was incapable of moving him an inch. Vampires were strong and evil. Jade was once again faced with the proof of that. "You can't do this to me. Humans are not to be harmed or abused. The contract is clear about that."

"It's not my intention to hurt you. Calm down and trust me," he assured, entwining his fingers with hers. He was motionless, almost frozen with a blank face and captivating blue eyes. His eyes were back to normal and that reassured her. He was also softly pressing his fingers against hers. "See, I'm not harming you."

"No, but you are creepily close," she complained, feeling helpless for the first time in a while.

"No crying, Jade," he hushed, pulling her against his body and using his hands to lift her hands up to his neck.

Subconsciously, she wound her arms around his neck and lost her breath with the intimacy of their contact.

"Honey, you should have understood by now that you belong to me. But since you are so unwilling to accept me, I have to do this a bit differently. I don't want us to fight, and I don't want you to be afraid of me. So, I'm not going to beat around the bush. I'm going to tell you the truth."

"What truth?"

"That you are mine, Jade. I knew it the moment I laid my eyes on you. You are mine."

"Are you crazy?" she asked, trying to keep her body from trembling. He couldn't be serious. His words were making him sound like a complete psycho.

"No." He smiled, brushing the hair away from her eyes and caressing it gently.

Jade was reluctant in letting her body relax against his. She mistrusted the creature, but she couldn't help feeling good inside his hug. It didn't help that he was so damn good-looking.

"Kiss me again and you'll see," he said.

"I won't."

"And if I kiss you?"

"I—just let me go!"

"One week, Jade. Give me one week to make you fall in love. If, by then, you won't change your mind about me, I'll let you go."

"This is ridiculous! I want to go home," she said, sobbing. *What kind of a twisted game is he playing?* He sounded deranged. She wanted him to stop touching her. Why couldn't she just go home and forget all about tonight? "My brother needs me..."

"I need you more than him."

"He is sick!"

"I know all about that," he whispered and kissed her on the forehead.

She closed her eyes without thinking. Her legs turned to jelly as a shiver ran through her body. "How can you possibly know?"

"I know a lot of other things, too."

"Then you know that I need to get back to my brother."

"I swear," he mumbled, drawing her attention to him as his soft voice caressed her face, "he will be taken care of. So, just relax and trust me."

"Why should I trust you?"

"Because I told you, Jade, you are mine, and I won't let anything or anyone ever harm you again."

"You are—" She sighed and looked away. Calling him crazy wouldn't help.

"Trust me."

"You're freaking me out."

He turned her face toward him. His eyes were shining, and she couldn't help but feel completely enthralled. He looked nice, he smelled nice, and she knew he tasted nice, too. She wanted to slap herself for even thinking about kissing that being a second time. It was bad enough that she was letting him hug her. She needed to push him back.

"What are you thinking?" he asked.

"That you aren't making any sense."

"Do you have any idea how long I've been waiting to meet you?"

"You say the strangest things."

"You need to understand this."

Jade's voice trembled. "You are scaring me."

"Maybe, but you need to understand that I didn't choose you randomly."

Sighing deeply, she said, "You chose me because you probably thought it would be funny to tease and annoy me. Now you think I'm some kind of challenge and you feel the urge to prove to yourself that you are able to seduce me like all of the other stupid girls you date."

"Interesting," he said with a lopsided grin. Shaking his head, he clarified, "But no, I chose you because we are meant to be together."

"I don't believe in that bullshit of love at first sight," she grumbled.

"You're such a bad liar." He sneered at her words, and she scowled. "Now, stop fighting and admit it. You feel the attraction, too."

A frown formed on her brow. "Why would I say that? Why would I be attracted to you?"

"I've already told you why. You are mine."

"People aren't a property to be owned. Only an egocentric maniac wouldn't think that."

"Well, maybe they aren't, but some are born to complete others, and you were born to be mine...as I was born to be yours."

Jade tilted her head, unsure if she was hearing him properly. He couldn't possibly be saying what she thought he was saying. "No," she mumbled, "you are mistaken."

The vampire shook his head, attentive to her reactions.

She blinked fast several times, swallowed, and breathed in until her lungs were ready to burst. Her panic began to surface, lacing her words. "How can you tell?"

"It's hard to explain."

"Nah, you're just crazy."

"You've already said that. You need to broaden your range of insults."

"And you need to let me go."

"Only after you kiss me," he bargained.

She lost her calm. "Are you seriously expecting me to kiss you when we've just met and you are practically forcing me into it again?"

"Pretty much, yes." He finished his sentence

with a mischievous grin.

"You're sick!" she complained, not finding it funny. She didn't understand how he could smirk and be sarcastic like that. *The jerk!*

"I thought you liked straightforward guys," he teased.

Jade's eyes opened wide.

"You have a profile online," he began. "I've done my homework on you."

"Oh! Now you're a stalker, too!"

"No, honey. I'm your future husband." Before she could say anything, leaning close to her ear, he whispered, "You can't deny the attraction between us. You are not indifferent to me. You can feel the pull, can't you?"

"Whatever happened back there, it was a mistake." Jade noticed how he lost his smile and removed his hand from her waist. She went cold without his touch.

He drew away. "You'll learn to like it here and you'll like me."

"Do you understand how deranged you sound?"

"You weren't complaining when you were kissing me."

Fisting her hands in protest, she said, "You kissed me against my will!"

His eyes turned black as he clenched his jaw.

She felt her cheeks burn because she knew it wasn't entirely the truth. She wanted to reduce the tension—and quickly. "I want to call Jenna, so I can check on my brother."

"You'll do that tomorrow. Now, you will go to your bedroom and be a good girl."

"What the hell is that supposed to mean?"

"I have some things that I have to take care of, so you'll have to be alone for a moment," he explained, opening a door to his left. He showed her a bedroom with gray painted walls and golden ancient-looking furniture with a rose leather headboard bed.

The bedroom was fascinating and it was suited for a princess. The décor was delicate and enticing with numerous pillows and rose-shaped white cushions. The highly ornamented golden furniture was like a piece of art. She had never seen a bedroom so captivating. It was romantic—a room she had dreamed of when she was a little girl.

She didn't have much time to drool over the bedroom because he turned her on her heels, bringing them face-to-face.

"Get some rest," he whispered, caressing her hair and hugging her by the waist. "We'll talk later."

"Are you going to leave me here alone?"

"I need to. Plus, I thought you didn't like me being around."

"You can't just leave me here. I need to eat and drink."

"I know. My people will take care of you. Now, kiss me."

"I don't want to kiss you," she said, leaning back to evade him in case he attempted something. She continued, “I thought we were over that already.”

“Fine. Then let me kiss you.”

“What’s the difference?” she asked, rolling her eyes.

He teased her with a sly and devilish smirk.

THERE WAS AN IRRITATING voice in Daniel’s ear, urging him to leave the girl, so they could talk. Jack, the director, wasn’t happy with him because he didn’t want cameras inside the limousine to film them at that moment. He couldn’t care less. He needed privacy so that the girl would trust him.

Suddenly, he wished that he lived farther away from the nightclub, so they could have more time to be together. He nibbled on his lip, remembering how she tasted. Her mouth was the softest and most desirable thing. He needed another taste before leaving, but she was still confused about their attraction. He was also stunned by how much he craved her. The blood lust was real—incapacitating. He had to endure and fight against it, so he wouldn’t lose control.

“Let me kiss you before I go, honey.” He understood that it was more of a plea than a request, and it made him realize that it was something he wasn’t used to doing.

“No,” she said, pushing him away and crossing her arms. “Stop!”

He pursed his lips and stepped back as he

rubbed the back of his neck. She was stubborn. He was, too.

“Don’t be afraid,” he urged after a moment, offering her his hands.

Jade shook her head.

“Come on, I’m not going to hurt you.”

“I’m sure that you’re used to having what you want, but you need to understand that I have no wish to be with you.”

He sighed before tilting his head to watch her. “Are you sure about that?”

She arched an eyebrow, and he fought the urge to grin at her again. Her presence sent flames surging through his body. Controlling the bloodlust was going to be a challenge as long as he was around her. Her constant denial to surrender to their attraction crushed his soul.

“And if I kiss you and let you continue to pretend that you don’t like me—” he wondered aloud, “—would it make you feel better?”

Jade rolled her eyes. “But I really don’t like you!”

“You’ll change your mind,” he replied, lowering his lips to hers.

He noticed that her eyes grew wider, but she didn’t try to dodge him when their lips locked. Kissing her softly, he played with her lips, waiting for her to pull back and tell him something hurtful.

She didn’t.

Instead, she shivered in his arms, mumbling something he didn’t understand. One thing was for sure, she wasn't rejecting his kiss, and so he deepened it. It was his time to moan when her hands massaged the back of his head and her tongue rubbed against his with the sweet sound of her surrender.

HIS FORCEFULNESS CAUSED her to step back toward the bedroom. She was unsure of what their kiss was going to lead to. He said that he needed to go, and she was mentally scolding herself for wanting him to stay tethered to her mouth. She wasn't ready for anything else to happen between them. But, by the way, her body was reacting to him, she wasn't sure if she might have been experiencing some sort of mind control—the kind that only vampires could use.

One thing was clear. He tasted and felt like a human. His skin was smooth and he smelled fresh. Putting her hand over his chest, she could feel his heartbeat. It might not be as strong as a human's, but it was there—a pulse under his skin. He was warm.

Her legs went weak from the sensation of his lips against hers. Heat spread down her body, impeding her will to push him back. She loathed his kind, so where did this attraction come from?

"Okay, honey, that's enough. I need to go. We'll see each other tomorrow night," he said between kisses. "I have something important to take care tonight, but I promise you that the rest of my nights will be yours." He removed her arms from around his neck and held her wrists, staring at her hazel eyes.

Jade blinked, her vision still blurred. “What do you mean, tomorrow night?”

“I’m a vampire. I’m asleep during the day,” he explained.

“And what am I supposed to do until then?”

“Sleep and wait.”

“You must be joking!”

“I wish I was,” he declared, kissing her again and nibbling on her lower lip before separating with a grimace. “Don’t be mad. You are safe here, and we’ll talk more tomorrow.”

“Safe from what?”

“The cameras, the nosy reporters, and whatever else that frightens you.”

“But will I be safe from you?”

“You are my beloved. There’s no need to be afraid.”

His eyes revealed his vulnerability. The tone of his voice was soft and sweet. Jade wanted to believe him, but her rationality was warning her about the insanity of everything that was happening. He was a vampire. They couldn’t be trusted. Maybe she could manipulate him, though.

“Give me my phone back. Your bodyguards took it from me when they dragged me to you.”

“I can’t. It’s in the contract that you can’t have contact with the outside world. Not having a device helps with that. I can’t let you—” Jade tried to interrupt him, but he hushed her. “Let me finish, Jade. You can’t contact them, but I’ll contact Jenna for you. I promise.”

She felt vulnerable when she asked, “Do you promise?”

“I do. Now get some rest. Tomorrow, we’ll have a busy night,” he said, caressing her hair and kissing her lips. He spoke into her ear. “I’m pretty sure that you hate kissing me as much as I hate kissing you.”

Jade was lightheaded and her body was immobile, resting against the wall. She didn’t know how to stop her body from trembling and her mouth from tingling. She wanted more of him. His sarcasm wasn’t making her feel better about her weakness, though. Kicking him wouldn’t help her case, and she didn’t want to hurt him. Even if he was an insufferable jerk.

“You don’t need to say anything, Jade,” he said, trailing soft kisses on her face. “I’m also confused about the deadly attraction between us.”

“I’m not attracted to you. You are a bloodsucking jerk,” she muttered, pushing him back and looking at her fancy holding cell. Tears stung her eyes. “If anything happens to my brother while I’m here, I’ll hate you for all eternity.”

“Duly noted,” he declared. “Goodnight.” He kissed her on the cheek and left.

After the door closed, she heard a key being slotted into the lock, and she ran toward it. She tried to open it, but the damn thing wouldn’t budge. Not giving up, she knocked and begged for him to open it. But there was no reply. Falling to the ground, she faced her room. It was big enough, sure, but it still made her a little claustrophobic. After all, she was trapped for God-knows-how-long in a vampire's house.

Tears tingled her eyes, and she let them fall. She should have stayed at home.

# CHAPTER FIVE: THE TERMS OF THE DEAL

**SOMETIME AFTER THE AUTOMATIC** blinds opened to reveal that it was getting dark outside, three women rushed inside Jade's bedroom. They grabbed her and dressed her in a silky, red mermaid dress. They also gave her an elegant hairstyle and makeup to complement her ensemble. She was looking rather sophisticated—or so she thought while staring at herself in the mirror.

Jade would never have been able to buy such an elegant gown with her waitress salary. But the dress wasn't the only thing she received as a gift. Other maids had filled the closet of the bedroom with plenty of new clothes for her to wear while the hairdressers were styling her hair.

She didn't have time to browse the new clothes. The maids left once she was dressed, and a man in a well-tailored gray suit entered the bedroom with a digital reader in his hand and a pair of hovering cameras following close behind him. Two other women entered, carrying production equipment.

Jade opened her eyes wide, and she felt herself recoiling. Her fear was from the cameras and all the unwanted attention of the viewers.

*Where in the hell is the vampire? And why is that man in my bedroom with cameras pointed at my face?*

The man asked her in a high-pitched voice, "How do you feel to be chosen to compete for the heart of the number one bachelor vampire in the United States?"

"Hum, I don't know."

"Did you ever think in your whole life that you would be chosen by a vampire to possibly be his beloved?" he asked, overly excited.

"No." She fought the wish to roll her eyes.

"What are you going to do tonight to try to win his heart and make him choose you to have a date tomorrow night?"

"What?" Confusion spread over her face. She squinted and clenched her teeth.

"What will set you apart from the other contestants?" he rephrased the question.

"Out!"

The order was clear and simple and made everybody tremble and stare at the door.

Despite the command in his voice when the vampire's gaze met Jade's, she felt her insides melting and her heartbeat increasing. He was so damn captivating that it was difficult to stare at anything else but him. He wore a black suit with a light blue tie that matched his stunning eyes. It made him look dashing, almost ethereal because of his light skin complexion.

A sense of security and warmth washed over her. She blinked, and he appeared in front of her face in a split second. Then, he grabbed her hand and brought it to his lips. His kiss sent thousands of shivers down her spine and made her lips curve into a half-smile.

“Do I have to ask again?” He looked back, clearly upset with the entourage inside the bedroom. One glare of those eyes and everybody got out, almost falling over one another.

If she weren’t so enthralled, she would be fighting an urge to giggle. But, she continued staring at him and feeling too flustered to care about the buzzing sound of the cameras leaving and the door closing.

Once she realized they were alone, the delightful warmth from seeing him was replaced with anger. After all, he did leave her locked up in that bedroom.

“What the hell were you thinking when you trapped me in this bedroom until now? Do you want me to die of boredom?” Her anger shook her voice as she evaded his touch and took back her hand from his.

“It was the best way to keep you safe and to prevent you from running away,” he answered with a lopsided grin that made him look like a mischievous, sexy demon. “Besides, my staff fed you, and you had the TV to keep you company.”

She had to breathe deep and stare at the floor to be able to reply to him with calmness. “We have a contract. I wouldn’t run away. I can’t afford the compensation you’re asking for if I break the deal.”

“About that, let’s talk about the terms of this deal.”

“Yes, let's!”

“Hold the sarcasm, darling,” he demanded, taking her to the bed and seating her next to him.

"You were worried about your job and your family. So, you need to know that for every day—no, night—you spend here with me, ten thousand dollars will be deposited into your bank account."

"What?" She stared at him in disbelief.

He frowned before he asked, "Do you think you should be paid more for your time?"

Jade kept her mouth shut. She didn't know how to answer him without feeling the urge to rip his head off. Was he treating her like a call girl or was that the standard fee they paid the girls who participated in the show? She was unsure.

"What are you thinking?" His eyes seemed to be evaluating her every action. "Jade," he whispered alluringly.

She shivered because of the softness of his breath stroking her face.

"You need to understand that I want you here with me. If you decide that we're meant to be, then you will never need to worry about money or anything else for that matter."

"You can keep your money and just let me go home, then," she blurted out.

He pursed his lips. "Stop being stubborn!"

Jade clenched her jaw at his scolding.

Sighing and curving his lips into that devilish smile that made her tummy flip, he added in a softer voice, "I've brought someone that I know you are dying to see, and you have another surprise waiting for you downstairs. You just need to relax and stop trying to find reasons to run away from me—from what we can have."

"I have no intentions of becoming a vampire," she declared with a serious face.

"And I have no intentions of letting you run away from me," he asserted, catching her chin when she stared at him full of sorrow. "I always get what I want, and I want you."

Before she could protest, he pressed his lips against hers. However, she pushed him back before it was too late for her to fight the attraction.

"Stop forcing yourself on me," she complained, annoyed by his unwillingness to listen to her. "You might think that I'll obey you if you kiss me, but I won't. I'm not a mindless girl with overactive hormones."

"Jade," he mumbled in a voice weighted with pain while holding on to her hands.

She dodged him so he wouldn't trap her inside his arms. "You can't make me kiss you back if I don't want to. You can't keep me in this room, either. And you can't force me to stay with you after the week is over. So, stop playing these mind games and tell me what the hell is going on outside? What were all those questions for? And what did he mean about the competition?"

The vampire contemplated his response and sighed. "You aren't going to like what I'm going to tell you."

"What else is new?"

It was a cold statement that made his eyes flutter with what seemed to be hurt. Jade tried to ignore it. She wasn't going to feel empathy for a vampire who was keeping her there against her will. They were attracted to each other, and she could give up and let go in his arms, but that was it. No empathy, no compassion, and no love. Especially no love. It would be so wrong to love a thing like him! She doubted that they could feel anything. *Could they?* Besides lust and hunger for blood, that is.

"Why do you hurt me on purpose?" he demanded, studying her.

"Why would my questions hurt you?"

"It's not the questions. It's the way you talk to me and the way you look at me as if I'm a monster of some sort."

"Aren't you?"

DANIEL TILTED HIS HEAD and narrowed his eyes. She was defying and judging him by what others may have done to her or her family. Or maybe she was biased because of what others thought about his race. He didn't know, but he had to change her mind about him. The fact that they were going to be surrounded by cameras during the week wouldn't help.

"Are you going to tell me that you've never sucked someone's blood and killed them in the process?"

"No, I'm not going to lie. However, things have changed. We don't need to kill people for blood. And even if I'm a vampire, that doesn't automatically make me a monster."

"Just an arrogant jerk who won't take no for an answer and keeps me here against my will."

He gave her a lopsided grin and touched her face with the tips of his fingers. She looked gorgeous. Too bad she seemed more upset than the night before.

His beloved pushed his hand away, denying the physical contact between them.

"Let's cut to the chase. Why am I dressed up and why all the cameras?"

"Jade...you have issues."

"I have issues?" Her high-pitched voice couldn't conceal her outrage. "I'm a person, and you aren't treating me as one. You keep saying that I'm your beloved, but you locked me in this bedroom and sent your servants with gifts without even showing your face to answer my question from last night."

"I was busy trying to make you happy."

Jade crossed her arms as her cheeks flushed with anger. "I'm not happy. Do you see me smiling? How can I be happy if you think that money and new clothes can fix my problems?"

"I'm sorry," he whispered, rubbing the back of his neck and looking at the bed. "I came to check on you in the afternoon. You were sleeping."

"The blinds were shut and there are no clocks in here. I have no idea when I fell asleep."

"The meeting with the director took longer than I thought. I spent the rest of the day trying to make your stay here a lot more pleasurable."

Jade frowned. "What did you do?"

He smiled. "I think I might deserve a kiss when I show you."

"I think you should just tell me what's going on and what's with the noise downstairs and all the cameras." Her face was showing that she wasn't sharing his happiness.

"The cameras will sometimes follow us. It's a contest's requirement. And the dress is because I wanted you to look nice for the other people waiting for us downstairs."

She arched an eyebrow. "Are we going to a party?"

"It's a private party. We need to go downstairs to meet the competition."

"Competition?"

"The other girls."

"What other girls?"

"The girls that are going to compete with you for my heart."

JADE FELT THE FLOOR SWIRLING under her new red ankle strap heels. "I'm sorry, what?"

She got up and paced in front of him. Then, she halted and glared at him.

He recoiled under her eyes. “I had to accept two more girls. It was part of the contract that I’d signed with the TV station. I wasn’t expecting to find you there. Now I have to stick with the terms, and I had to accept two other girls to spend the week with us. There is nothing I can do until the end of this week. After, I’ll send them away. I promise.”

She stepped back, processing everything. He was explaining himself to her. She didn’t know how to feel about it. Touched, appeased, ticked off? Maybe it was just a trick. He could be lying.

She stood before him. “You’re saying that I will have to participate in some stupid reality show with two other girls to win your heart?”

“Yes.”

She put her hands on her hips. “It’s easy then. I forfeit. I choose to lose. Can I go home now?”

His expression became serious as darkness flickered inside his eyes. “It doesn’t work like that.”

“Why not?” she asked, folding her arms and pursing her lips while fuming on the inside. Despite the anger, she couldn’t deny the pain that was clenching her heart because of her intention of leaving. It was insane, but her body was experiencing physical pain with the thought of leaving him. Mind control. That’s the only reason she could think of to explain that feeling. But, she was stronger than him.

“Because you are my beloved, I won’t let you forfeit.”

Jade noticed his sad expression; it was soothing her anger. He made her feel vulnerable and she didn't like that.

Swallowing hard, she mustered all of her free will to speak. "I don't want to compete with anyone for anything you have to offer and, especially, not for your heart. Give me a break! The last thing I would want is to be some douchebag vampire's beloved! Thanks, but I'll pass!" Raising her chin, she turned away from him to make her point.

The vampire put his hands on her shoulders. His touch sent a wave of heat down her arms and spine and made her stomach flip. "You are just upset. I know you don't mean it."

"Oh, but I do!"

Jade escaped his touch and walked to the closet where she had her old clothes. It was pointless to wear a fancy dress if she wasn't going to leave the room.

The vampire sighed loudly but didn't stopped her. "So, I guess I can send your brother home and go downstairs to receive the rest of the guests while you stay locked up in this bedroom for the rest of the week."

She stopped and spun around with wide eyes. "What?"

The vampire explained in a solemn voice. "You don't want to play the game. Fine. Then the punishment is to be locked up in this bedroom while the cameras are outside recording or go away and pay the sanction."

"You sick, twisted—"

In a flash, he was in front of her face, holding her wrists and breathing closer to her mouth. The sweetness was gone from his voice. “You might be my beloved, but that doesn’t mean that I will let you insult me! I’m being nice. I’m explaining to you what is happening. There is nothing I can do about this. I’m just trying to work with what I’ve got. I’m also hoping that you’re smart enough to realize that the other girls don’t mean anything to me now that I’ve found you. It’s time for you to decide. You come downstairs and play along or you stay here and…you lose me.”

“I don’t give a damn about you,” she stated with erratic breathing while tears stung her eyes.

Pinning her against the wall, she gasped as the blood drained from her face. Then, she realized that he didn’t exercise too much strength and didn’t hurt her.

She swallowed hard when he leaned his forehead against hers. “Stop being so stubborn. Just admit that you like me.”

“Never,” she muttered as her heart raced and her chest burned.

He laughed.

“It’s not funny.”

“I know. But, I can’t help being happy because I’ve found you, even if you’re always mad at me.”

She rolled her eyes. “You’re demented.”

“Maybe, but... Honey, you need to understand that I can’t send them away, and I want you with me downstairs.”

Jade pouted at the plea in his voice. Having him calling her 'honey' made everything seem a lot more intimate than it should be between them.

"You locked me in here," she accused him. "Now you expect me to act like nothing happened? Like I'm happy and carefree?"

"I did it for your own safety. You need to believe me."

"You have done nothing but bully and force yourself on me. Why should I believe you?"

"I never lied to you. I didn't hurt you, and I'm not going to hurt you."

"You hurt me by keeping me here against my will," she retorted, vulnerability flowing into her voice.

The vampire paused and looked into her eyes as if he wanted to read her mind.

She tried to release her wrists from his grasp.

Moments later, he let her go and stepped back. He raised his hands, so she would see that he was telling her the truth.

Jade relaxed against the wall and nibbled on her lower lip. His rich scent was still lingering around her nose, making heat spiral down her midriff.

His voice came out hoarse and sad. "I don't want you to leave me..." They stared at each other until he added, "I brought your brother to stay with us. You'll be able to take care of him."

Jade remained stubbornly silent.

"It's only for a week. You'll earn money that you can use to help your brother. Then, if you want to leave me...you can."

"Can I really?"

"Of course."

She tilted her head to eye him suspiciously.

"I give you my word, Jade."

Jade tucked a strand of hair behind her ear, caught inside his eyes and words. She had mixed feelings about the vampire. However, he had a point. She could use the money to help her brother. "Is my brother really here?"

"Yes."

She held her hands against her heart. "Is he scared?"

"No, he's excited. Sakura is with him. He adores her."

"Sakura?"

"My maker."

"The little girl," she deduced.

He nodded. "She's also eager to see you again. She finds you to be the most beautiful thing."

"Why?"

"Why what?" he asked.

"Why is she excited to see me?"

"Because you're my beloved. She's happy for us. You are now part of our family," he explained.

"Family... She looks extremely young."

"She was sixteen when she was turned, but she's older than me. She's quite friendly, and you'll like her a lot if you give her a chance."

"Okay."

"Are you still mad at me?"

Jade shrugged.

"Don't be. I'll do anything to make you happy," he said, leaning closer. She recoiled, and he halted. "I'm sorry. It's hard for me to stay away from you."

"What do you mean?"

"You smell better than anything in the world to me. I want to...touch you all the time."

She pursed her lips when her eyes landed on his lips. A new wave of heat spread throughout her body, and she fought back the attraction. She needed to stay away from him.

She was fully absorbed in her own thoughts when his next words shattered the turmoil inside her mind. "Let me come closer."

"No."

"Jade..."

She wanted to say his name back, but she suddenly realized that she had no idea what his name was. Calling him vampire dude wasn't wise or logical for that matter.

"What's wrong?" he asked.

"What's your name?"

He frowned. "Don't you already know me from the magazines and the internet?"

She rolled her eyes. “I don’t.”

He leaned forward, speaking near her mouth. “My name is Daniel. Start practicing it, so you’ll know what to moan when we are in my bedroom this dawn.”

Jade shoved him back. He was insufferable, and she needed to make things clear between them. “I may be stuck here, but I’m not sleeping with you.”

With a mischievous smirk, he teased, “You will. There’s no way in hell that I’ll spend another day away from you. We don’t want you to get bored, do we?”

Anger clouded her mind with the need to slap him and then kiss him.

Instead of being upset, she smirked. “I won’t. I’ll spend the rest of my days thinking about what I’ll do once I leave this place.”

He lost his smile. “If you don’t come to my bed, I’ll have to choose someone else. Do you want me to do that?”

“I don’t own you. You can do whatever you please but don’t expect me to want to touch you again, jerk!” She pushed him away and, this time, he stepped back and grinned with a proud expression.

Jade watched how he looked at her sideways. He was gorgeous and wicked. It was a deadly combination for sure, but she hated his guts because of his childish threat.

“The viewership ratings have to go up, so I need to take someone into my bedroom at the break of dawn," he said. "If you aren't willing to come with me, I'll have to find someone else who will."

She folded her arms and stared away. "Do whatever you please!"

"Then, I'll grab you and take you against your will." His dark words sent a shiver down her spine.

She glared at him. "You wouldn't dare."

"But I would."

"You said you weren't going to harm me!"

His eyes turned black, and he lost his smile. "Damn it, Jade, why will you always think the worst of me?"

"You're a vampire."

"So what? Are the words 'sexual molester' written on my forehead?"

"No." She pouted when answering.

Fisting his hands, he added, "I may be impulsive when it comes to you, but I won't hurt you. I give you my word."

"Yet you are forcing me to stay here." Her lips trembled and she hugged herself as she tried to hold on to the rest of her sanity.

"Having you here is the only way I got to convince you that we are meant to be."

"I could never..."

He put his hands in his pockets. "Love a monster like me?"

She pursed her lips and shrugged.

"That's why you need to stay here, so you stop thinking of me as a monster and see me as a being—a rational and emotional being that happens to have to drink blood to survive."

She gazed at him, unsure if he was teasing her or being sarcastic. It seemed that he wasn't being either. He had a straight face as he waited for her reaction, blue piercing eyes and perfect skin. He smelled like heaven and tasted wonderful. Their lips together were perfection.

*Why the crazy attraction? Why is it that one moment I want to kiss him and the next I want to rip his head off?*

Walking to the bed, she sat and gazed at her shoes with mixed feelings. "Why does my opinion bother you so much?"

"Because you are my beloved. You need to understand that I'm not lying or trying to trick you." He stepped closer with squinted eyes. "Doesn't that mean anything to you?"

She crossed her legs. "I don't believe in that bullshit. Vampires invented that to trick humans to beg and run to your nightclubs to be taken as willing prey. It's a scheme, nothing more, nothing less."

Daniel sat beside her and folded his hands above his lap. "Hmm, you really think the worst of us. If you have to know, it's extremely rare for a vampire to find his beloved, but it's not a lie."

"I'm not a vampire, so I don't know if you are telling me the truth or not."

"Fair enough, then let's go to plan B."

"What plan B?"

"The plan where I do everything to make you beg me to make you mine." He drew a smile, a teasing and annoying grin that made Jade wish to slap it off his face.

Getting up, she assured him, "That's not going to happen."

"You are stubborn, but I'm persistent. You will eventually realize that you can't live without me."

"Right..."

"See, you are already agreeing with me."

Jade growled and furrowed her eyebrows at him, wishing she had some pillow to smack him with.

"You are obnoxious and irritating. I just hate you," she hissed.

"No, you don't," he disagreed with a happy smile despite her insults.

"This is pointless." She folded her arms. "I want to see my brother. Take me to him."

"Will you behave downstairs and be nice to me?" He got up and fixed his tie.

Arching an eyebrow, she questioned, "Do I have any other choice?"

"No."

"Then, stop smiling like the Grinch and lead the way."

"I love it when you give me orders."

"You are insane."

"Maybe, but it's quite refreshing," he added, sighing and staring at her from top to bottom.

She glared. "Stop doing that."

"What?"

"Whatever you are doing."

"I was just congratulating myself on the choice of the perfect dress. It looks stunning on you. You look all grown-up." He sank his hands into his pockets with a proud expression while she looked down at her figure. "You'll just need to put more lipstick on."

Jade frowned. "Why?"

Daniel smirked. In a blink of an eye, he was in front of her face, whispering against her lips. "Because we are going to kiss." His lips stopped inches from hers, waiting for her permission.

"Keep dreaming about it. You'll need to deserve it. You don't." She stepped back and looked at the door. Smoothing the material of her dress down, she asked, "Are we going to attend the party or not?"

Daniel cleared his throat and offered his arm for her to hold. "Are you ready for your surprise?"

# CHAPTER SIX: THE COMPETITION

**AS JADE DESCENDED THE STAIRS** and noticed all the cameras and the crew members around them, the huge house started to look small and claustrophobic. Her face was being broadcasted everywhere, and she had never wished for that kind of attention.

"Are they broadcasting live?" Jade mumbled next to Daniel's ear. Despite him being a jerk, and definitely arrogant about what he thought he could obtain from her, having him by her side reassured her.

"No, it is just for the footage. We will have a special appearance at the show tomorrow night, but the original program records live the other vampires' lives. We are a special edition. They will assemble the best moments of our week and broadcast it during the weekend."

"You don't look like you need the money. Why are you doing this?"

"I owe a favor to one of the elder vampires, so I had to help him out with this. But when it's done, they will get out of my home, and we will be left alone."

Reaching the landing in the foyer, with a fake smile, she asked, "I have no plans to be left alone with you. I want all of this to end, so I can go back home."

"That is discrimination, Jade." He helped her descend another set of stairs.

"What?" She stared at him. He was such a tease and his annoying good looks made it hard to stay mad at him for long.

"You don't want to date me because I'm a vampire. But vampires have feelings, too. We are also—beings," he finished with a theatrical gesture that made her roll her eyes and realize that they were at the bottom of the stairs and there were other people in the room to their right, talking, drinking, and enjoying the party.

Jade stared at the other guests, intrigued by who they were. It was then that she noticed the seven well-dressed vampires, who starred in the reality show, were at that party with their new pets.

"I may have to leave you alone sometimes to talk to others, but you will have someone to keep you company."

"Where is my brother?" she asked, ignoring the party and remembering his words.

"You will see him after the party. Your surprise has seen you," he said, gazing at the party.

"Are you—" She had no time to finish her sentence because a screaming blonde girl ran to her and hugged her tightly. It was Jenna, to her utter disbelief, wearing a cute golden dress and looking stunning.

"What are you doing here?" Jade asked.

Daniel squeezed her arm and indicated that he was going to join the party and greet the guests.

She just nodded and gave her full attention to her best friend.

"The director liked me so much that he chose me to participate in the special program. So now I'm one of the contestants to win the bachelor's heart," Jenna explained proudly.

"What?"

"We are going to compete against each other and another girl for Daniel's heart. Isn't it great?"

Jade's heart seemed to stop and all color ran from her face. The world was spinning around her at an unwelcome speed.

"Are you all right?" she asked, frowning.

Jade felt like she wanted to run away and hide.

"Anyway," Jenna continued, grabbing her arm and urging her to enter the living room where everybody was busy talking and some even making out in the couches. The people became blurs to her. Jade was too shocked to pay attention to her surroundings. "I was thinking," Jenna went on, "that we could team up against the other girl, and you could help me win Daniel's heart. You don't want all this, so I'm glad you are here to help me."

"Help you?" Jade asked, baffled. *Is she crazy?* "You said you were going to take care of Stevie!"

"He's fine. Daniel's employees took care of everything. They even took him to his treatment, and he is upstairs with Sakura. He loves her. He thinks she is the most beautiful girl he has ever seen."

"Great, just great," Jade hissed.

"Seth is here. He's been checking me out. He even smiled at me," her friend whispered in her ear, and Jade snapped her head to stare at her blue eyes. "He is so charming! He looks like an angel, Jade!"

"He has a pet," Jade muttered.

"His pet is an annoying girl, and it seems he can't stand her. I would gladly trade places with her, so I could be next to him."

"You've just told me that you wanted my help to win Daniel's heart!"

"Oh, don't look at me like you are judging me! I just want to have someone who loves me."

"Nice place to look for it—in a vampire's lair and with vampire men," Jade said, rolling her eyes.

They sat on an empty couch, and Jade browsed the living room, looking for Daniel. It was automatic. Her eyes were seeking him out against her best judgment.

"So, do you like him more today?" Jenna asked after pouting a bit.

"Who?"

"Daniel."

"He is not so bad," she confessed, nibbling on her lower lip and remembering their time alone. Daniel was as intriguing as he was overwhelming. Besides, there was no point in lying to her best friend about her feelings. Jenna would, eventually, see right through her. Moreover, she didn't want to compete against her best friend for a guy's attention.

"That's cool. We always tend to fall for the same guys." She giggled, and Jade stared at her sideways. "Oh, come on! We can share him."

"No, we can't," she said seriously.

Jenna burst into laughter, putting her hands on her shoulders. "There you go. You have finally admitted it. Was that so hard?"

The patronizing tone in her voice rattled Jade. "I've admitted *what*?"

"That you like the guy. I was teasing you, waiting for you to confess. You can be stubborn. Besides, Daniel seems nice, and I've joined to be next to you and... Who knows, maybe I'll meet Seth." She smirked and wiggled her eyebrows, making Jade laugh.

"Does that mean you are leaving Daniel alone?"

"He's gorgeous, and he's going to great lengths to make you happy. I'm pretty sure that he's extremely interested in you. Besides, I saw how you two were acting while coming down the stairs. Also, you let him touch you! Thus, I'm guessing that the animosities between you two are over."

"Oh, no. I still think he's insufferable," Jade said, breathing out dramatically.

"Oh, you so have a crush on him!" Jenna squealed.

Jade palmed Jenna's face and growled, pulling her back. Her best friend shouldn't say that out loud, and she shouldn't be finding it hilarious.

"Where is he anyway?"

Shrugging, Jade scanned for him one more time to see if she could locate him.

“Outside with the brunette,” a husky and soft voice whispered in her ear, startling her. She turned her head to see who was talking so close.

Jade’s eyes widened. Seth, the vampire hottie, was talking to her in person.

“Hi, I’m Seth,” he said with a dreamy smile, taking her hand and kissing it softly.

Her temperature rose and her stomach dropped. “I’m J-Jade.”

“And, I’m Jenna,” her best friend interrupted.

“So, you are both my brother’s guests for the week,” he stated, smiling mischievously. “He has great taste. I’m jealous.”

“Brother?” Jade asked, frowning.

“We have the same vampire parents. I’m the youngest, though. Are you ladies having fun?”

“Yes!” Jenna cut Jade’s turn to speak.

Meanwhile, Jade stared at the balcony to see if she could find Daniel. The word ‘brunette’ was floating inside her mind, leaving a rash of jealousy on her skin.

“Do you want to know against whom you are competing?” Seth asked with a hint of gossip and amusement in his voice.

“Oh, I would love to know who the third girl is,” Jenna declared.

“It’s someone you two probably know. She is rather famous.”

Jenna’s eyes grew bigger.

"Who is it?"

"It's Emma Dawson." He used the same tone of voice that a TV host would use to reveal the winner of an important prize.

As if on cue, Jenna's mouth fell open. She slapped her hands to her cheeks.

"They used to date," Seth continued, sitting in the middle of them as if they were longtime friends who were sharing the latest gossip.

Jenna never looked more excited, and Jade more puzzled.

"I know!" Jenna nodded repeatedly.

Jade didn't. Though she knew who the actress was, she had no clue of what was going on with the stars, the vampires, and so on. She had real problems to worry about. Emma was a famous actress and was gorgeous with an endless number of fans who would worship the ground she walked on. In a way, it made sense. A rich and good-looking vampire like Daniel should have a long list of actresses and models as his ex-girlfriends.

Jade tried to focus on Seth's information. She needed to know what she was getting herself into.

"The producer was looking for a media sensation to enter the show against the one he would choose and the one the producer would cast. It seems that Emma did everything she could to enter the competition. She is probably regretting breaking up with him."

"And they dated for a year or two, and everybody thought they were going to get married," Jenna filled in the blanks.

Jade began to feel sick. Her stomach was doing flips inside her tummy. She cut into their conversation, asking, “What is your deal, Seth?”

“I wanted to warn you about what you were going to play against. I don’t think it will be a fair competition. Besides, you two look neglected over here. Isn’t my brother giving you the proper attention?”

“Don’t you have a pet to take care of?” Daniel’s voice came from behind them, taking the words right out of Jade’s mind.

“Yes, but I wanted to talk to your girls. They are extremely friendly, and I wanted to meet the girl that can be my future sister-in-law,” he replied, turning around with a sizzling smile.

Daniel was not smiling, though. “Stay away from them and move along.”

Seth lost his smile. “Always rude, brother.” He got up and studied Jade and Jenna. “We will talk later. Come and join me whenever you feel bored.”

“I’m bored already,” Jenna said, getting up. “I would love to go with you.”

“Let’s go and see the garden then,” he proposed, and she grabbed his arm, leaving the others behind.

Jade’s eyes were on her lap. She was feeling restless. It wasn’t helping that Jenna was playing with fire and wanted to get burned. But, she was a big girl, and Jade didn’t want to ruin her fun. She was sure her friend was going to try to make out with Seth, and the garden seemed like a good place for them to do that. Nonetheless, Jade was sure that Seth had his own agenda.

"What lies was my brother telling?" Daniel moved around the couch and sat next to her. "It must be something bad to make you lose your smile."

"I want to see my brother," Jade said, facing him.

He was staring at her with big blue eyes and an inquisitive expression. "Aren't you happy to have your best friend joining us?"

"I would be happier if this nightmare was over."

He leaned forward and whispered in her ear, "It doesn't have to be a nightmare. It can become a hot and pleasant dream."

Her blood raced through her veins and her cheeks burned. Even if her traitorous body liked what he was implying, her reason was not so keen on surrendering and falling for his promising words.

"I've heard your ex is coming to join us for the week. How are you planning to handle that?" She put in the effort to grin evilly, but she was feeling distraught to have to compete with freaking Emma 'Gorgeous' Dawson for Daniel's attention.

"I plan to treat her with respect. We've remained friends. However, I'm not planning on picking up where we have left off."

Jade's shoulders relaxed.

"Feeling less jealous now?" he asked, grinning.

Jade felt the need to choke him with one of the cushions that were behind her back. But, she simply looked away.

“In my defense,” he added, “I didn’t want her here. They are only doing this to increase the ratings.”

Jade shrugged, focusing on the other guests and perceiving the hovering cameras around them.

He leaned in until his breath brushed her ear. “If I let you see your brother, would you look less bored after?”

A frisson of excitement caressed her neck, and she partially closed her eyes.

“It would be so much better if we had stayed locked inside your bedroom,” he continued, leaving her even more fragile under his spell.

Jade couldn’t help but nibble on her lip as her mouth went dry.

“Afterwards, you must come back and mingle with the rest of the guests.” He brushed his finger along her neck, leaving a trail of fire behind.

“Okay.” She turned her head and met his tender eyes. She could get used to getting lost in them if she didn’t have so much at stake and so much more to lose. After all, Jade had her brother to take care and her mortality to treasure.

Daniel smiled, pleased, and she smiled back. They moved away from the crowd and went upstairs, so she could see her brother. Daniel had a strange power of making everything seem interesting, dangerous, and exciting. But, she knew better than to trust him. Like all men—vampire or human—they had only one thing in mind: women and how many more they could sleep with. Jade was merely another challenge to him.

# CHAPTER SEVEN: A BLOODY KISS

**AS SOON AS DANIEL OPENED** the wooden French door that led them to a beautiful sitting room with a view of a private pool, Jade saw Stevie playing a game with Sakura.

Sakura looked like a life-size anime figurine. Her gorgeous blonde hair was perfectly curled, and she wore a white and blue corset princess dress. She had a peculiar taste in clothes, but she was beautiful like a walking and talking doll.

Stevie had his eyes glowing, and he didn't seem to be afraid of her. Maybe he had no clue that she was a vampire. He was aware of their existence and that he shouldn't trust them. Yet, the blonde girl had won the little boy's heart, and she looked harmless enough. Looks could be deceiving, though.

"It's so unfair," Stevie complained as his enormous milky brown eyes focused on Sakura. His pouting face was enough to make anyone melt, and Sakura was the target of it. "You always win!"

"You need to be faster," Sakura said playfully, tugging at his messy hair and making him smile. "Your sister is here, big boy. Don't you want to hug her?"

Stevie's head snapped in his sister's direction. His eyes grew bigger and he broke into a wide smile. He was Jade's angel, her gorgeous, sweet angel as well as her only living family. She loved him so much that her heart hurt inside her chest. There he was, her little Tasmanian devil as she liked to call him. In her defense, he was hyperactive and would always make a mess at home.

"Sis!" he squealed, getting up from the floor, and ran to her with his arms opened wide.

Jade crouched down and took him into a bear hug. She had missed him terribly. It had been years since they were apart for so long.

"You have to see my new room," he said. "It's huge, and Daniel said he was going to buy me a train. Do you believe that, Jade? A real train like the one we had at Christmas time in Jenna's grandmother's home."

"Are you okay, Stevie?" She was overwhelmed by the sadness and happiness brought on by seeing him and being able to hold him. She had cried the entire day when she was locked in that bedroom because she was worried about him and the bills she had to pay, so he could get his treatment. He depended on her and her income to keep living. He was her responsibility since their parents were killed. She couldn't lose her job.

"I'm okay. You don't need to worry." He smiled, putting his tiny hands on her face. "Daniel and Sakura were kind to me. And, a nice lady took me to the hospital, so I could take my shot."

"I'm glad, baby," Jade whispered, her voice laced with emotion. She was barely holding on to her tears. She was a lot more relieved now that she knew that Daniel had taken care of her little Taz. Maybe that vamp was not so bad, after all. He took his time to care about what Jade had been concerned with the night before. And, he brought her brother to live with them in that house. That was astonishing and unexpected.

"Why are we going to live here now?" His big brown eyes were attentive to her expressions. He was young, but he wasn't stupid. In fact, he was a bright and curious boy at the age of five.

"I've already explained it to you," Daniel intervened, and Jade frowned at him because she didn't like the fact he had promised a train to Stevie and now she was finding out that he had talked to Stevie about them all living together.

"Is Daniel your boyfriend?" Stevie asked.

Jade gasped in disbelief as she straightened up with her brother in her arms and looked at Daniel. *What story has this crazy vampire told my brother?*

"Daniel is my friend, not my boyfriend."

"We will be boyfriend and girlfriend," Daniel said.

Stevie chuckled and shook his head. "Jade doesn't date boys. She says boys are stupid, and I am the only man in her life."

"Well then, I guess you will have to learn how to share her," Daniel teased, and Stevie's brows furrowed in a possessive grimace.

Jade couldn't help but chuckle. She bet Daniel was not expecting that. *Serves him right.*

"Stop saying nonsense, Daniel," she muttered.

The vampire gave her a lopsided grin.

Arching an eyebrow, she questioned, "What?"

"I like the sound of my name coming from your mouth," he whispered.

She frowned at him and shook her head. *The*

*nerve the guy has!*

“So, is he really your boyfriend?” Stevie gripped harder his tiny arms around his sister’s neck, almost choking her in the process.

“No, baby. He is not.”

“I will be,” Daniel intervened.

Jade turned around and glared at him. “You are terrible with kids. Don’t upset him.”

Daniel shrugged. “I let him play with Sakura, so he shouldn’t be so possessive with you.”

“He is five! I’m his only family.”

“We are your family now. We will take care of you,” Daniel said in a soft voice.

Even if Jade didn’t believe his words, they had the weird effect of making her heart melt. Her eyes met his while her voice felt trapped in her throat. She looked at her brother and noticed how confused he was.

“This is just temporary. I have some...business to take care of here. We’ll go back home next week. Okay?”

Stevie nodded and stuck out his tongue at Daniel.

“Don’t be rude, Stevie,” Jade reproached him.

He pouted. “I’m sorry.”

Jade patted his hair. “Are you going to be okay here?”

He nodded with a smile.

Daniel placed his right hand on her lower back.

"You have my word. He will be well cared for."

"Don't worry, Jade. We will take care of Stevie and pay for his treatments while you are here," Sakura intervened, moving closer. "I didn't have an opportunity to properly introduce myself to you. I'm Sakura, Daniel's sister."

"Daniel said you were his mother," Jade said as Stevie laid his head on her shoulder with heavy eyelids.

Sakura twisted a lock of golden hair around her finger and smiled with bright red cheeks. "I look so much younger than him. I feel that people don't take me seriously when I say I'm his mother." She giggled, and Jade's lips curled into a smile.

Sakura was pretty, so beautiful that it was impossible not to like her when she was being friendly.

"Stevie, do you want to watch cartoons with me?" Sakura began. "Jade and Daniel need to go back downstairs to the party."

Stevie raised his head and nodded. It amazed Jade when he left her arms and ran into Sakura's. There weren't a lot of people he liked to hug. He was special, different, and too smart for his own good at that age. Trusting for him was an issue. Well, for the both of them, actually.

"Could you please read him a story before he goes to bed? It's past his bedtime, but he can't sleep without someone reading to him," Jade requested.

Sakura nodded, and Daniel placed his warm hands on Jade's naked shoulders, rubbing them softly.

"He will be fine. Sakura is talented with children. You'll have plenty of opportunities to talk and be with him." He leaned in, gently massaging her tense muscles. "No crying."

Jade was too emotional to speak. She nodded and bit her lip, staring at Stevie disappearing with Sakura into another room. Suddenly, her entire body melted as she felt Daniel's hands running up and down her arms and his chest against her back. Jade's breath hitched, her heartbeat increased, and his scent clouded her senses with hot thoughts of kisses and gripping hands. She was feeling so vulnerable that it was even ridiculous to try keeping her eyes opened. Jade closed them and sighed when his lips touched the crook of her neck and his hands pulled her closer to him by snaking around her waist.

"I wish it was already dawn, so I could be left alone with you," he whispered against her skin, making her want to turn around and kiss him.

"Who said I would accept going with you to your bedroom?" Jade tried to fight him back, to make him doubt his power over her.

"Who said you had a choice?"

Jade's eyes flew open. His arrogance and the disrespect he had for her feelings and desires had her body trembling with exasperation. "I don't like it when you say that."

"And I don't like when you deny me things." He softly kissed her neck which caused shivers to run down her spine.

Jade wanted to groan at his words, but she was completely weak against his mouth on her skin. Already, her arms reached up, seeking to play with his soft hair. "We need to go back to the party."

"Fuck the damn party." Daniel turned her around to face him and cupped her cheeks. In a raspy voice, he said, "I believe I deserve a reward."

Jade pursed her lips and tried to appease her fluttering heart.

Daniel's eyes were flickering between blue and black. His hands were securing her as he leaned down. He waited for a moment before asking, "Do you still fear me?"

Jade shook her head and closed her eyes as she raised her lips to meet his.

"Be careful not to cut your tongue then," he warned with husky voice before his lips softly brushed hers.

Seconds later, Jade moaned when their tongues entwined. She touched his fangs, exploring and teasing him. Their bodies melted into each other, and she could feel his arousal against her stomach. That was unexpected. She had no idea that he was so turned on by her. However, his kiss was slow and enticing. It was making her want to beg for more. Everything seemed perfect. All she could hear was the pounding of her heart while experiencing the blissful sensation of peace and pleasure. He was a great kisser. Years of practice, she assumed.

He broke the kiss, staring at her intently. "Jade, stay away from Seth. He wants everything that is mine, and I don't want you to fall for his lies. He is jealous."

She nodded, barely keeping her eyes open or registering his request. "Jenna is with him."

"He doesn't care about her. He knows that you are mine, so he will do anything to ruin what we have."

"There's nothing between us."

"Do I have to kiss you again to make you stop saying nonsense?" he asked, trying not to look annoyed, but she knew he was.

Jade bobbed her head, and he chuckled.

"Clever girl." He kissed her again, his tongue offering tormenting pleasure as her hands gripped his shoulders. When he moved her head to deepen their kiss, she was lost.

Things got intense when he sucked gently on the pulse throbbing at the base of her throat. Fear and lust coiled around her body. She dared to place her hands on his chest, perceiving the movements of his breathing. His pulse vibrated under her palms. Her lips parted to suck on air. Then, she felt the tip of his tongue tracing her bottom lip. Another heart stopping kiss, and she was helpless in his arms. Moments later, she felt the taste of iron in her mouth and her lower lip tingled as Daniel's teeth were sucking on it. Heat spread to her cheeks and panic took over her. She pushed the vampire away.

"Why did you do that?" She touched her bloody lip.

"Don't," he begged in a hoarse voice. His eyes had gone dark. "Don't touch it, Jade. I'll fix it. I promise."

Jade hesitated, but, eventually, moved forward with parted lips while the blood dripped down her chin.

"You taste like heaven. Have you been bitten before?"

"No," she whispered. She should be freaking out because he was engulfing her lip and tasting her blood, drinking from her.

"I won't do it again without your permission. I just...needed to have you in my bloodstream to calm down. You smell better than anyone else, and your blood is...enticing," he said against her lips before leaning back and sucking in a breath.

"Should I be worried?"

The vampire shook his head as he licked his own lips.

Jade felt her cheeks blush. Her eyes followed every movement of his tongue. She realized that she was barely breathing.

Her lip stung, but she wanted to kiss him again. So, she pressed her bloody lips against his and smiled when Daniel closed his eyes and replied with fierce passion.

"God, you taste like candy... I've never tasted anything like you before," he said softly.

His words made her feel proud. She shouldn't be. This type of conduct was highly grotesque by her standards, but her priorities started being rewritten since she met Daniel.

His mouth kept tempting her. Yearning for

further contact, she lazily moved her tongue along his lower lip, shivering when his hands gripped her waist harder and his body fully pressed against hers. She moaned loudly when he tugged her lip into his mouth and began to suck on it. It was scary and sexy at the same time.

"I have to seal your wound," he mumbled.

She opened her eyes and raised her chin as she parted her lips.

Daniel licked her wound and it stung. She released a moan of complaint, but it stopped hurting immediately. Her fingers touched her lip. The wound was gone.

"It's healed now. We need to get back to the party, but we'll resume the foreplay later," he whispered into her ear and moved away before she could register the implied invitation in his words.

# CHAPTER EIGHT: THE MOVIE STAR

**THE PARTY WAS LOUD**, and everybody seemed to be already intoxicated. Even the vampires had feasted on too much blood laced with whiskey or some other strong beverage. Jade was in a corner, watching the vampires making out with their pets and the crew members recording everything like their lives depended on it. Who in their right mind would make out in front of a camera while not being bothered by it?

Meanwhile, Daniel was talking with the director and the producer of the show. He didn't look pleased, and she wished she had superhuman hearing, so she could find out why. To make matters worse, Jenna was nowhere to be found, and Jade was still trying to figure out if the hot movie star was going to join the party or not. The suspense was killing her.

Her question was answered when the actress walked in from the balcony wearing a rose gold, long sleeved, embroidered dress. The stunning cocktail look was completed with matching pumps and pink drop earrings. She looked like a goddess.

Everyone stopped what they were doing to look at her—even Daniel.

A girl immediately started to scream from excitement and ran towards the actress to tell her how much she loved her and that she had seen all of her movies. She finished by rambling about something else, but Jade chose not to hear it. She was busy evaluating Daniel's reaction to the arrival of his ex. He soon resumed his speech and paid no more attention to the brunette. Jade smiled, pleased, as she stared at her glass while sucking the liquid through the straw.

"Take five, people," the director shouted.

Immediately, all the cameras were put down, and the vampires got up and went inside the house while their pets relaxed on the couches or headed to the garden.

Jade stared at everything with curiosity, noticing how Emma was pretending to be friendly with the fangirls, but she was also stealing glances at Daniel out of the corner of her eye. He was talking with one of the seven vampires who starred in the reality show.

"I don't want you harassing the star," the director said, motioning the girls to move along and leave Emma alone. "I'm so glad you were able to come, Emma." He softened his voice when he sat next to her.

"I wouldn't miss this for anything in the world," she said with a smile.

"I have your script right here." He showed her a digital tablet.

Jade frowned.

*Why does she need a script in a reality show where things are supposed to happen naturally?*

"Why isn't Daniel choosing me today?" she asked, glaring at the screen. "You told me that you had this covered. I don't want to lose my time. I need the publicity, and I need to have a key part in all of this. Besides, everybody is waiting anxiously for us to get back together. It will sell magazines and should be good for my upcoming movies."

"He is being stubborn about it. There's nothing I can do to fix this."

Emma fumed. "Just call Dominic then. He will convince him."

"Emma..." The director was going to say something else but noticed that Jade was staring at them. His green eyes shifted to golden, and Jade's eyes widened in fear.

*What the hell is he?*

He wasn't a vampire, but he wasn't a human either. Maybe he was a werewolf.

"Jade, could you give us some privacy, please?"

"Sure," she said, getting up and moving away.

"Is that his new toy?" Emma asked with a hint of amusement.

"Yes, he is being stubborn because of her."

"What was Daniel thinking when he chose her last night? She clearly didn't want to be here." Emma continued, apparently not caring if Jade overheard them or not.

"She has cleaned up nicely," the director said. His words made Jade pause before leaving for the balcony. He continued, "And people are dying to know if he can tame her or not. Some are sympathetic, others are simply curious about what will happen. It's a money machine."

"I'm not liking that she's stealing my spotlight.

This show should be about me getting back with Daniel, not about Daniel and her," Emma grumbled, tossing the device onto the director's lap. "I'll call Dominic myself." She took out her cell phone and moved away to make the call in private.

The director got up as Jade turned around and strolled toward the balcony. Once outside, Jade casually leaned against the balustrade. She pretended that she was looking at the garden and hadn't heard their conversation. To her surprise, the director joined her.

"Jade, I didn't have the opportunity to talk to you yet," he said, trying to get her attention.

She stared back at him. He was a young man in his early thirties and had a nice smile, even if Jade wasn't buying his friendly façade.

"I'm Jake, the director of this show. I'm going to spend some time with you in this house, telling you what to do and how to act. I would appreciate if you would come to me if you have any problems or concerns about the show. I'm here to address any issues you might have," he explained, taking her hands between his and staring deeply into her eyes.

"Thanks, but I'm okay." She took her hand back, not liking the invasion of her personal space.

"Do you like being here?"

She answered with a shrug. "It's nice."

"Is Daniel treating you right? I know he can be...overwhelming."

"I don't understand what you mean by that. Everything is fine." Jade grasped the balcony railing while staring at the lights illuminating the garden. She sipped on her cold drink, trying to clear her throat.

"I know Daniel is very fond of you. You need to understand that this is a show, and we need to entertain our audience. So, we are going to have some games that you and the other contestants need to play. The winner of those games will have the opportunity to spend extra time with Daniel."

"Games?"

"Yes, it was our team's idea to add an extra allure to the show and increase the competition. It is also a way to portray who is really interested in winning Daniel's heart."

"I see."

"You are stunning. Have you ever considered modeling or a career on TV? I would love to work with you when this show is over. There will be a lot of opportunities for you after. Here." He grinned as he handed her a business card that she reluctantly accepted. "That's my personal number. Call me, and we can go out and discuss some career opportunities for you."

Jade looked with little interest at his business card. "Thanks, Jake, and don't get me wrong, but I don't want to be famous. I didn't even want to be here."

"You simply need to make an effort to survive through this week. Be pleasant; be smart. Daniel always gets what he wants, and he is set on breaking you to his will because he thinks you are a good challenge. However, don't mistake sexual yearning with love. You are a sweet girl, but you have no real chance with him. He will get what he wants and then he'll leave you like he's left the girls before you. Just enjoy the fame and try to use it to your advantage."

"And why are you telling me all this?" Jade asked, finding it odd how he was so keen in warning her about Daniel's womanizing reputation.

"Because in the end, Daniel and Emma will get back together, and you will be forgotten. They've been on and off for years. All this was a publicity stunt to get the viewer numbers to go up."

"Daniel said..."

"Daniel says a lot of things. You and I know better than to trust a vampire, don't we?" he asked darkly, and his eyes shifted again, making Jade tense.

"Are you a wolf?"

"That's not important right now. Just keep my number in case something bad happens to you. Rest assured, I know everything that happened to you and your family. You have every right to feel trapped and to mistrust his kind." He walked back to the living room where Emma was calling for him.

Jade stood there, unhappy with the fact that they went digging into her private life and could use it against her. She had no intentions of sharing it with the rest of the world and having people judging and looking at her differently. She wanted to be normal and leave the past behind.

In the living room, Emma was making her demands known to Jake.

Jade brushed their talk aside, deep in her own problems.

"You are out of your league, aren't you?" a smooth and creepy voice whispered next to Jade, startling her.

"Seth, you need to stop doing that," she complained, placing her hand on her chest.

"Why? It's so much fun to be able to catch people when they're distracted."

"Where is Jenna?"

"I left her with the other girls in the pool. They're drinking and partying."

"What pool?"

He gestured with his hands as he said, "There's a pool at the back of the house. They are serving drinks, and the girls decided to go swimming. You should join them. I bet there are a lot of nice curves beneath that dress."

Jade glared at him.

"I'm not normally a jerk if that's what you're thinking. I just like to tease. Anyway, I came back here to see how things were going with Daniel and Cleopatra."

Jade frowned. "What are you talking about?"

He pointed to Emma, and she chuckled at his comparison.

Seth added, "She can be a drama queen and a diva. Scratch that, she is. They would get in the craziest and most heated discussions. Mom and I were glad when they broke up."

"I think she wants him back." Jade looked at her hands, pouting.

"Yes, she likes money and the attention that dating him brings."

"Why are you defending him now?"

"I'm not. I'm only telling you what's really going on. I didn't want you to crucify Daniel because a crazy bitch thinks Daniel is her toy. Emma plays with other people's feelings. So, don't let her get to you."

"Doesn't Daniel think that all women are toys or pets? Don't you have a lot of pets, Seth?"

He rubbed the back of his neck with a boyish grin. "It's just a show, Jade. It's a way to get me to another place in the showbiz industry. Being a vampire bachelor doesn't define me as a person."

"You are not a person."

"Yes, I am. I was turned into a vampire, but I'm still a person. I still have dreams. My life changed when I became this, but now I have the opportunity to do what I was born to do."

"And what is that?"

"To sing and act. I want to be a serious actor and keep singing."

"Don't you people want to do something else with your lives? There are plenty of other career options that can be fulfilling."

"Like what, being a doctor?"

Jade rolled her eyes. "Yes, and so many other things."

“Well, I would rather be a singer who cures hearts and souls than a doctor who fixes bodies.”

“That was deep, brother,” Daniel joked, coming in from the balcony with a glass of bourbon in his hand.

Jade felt her cheeks turn red because he looked rather dashing in his black tuxedo with ruffled hair. His eyes were so deep and blue that it was impossible not to get lost in them. Besides, his sense of humor was a plus, even if Jade would rather deny it and pretend that he couldn’t make her smile.

“Has Cleo given you her demands for participation?” Seth teased back, giving a lopsided grin that made Jade crack a smile. It was rather funny to see those two acting evil to one another.

“She did.” He slipped one hand into his pocket.

“What does she want?”

“She wants me to choose her to spend the first day in my bedroom,” he said, staring directly at Jade who narrowed her eyes and gripped her glass tighter.

“Are you going to comply with that?”

“No, I’ve already promised someone else I would choose her.”

“Don’t refuse something that extraordinary because of me,” Jade said, her blood boiling in her veins. It crossed her mind that Daniel wanted something new to play with and was leaving the old fun for later.

“She is nothing extraordinary. Besides, she

wants publicity and all I want is to stay away from her. And Jade—" He stepped forward, touching her face. "You know you are my number one."

"Cheesy brother, really cheesy." Seth laughed, shaking his head. "I'll go back to the pool and join the party," he added, disappearing in a flash from their side.

"I'm not cheesy," he complained with a beaming smile that made Jade laugh.

"I have to agree with Seth on this. It sounded cheesy."

Daniel sighed deeply. "Emma is trying to convince the director to force me into choosing her."

"Can she do that?"

He shrugged. "I should have killed the bitch!"

"Daniel..." Jade lost her breath at his words. She didn't know if he was serious or being mean, but it was not a nice thing to say.

Leaning forward, he said, "I need to know that you trust me."

"Well, I don't," she said bluntly, making him smirk.

"Daniel, we need you inside," the director yelled to get his attention.

"I have to get back to work. Don't go wandering around. I don't like it when I can't see you." He brushed his lips against hers and disappeared into the living room.

Jade turned around and stared at the moon, feeling uncomfortable. Her life was a mess and her heart was being hijacked by unwanted feelings. She wasn't going to fall so easily for a vampire, was she?

"Hi," a girl's voice brought Jade's attention to the actress. "I'm Emma."

"I'm Jade."

"I wanted to come here and introduce myself to you. Do you know where the other girl is?"

"Jenna is in the pool," Jade replied.

"Look, I don't want to be treated differently by you. I know I'm famous and all, but this is just a TV show, and we all know that Daniel is a jerk," Emma said.

Jade stared at her, not sure what this girl wanted from her or why she was here in the first place.

"We have a contract," Emma said.

"Yes, I have one of those, too, but I didn't know what I was getting myself into."

"He chose you."

"Yes."

"I saw the special."

"What special?" Jade asked.

"It was a live show. I saw when he chose you. You didn't want to come. I felt sorry for you."

"Thanks, I guess."

"I wanted you to know that I'm here if you need someone to talk to. You don't need to be afraid. Daniel isn't evil; he would never hurt you."

"I know that now."

"And don't fall for his act. He tells all his girls that they are his beloved," she added with a grin and walked away, leaving Jade frozen by her words under the moonlight.

# CHAPTER NINE: THE HOT STRANGER

**JADE SAT ON ONE OF THE BENCHES** near the pool while the other human guests were in their underwear—diving, screaming, and playing crazy water games with the vampires. They were having fun, and Jade was watching them play even if she was not in the mood to participate.

Her mind was a mess. A lot of doubts and unhappy thoughts were running around her head, making her feel gloomy and stupid.

If she could, she would grab her brother and leave that place. If she could, she would disappear and never look at Daniel again. And to think she was starting to fall for his charming fake personality.

"Come on, Jade, the water is great," Jenna yelled, splashing water at her.

"I'm fine with watching you act like kids."

"Can someone give me a towel?" Jenna requested to one of the assistants who belonged to the show. She got out of the pool and sat next to her friend, wrapped in the towel. "What's wrong? I'm trying to have fun, but I can't keep ignoring your unhappy face. What happened? You were happier when I left you with Daniel. Are you still worried about what I said about wanting to compete with you? I was kidding. If you want him, then go for it. We both know that you are in desperate need of getting laid!"

"Shut up!" Jade complained, looking around and noticing the hovering cameras focusing their attention on the pool. She didn't want the whole world to know about her non-existent sex life.

Jenna pushed her further with an empathic face. "How long has it been since the last time?"

"What last time?" Jade asked, making her friend giggle.

Jenna suddenly frowned. "Are you falling for him?"

Jade shrugged.

"It's one thing to have fun, Jade, and another to give your heart to him."

"I barely know the guy!"

"It doesn't take much to fall in love. But not everybody is the best option with all that's happened to you and all the hate you have for vampires. You need to be careful. Besides, we all know that Daniel is a player. He is well known for collecting girls and breaking their hearts."

Jenna's words imprinted on her mind along with Jake and Emma's previous warnings. She was feeling stupid beyond words. "I don't know Daniel. I don't read gossip magazines, and I sure don't watch any reality shows."

"Well, he is. But we can't believe everything we read in the magazines. He may be different, or he may truly fall for you."

"And pigs may fly," Jade added, rolling her eyes. "Now, enough about me. My life is depressing. What happened between you and Seth?"

"It was fine." She shrugged with a certain amount of disinterest that made Jade wonder.

"That bad?"

"Don't get me wrong, I was up for it. I was eager to be able to say to everybody that I had banged Seth."

"What a manly thing to say, Jenna!" Jade knew Jenna, and she was all about equal rights, even if it was to hook up randomly.

Jenna giggled and eventually rolled her eyes. "The guy just talked and talked and ranted about his life, being a vampire, and wanting to pursue a more serious career in the movie industry. He basically bored me to death since I wasn't there to listen to his insecurities and fears. I just wanted to fuck."

"So, Seth is a nice guy?"

"Yeah, I guess he is."

"Don't you feel bad for wanting to use him?"

Jenna arched an eyebrow. "Are you joking?"

"Yeah." Jade snorted, and Jenna burst into laughter.

They laughed until their sides hurt. Not because it was that funny, but because they needed to forget their troubles.

"If I were you, I would totally bang Daniel if he wanted to," Jenna said after a while of welcoming silence. "He is insanely hot. And so what if he's just trying to seduce you and get you into bed? He probably has a nice bed, and he'd show you a good time. You don't need to get married to every guy you fuck. Just let go and have some fun."

Jade shook her head. "You are a terrible adviser!"

"But an awesome friend!" She clapped her hands with a beaming smile.

"I don't know why I put up with you."

"Because you love me, and I'm the only one who won't let you down. Not even for a man. Fuck men! I have your back and you have mine. We will grow wrinkly together and keep each other company. Just like in 'Sex and the City'."

"That's a really old show. How did you even think of it?"

"Well, I've realized that I probably won't become a vampire and will have to stay human and get old. I don't mind, though. Vampire lives seem too sad."

"You're noticing this just now, are you?" Jade smirked at her best friend's epiphany.

"Well, I always liked the idea of staying young and maybe finding a mate for an eternity. But I don't think I can fall in love with just one person and be exclusive. I want to have fun. I want to live free and go to orgies!"

"What did you have to drink?" Jade asked with a concerned expression.

"Pool water! And it is time for you to have some, too!" Jenna yelped with excitement. Moving too fast for Jade to protect herself, Jenna pushed her into the pool.

A splash doused the poolside when her body hit the water. Jade struggled to swim to the surface and to breathe. Before she could drown, arms grasped her around the waist and she was rescued.

She gasped and coughed, climbing onto the edge, helped by the hands of a stranger. Someone was drawing circles on her back, asking her to breathe with a husky foreign accent. It was a guy, but it was not Daniel.

“I thought you could swim,” Jenna said next to her with a worried face.

Jade sucked in a deep breath. “I can, but my dress pulled me under.”

“She'll be okay,” the guy said next to her, pulling himself out of the pool and offering her his hand.

Jade lifted her eyes at the male figure and lost what little breath she had in her lungs. In front of her stood a gorgeous blond guy with all the enticing features of a Greek God. He was dripping water from his rather expensive tuxedo.

She blushed from head to toe. It was hard for her to find her voice and thank him for saving her.

“Did you bump your head?” he asked, arching an eyebrow when she didn't give him her hand and simply stood there gaping at him.

She shook her head and put her hand in his.

“I'm sorry, Jade. I thought it would be funny,” Jenna said with guilt shining in her eyes.

“That's okay, but the water is freezing!” she complained. Suddenly, she was swooped up from the pool as if she were a feather.

As all five foot ten of her stood soaking wet before the guy, she felt rather small. He was huge with broad shoulders. To add to his features, he was also extremely handsome with blue eyes and radiant blond hair. He was probably six foot four, but she couldn't say for sure because she was too busy staring at his gorgeous face.

"I'm Dominic," he introduced himself, leaning his face closer to hers. "Are you okay?"

"I'm fine, thanks," she replied, stepping back and almost falling into the pool once again.

Dominic grabbed her by the waist before she could fall, smiling.

Jade blushed at her lack of grace.

"She'll be even better when you take your hands off her," Daniel shouted, arriving next to them and pulling Jade from Dominic's grasp into his arms. "What happened?"

Jade looked into his eyes with blurred vision. He seemed concerned and jealousy was definitely the reason why he was rude to that other guy because his eyes were shifting.

"I pushed her," Jenna explained.

"And I saved her," Dominic added with a playful smirk.

"Thank you, but I'll take it from here." Daniel walked Jade to the mansion. It seemed like he was running from something, and he was definitely not happy.

"Who was that?" Jade tried to keep up with his strides, noticing she was leaving a trail of water behind.

"Someone who shouldn't be here. Forget all

about him. Let's get you dry. You have new clothes in your bedroom, and Jenna brought some of your old things."

"Daniel," she said, holding her ground and preventing him from walking further. "We need to talk." She put her hands on her waist.

He stared at her through narrowed eyes. He didn't look pleased. But she didn't like being around him anymore. His grip around her waist felt odd. She wasn't finding their kissing sessions that hot, either. If anything, she was feeling silly about letting him kiss her and for enjoying it so much. She felt stupid for believing his words about her being his beloved. Even if she'd said she didn't believe him. Yet, deep down, she was as romantic and stupid as any other girl. It seemed like he had preyed on that.

He leaned forward, and she stepped back.

"You can't kiss this away," she declared.

The emotion behind Jade's words caused him to lean back and better analyze her reactions. Something was *off*.

He grew impatient. All those people and their drama were making it harder and harder for him to win Jade's trust.

"I'm going to save us both a lot of time and simply ask, what's going on? I don't like guessing. So, spill it. What happened or did anyone say anything to make you recoil back into your shell and stop trusting me?”

“I just want to go home. That’s all,” she mumbled, and he knew she was lying.

Daniel noticed her shivering body and the goose bumps. She was cold and her eyes were analyzing her surroundings. He also looked around, searching for cameras and people who might be eavesdropping on their conversation.

He softened his voice. “This is your home now.”

“I don’t belong here.”

“You are mine, therefore, you belong here.”

She glared at him. “For how long?”

# CHAPTER TEN: DECEIVED

**JADE WANTED TO SCREAM**. She was mad at him for being such a player and a liar. She was mad for falling for his deceitful, charming personality.

Daniel questioned, “For how long what?”

“A week, two months, a year?” she demanded. “Until you get tired and find a new toy?”

“Hold on,” he asked, motioning for her to calm down with his hands. “Where is this coming from?”

Jade pursed her lips and crossed her arms over her chest.

“I don’t understand, Jade. Until now, you have told me that you didn’t want to be with me. That you wanted to go home. Now, you are accusing me of wanting to send you away?”

“Because you lied to me!”

“When?”

“Yesterday and today in my bedroom. You are still lying to me. You are an arrogant, conceited bastard who thinks he can sleep around with anyone he wants and play with other people’s feelings.”

“Well, first, I can do that. Second, I normally do that. Third, I can be arrogant and conceited, but I’m not a bastard. Women know what to expect from me when they decide to spend time in my bed.”

Jade looked at him unsure if he was being sarcastic or delusional. Her stomach was clenching and her eyes were stinging. “Well if it is that easy for you, why are you wasting your time with me? I clearly didn’t want to be here. I specifically asked to be sent away, and I had no intentions of sleeping with you.”

“*Had*? You *had* no intentions?” His wicked grin made her growl.

Jade turned her back on him and left for her bedroom, huffing at the way that the conversation was heading. Talking to him was useless. The more she did, the more she understood that he was insufferable and didn’t give a damn about other people’s feelings—about her feelings. He was bored, and he wanted to play with her heart. But she wasn’t going to let some arrogant vampire make her lower her guard and make her into his new sex toy. To Daniel, she was yet another score in his huge list of sex partners and not as special as he wanted her to believe.

FOR A MOMENT, Jade thought he wouldn’t let her go or would make an effort to follow her into her bedroom and talk her out of it. She thought he would, at least, try and persuade her that it wasn’t true—that she was special. Watching too many romantic movies would do that to a person.

She used to be proud of thinking that she was not a gullible girl. However, she was beginning to understand that the right guy with the right words was enough to convince any girl to trust them only to get burned in the process.

Maybe Jenna was right. It was stupid to think that love was the solution to all of the problems. Perhaps it was nothing more than lust that was making the world keep turning, stupid and meaningless lust. That was what she was to guys—a piece of meat, a nice package, a pretty face. Someone they could bang and have a good time with. And that prick was old enough to know what words made naive girls lower their guard and let him take away the rest of their innocence.

After getting out of her wet clothes and showering, Jade started throwing her belongings into a bag with teary eyes.

*Why am I crying?*

She should be mad and break everything in that damn bedroom. Sadness was for the weak. She was strong, she was independent, and she would get over it! There was more to life than love, passion, and a feeling of belonging. Wasn't there?

Someone knocked on the door, and Jade froze for a moment. Could it be Daniel? And, if it was, what was she going to say to him?

She wiped her tears and opened the door.

It was Jenna.

Any remaining hope she had definitely died right about then.

Wide-eyed, Jenna was panting. "Where have you been? It was crazy downstairs."

"What do you mean?" Jade asked, trying to conceal her sadness.

"Have you been crying?" Jenna questioned,

getting in and closing the door behind. "Why are you packing your things?"

Jade indulged her curiosity. "Because I want to leave. Because I'm angry and stupid. Even though I know I can't leave, I wish I could."

"You aren't making any sense! And Daniel went crazy downstairs and got into a fight with Seth. They broke things, and it was insane how fast they were and how they shattered glasses, chairs, and tables. Daniel was so angry with Seth! He kept asking what he had done. But Seth didn't know why he was mad at him, so Dominic had to break the fight. Then, Daniel punched Dominic right on his face, and Dominic punched him back and... Well, it was a mess." Jenna stopped gesticulating and mimicking punches to describe the scene and dropped her hands along her body with a shrug.

Jade's heart pounded faster because of everything Jenna was telling her.

"Is Daniel all right?" Jade asked, putting both hands against her chest.

"Just some minor bruises. He will heal. Sakura took him to his bedroom and the party ended. Everybody went back to their own places and the crew was sent away. We were told to go to our bedrooms, but I was worried about you."

"I'm fine."

"Did the fight have anything to do with you? Did Seth make a pass at you? Daniel was extremely jealous of Dominic downstairs!"

"I don't know why he fought with his brother. And I really don't care," Jade lied. "Now, I need to lie down and rest. I have a headache."

It was not entirely a lie, but Jade needed to be alone.

Jenna told her to take an aspirin and rest. She would wake her up the next day, and they would spend some time near the pool to have fun.

Jade nodded and closed the door.

Her stomach was upset because she was feeling guilty. She was also worried about Daniel. *Why did he attack his brother?* Seth was nothing but nice to her.

Another soft knock on the door woke her up from her thoughts. Jenna probably wanted to talk to her and make sure she was okay. But when she opened the door, it wasn't Jenna on the other side. It was Daniel, with his white shirt unbuttoned, showing his perfect torso. He had a bag of ice against his eyebrow. He was bruised and bled from his left eyebrow. Even if it was nice to check out Daniel's torso and get a little flustered, she was more concerned with understanding what he was doing there.

"What do you want?" she asked, trying to sound nonchalant.

# CHAPTER ELEVEN: THE WEB OF LIES

**DANIEL RUBBED THE BACK** of his neck at her cold reply.

"To apologize." The answer made Jade stare at him with an arched eyebrow and folded arms. She was defensive, and he still didn't know what he had done to make her hate his guts, *again*.

"About what?"

"I don't know. You tell me. Seth swears he didn't do anything. I may not trust the guy, but I know when he is saying the truth. So, who was it?"

"Who was what?"

"Really, Jade? Are you going to play dumb?" he asked, losing his cool. "Can't you see I'm hurt and this stings like hell?"

Jade placed a hand on her hip. "Do you want me to feel sorry for you?"

"It would be a start. And then you could kiss me to make all of the pain go away," he added with a mischievous grin.

Jade's eyes narrowed, and she grabbed the door. He stopped her before she could close it in his face.

"You're a vampire. It will heal quickly."

"You could still kiss me to make me feel better."

"I could, but then I would have to throw up," she added.

It was his time to arch an eyebrow. "Is kissing me so bad?"

"I think it's worse than you imagine."

"And why is that happening?"

"Because you lied to me!" she snapped.

"Maybe if you elaborate a bit more I can defend myself," he proposed, and she growled at him. "That is sexy and all, but I would like to know what is going on and why you are mad at me."

Jade indulged his curiosity with a sarcastic comeback. "Why don't you go and ask your ex?"

Daniel frowned. "What does Emma have to do with this?"

"She said you pull this stunt on every girl you want to fuck."

"What stunt?" he asked, trying to stay calm but blood was boiling in his veins. Jade took too long to answer. "Okay, that is it! We are going to the source of the problem, and I'll ask her what she's done." He tossed the ice bag on the floor, grabbing Jade's wrist and walking down the corridor to where Emma was staying.

"Daniel, stop! Just stop. Please," she pleaded. "You're hurting me!"

"Well, I'm trying not to hurt you, but it is hard when you're fighting to escape from my grasp. Just follow me."

"You don't need to go after her. I'll tell you," she said. "Stop! There's no need to make another scene."

JADE HAD NO IDEA what Daniel would do to the other girl. He had hit Seth because he thought it was his fault. She didn't want anyone else getting hurt. He eventually stopped midway and let go of her.

"You really are a jerk! Do you know that?"

"Yes, people keep telling me that. For what it's worth, I've been trying not to be a jerk with you and things are not going my way, are they? So, I don't have any other choice than to act like a jerk."

"That reasoning is stupid," Jade complained, rubbing her wrist where it hurt.

"It's the only one I've got."

"Well, it's ridiculous." Her voice shook and her eyes sparkled with unshed tears. "You are stupid, and I'm sick of stupid people."

"News flash, Jade! People are stupid. People are idiots."

"News flash, Daniel! I don't give a fuck about people, and I sure don't give a fuck about you. You can rot in hell for all I care. You can keep your stupid romantic words and your stupid lies for the other girls. I'm tired, I'm pissed, and I don't want to see your face anymore today!"

"Really?" He smirked, folding his arms across his chest and making Jade's eyes narrow with disbelief. "You are mad at me, but you don't care about me? *Interesting.*"

"I'm mad because you lied."

"And you won't tell me what lie that was. I'm waiting. Tell me before I do something really stupid like break that goddamned door and ask that fucking liar what she did this time to ruin my life!"

Jade pulled him before he could do that.

"You told me that I was your beloved, but you lied. You say that to all the girls. You said that to her." Jade felt the tears wanting to roll down her eyes and the pain obstructed her throat.

Before she could breathe, Daniel grabbed her against him and sped his way down the corridor, stopping inside her bedroom. He threw her onto the bed. She complained as she sat up and held on to her dizzy head. He locked the door and stood in front of the bed staring down at her menacingly.

Jade gasped, confused by his actions. She was afraid of what he was going to do. It was no use to scream. His black eyes and extended fangs weren't helping her to calm down.

Daniel spoke with a serious face. "Let's get this straight. I don't go around saying that to women. I have never said that to Emma. Why on earth would you share that information with her when you know that she is here just to spread her venom?"

"I don't know anything of the sort. I didn't tell her anything. She told me that herself, and you've told me that inside your home, away from the cameras. How could she have known anything about that?"

"How the hell should I know?"

Suddenly, Daniel stopped cursing and became pensive. Jade caught her breath and kneeled on the bed. Her hair was still wet from the shower, and she was wearing a short-sleeved cotton pajama top with shorts.

"That sneaky, lying, rotten bastard," Daniel whispered through his clenched teeth. "He put cameras inside my house when I told him not to. I'm going to snap his neck and bury his wolf ass in the ground!"

"Did he record us when we were in the bedroom?" Jade panicked, remembering what they did, the things they said to one another, and the kisses.

She put her hands on her cheeks, ashamed and humiliated. Tears ran down her cheeks, making Daniel take a seat next to her and pull her into his arms. Her tears and pain seemed to be enough to calm him down.

"Come on, baby, don't cry. I'm going to fix it. Besides, it wouldn't do him any good if he were to broadcast to the nation that you're my beloved. His show would be ruined. He gains a lot more by turning you against me and making me go crazy. I tend to lose my mind," he said sweetly into her ear, caressing her hair, and clearing the tears with his thumbs. "He must have told Emma, so she would use that against us. She wanted to make you jealous, so she could make her move. I've told you not to believe others, didn't I, Jade?"

Sobbing, she asked, "Why would they be that mean to me?"

"Because there is a lot of money at stake. Jake is going to lose his position as a director of this show if he doesn't increase the ratings. And Emma is losing a lot of leading roles in movies because she's getting older. She wants to be turned into a vampire. The only way she can become one is if a vampire accepts her to be his bride for eternity or, at least, for a lot more time than five years. There are strict laws among our kind. There are strict laws among humans."

"Daniel, if I find out that you are lying to me, I'll put a damn stake through your heart," Jade whispered against his chest, gripping his arms.

His scent was calming her down and his voice was making her strong again. But, even if she wanted to believe his words, she was not going to let him trick her. He had been warned.

"Don't be mean, Jade. You shouldn't threaten the person who will love you more than life."

Jade hid her face in the crook of his neck. "If you break my heart, I don't need your love, do I?"

"And if you break mine?"

"You have no heart to break."

JADE'S WORDS STUNG. Trying to lighten the mood, Daniel joked, "Of course I do. I've just been ignoring it too well until I met you."

"Why do you have to joke about everything?"

"Because life is boring, so we need to joke about things. Besides, I may be kidding around, but I'm scared."

"Of what?"

"Of someone else trying to take you away from me or trying to make you hate me."

Jade looked up to meet his eyes, and he noticed how her cheeks warmed and flushed at his confession. He could feel his heart fluttering in his chest as a pleasant sensation spread throughout his body.

"I still won't sleep with you," she declared when he was leaning down to kiss her.

Her words were like a bucket of cold water over Daniel's head. "Come on, give me a break! I'm a nice guy!"

"Not really, no."

He smirked which made her smile back at him. "I can convince you differently if I try harder."

Her voice came out vulnerable when she retorted, "Maybe, but then I would regret it tomorrow and hate your guts."

"I seriously doubt that you would regret it. It would be the best sex you've ever had."

Jade tore her eyes away and stared at the wall behind them with pouting lips. Daniel felt her body tensing. He furrowed his eyebrows. *No way!* He smiled and placed his nose in the crook of her neck, inhaling her scent.

He touched her skin with his words. "So what do you want to do if we can't have sex now? It is still early for me to sleep. The sun hasn't come up yet."

"I'm starving," she whispered, staring back at his baby blue eyes.

"Then let's go downstairs. I can cook something for you, and we can stay on the couch, watching reruns of old movies on TV."

She nodded with a huge smile that made Daniel's eyes sparkle. It made him happy to see such a reaction on her face. "And then we can have sex!"

Jade's smile faltered, and she moved her hand to slap him.

"I'm kidding." He chuckled, taking hold of her hand. "Can we at least kiss?"

She nodded fast enough for him to crack a smile. Once he kissed her, he sped downstairs with her in his arms.

# CHAPTER TWELVE: DANIEL'S BEDROOM

**DANIEL WOKE UP LAZILY** when the lights in his bedroom turned on. They were automatic, and he used them to wake up and start his workday, which didn't necessarily mean that he left the bedroom. On the contrary, he had everything he needed in one room.

He sighed and blinked several times, stroking Jade's hair. She had her head resting on his chest, and her arms were wrapped around his torso.

She complained about the sudden bright lights.

He kissed the top of her head and looked across the bedroom to his work desk that had electronic devices and computer paraphernalia.

His bedroom consisted of four white walls and LCD lights in the ceiling mimicking the sun rays and the blue sky outside. It had a royal king size bed and a closet. Next to the desk was a corridor that led to a full bathroom with a huge tub and shower combo with custom porcelain and a wood vanity with a matching mirror. It wasn't much, but he didn't need much to live. He had his own office for when it was night. During the day hours, he preferred to work from his bedroom and give instructions to his employees from there.

Jade squirmed, warning him that she might wake up.

Daniel didn't want to move to turn off the lights. It would wake her up. But the lights were waking her, too. He was faced with a dilemma. Her movements made the strap of her nightclothes slip and revealed the perfection of her breasts. Her skin was soft, silky, and warm. The sound of her beating heart was soothing and not agonizing as he might have expected because of the blood lust. It had calmed down since he tasted her blood. There was one thing he craved more than her blood—her trust.

Stroking her hair, he inhaled her perfume, utterly captivated by her innocence and beauty.

Her eyelids fluttered open. She turned her head to face Daniel, studying him with her hazel eyes.

His lips automatically curled into a smile and his gaze softened.

Registering a sudden increase in her heartbeat, he realized that she was assessing where she was as her eyes focused on the unfamiliar place. Closing her eyes, she relaxed and inhaled deeply.

"How did I end up here?" she mumbled after clearing her throat. She rolled over and stretched, blinking up at the sky-blue ceiling. "Why is it so bright in here?"

Daniel propped his head up, watching her as she adjusted her pajamas to make sure she was fully clothed. He smirked before answering. "You fell asleep on the couch, and I brought you here."

"You could have taken me to my bedroom instead."

"I had promised you that you would end up sleeping in my bedroom before the end of the night," he teased, turning on his back and flashing a mischievous grin while flexing his arms behind his head.

JADE STRETCHED HER sore neck and sat up a bit straighter. Her gaze fell on his shirt. It was unbuttoned and was showing his naked torso gleaming in the artificial light. He was ridiculously attractive—she couldn't deny that.

It was extremely bright inside the bedroom. She stared at the ceiling once again and realized that it was made of liquid crystal displays that were imitating a clear blue sky with rays of sunshine. That was where the light was coming from and illuminating the bedroom as if it was morning. She felt a mix of sadness and tenderness for Daniel. He couldn't face sunlight, but he craved it so much that he made his bedroom look like it was set in an open space outdoors.

It was beautiful and gloomy at the same time.

Jade relaxed and stared at him. For the first time, Daniel averted his eyes and shifted uncomfortably on the bed before he completely got up and trailed his way to the left side of the spacious bedroom. He sat in front of the huge computer desk that had a lot of black screens, keyboards, and headphones.

Daniel seemed troubled as if he had guessed her thoughts and they angered him.

Jade sighed and stared at his back, hoping he would look back at her. He didn't. He turned on the computers with the press of a button, and a colorful display of streets and places showed up on the screens. It was like he was seeing life through someone else's eyes. It was his window to the outside world during the day.

"What do you want to have for breakfast?" he asked, without turning around. He put a set of headphones over his ears and adjusted the sound.

"Black coffee will be fine," she answered, unsure if he had heard her.

He did because seconds later he spoke to someone and placed her order.

Jade got up and stood behind his back. "What is all of this?"

"These are my eyes and ears in the world when it's daytime and I can't get out of here."

"Clever." She stretched out her arms. "What time is it? I have to check on Stevie and get him ready for school."

"He's already at school. I hired someone to take care of that. You have slept for several hours. Plus, you are on a sort of vacation from your normal life while you are spending time here with me."

"I always kiss Stevie before he goes to school." She pouted, guilt taking over her expression. Her brother must be feeling abandoned while she's been busy with Daniel. She had to make up for losing the track of time. Stevie was her responsibility, and he wasn't used to being left alone with strangers.

"You can talk to him when he comes back. It will be in an hour. In the meantime, you will eat breakfast and then you can join the girls in the pool."

"What?" She stared at the screen that Daniel was pointing at.

The evil Emma and her friend, Jenna, were sunbathing near the pool without any care in the world while talking about something that Jade couldn't hear.

"I have no intentions of talking to that lying bitch without smacking her down."

"That would be something worth seeing." Daniel chuckled. "But weren't you the one who didn't want me to hurt her last night?"

"It wouldn't look good if you hurt her, would it? I, on the other hand, have nothing to lose," she declared, folding her arms.

"You're worried about my reputation, are you?" He turned around in his chair and pulled her against him.

Placing his head against her stomach, Jade's body quivered in response to his touch. Instead of recoiling, she unfolded her arms and placed one hand on his shoulder and the other on his head, caressing it.

"I'm growing on you, am I not?" he questioned with a grin.

"Maybe."

Daniel nibbled on his lower lip. "Just be smarter and pretend you've believed everything she told you."

"So you don't want me to punch her?"

Daniel chuckled and nuzzled his nose against her stomach, bringing out a giggle from her. “It's cool that you would hit her for me, but I just want you to put on a pretty bikini and show them how gorgeous you are beneath these clothes. Then, I want you to put some sun block on and sunbathe for an hour or two, so I can smell the sun on you and lick it from your skin.”

“That's gross,” she complained as his hands gripped her hips.

“That would be anything but gross, trust me.” He lifted his head to look at her with lustful eyes.

“Perv,” she whispered, rolling her eyes.

Daniel wiggled his eyebrows, and she laughed before covering his face with her palm. He used his strength to rise from his chair with her in his arms. Lifting her feet off the ground, Daniel sped his way to the bed where he laid her down.

His movements didn't frighten her. She was beginning to trust him. Daniel had become more caring after they made peace.

Jade used her elbows to raise her upper body, trying to figure out his intentions. She shivered in anticipation as his lips hovered over hers, and she could perceive the heat that was coming from his body, almost touching her.

“What?” She stroked his face, curious about his indecipherable gaze.

“You're beautiful.”

“I think the light is damaging your ability to see properly.”

"I don't need to see to know that you are a beautiful and brave person. I can't tell you how much I love the fact that you are real and courageous. You've been taking care of your little brother—all by yourself—while working and studying. That's brave, that makes me respect you, and that makes you beautiful."

"Why are you saying all of that?" she asked softly, caught in his eyes and captivated by his words.

"Because I want you to take me seriously." He lowered his lips to her forehead, placing a kiss there. "I want you to understand that you are no longer alone." He landed a kiss on her cheek and another on the tip of her nose.

Jade was following his movements with parted lips. Her breath hitched.

"I'll prove that you can trust me, but I need you to see me for who I truly am and not for what other people think I am."

Jade nodded, lifting up her head, so she could brush her lips against his.

He smiled. "And, baby," he whispered with a glint of naughtiness in his stare, "there's nothing gross or perverted about licking and kissing your skin. I'm going to give you a demonstration and then you'll have to work for more."

Jade furrowed her brows, unsure of what he was talking about.

Daniel grinned, and she stopped breathing when his lips crashed against hers.

It was a demanding and hungry kiss where their tongues touched and danced to a rhythm of their own urgency for contact and relief. Jade fell back on the mattress, using her hands to tangle her fingers in his hair. She pulled his head back, so she could deepen the kiss. Their lips moved back and forth, each trying to consume the other. She always felt close to him when they were kissing. It wasn't just a physical thing. It was almost mental as if she could feel him inside her mind, tearing apart her defensive walls and all of her fears of letting someone get close to her.

The heat of their kiss seared its way from her breasts and down to her core. She gasped when he plastered his solid body against her soft one and moaned when his fingers brushed her skin, stretching the fabric of the singlet to let her cleavage show. His mouth trailed kisses down her neck and his tongue flicked between her breasts, making her shift and moan from lust while pinned under him.

Desire washed over her like a wave of fire, clouding her mind. Her breasts tingled as she hungered for his touch. His mouth didn't give her the relief she longed for as he trailed it up her chest and neck. His tongue licked the tender spot below her left earlobe while his hands sustained the weight of his body.

Somehow, the vampire managed to get up and move away from her. She opened her eyes in a daze, adjusting to the sudden change.

She wanted more.

"The demonstration is over," he said, smiling mischievously. "Do you still think it's gross?" He offered her his hand.

Jade shook her head, flustered as she got up and tried to balance on her feet.

"Now be a good girl, go eat your breakfast, and have fun by the pool. I have some urgent businesses to take care of, but I promise that this night will be for the two of us," he spoke tenderly, his eyes flickering black.

Jade gulped and sucked on her bottom lip while trying to calm herself. Every fiber of her body wanted to go back to Daniel's arms and continue what they were doing. Staring at his perfectly shaped, slim torso wasn't helping her ability to stay away. She found her body moving involuntarily toward Daniel, and her mouth met his, so she could taste his kiss one more time.

Moments after, she pressed her forehead against his to recover her breath and soothe her racing heart. She smiled, stroking his lips with her fingers.

"What are you thinking?" Daniel asked.

"You can be sweet when you want to."

"Just don't tell anyone about that. It would ruin my bad boy reputation," he whispered.

She chuckled.

"I've got to work now. One of my employees will bring you coffee. Stevie will be home in an hour, and I would like it if you had some fun with your brother and friend while sunbathing for me."

"Okay. I'll leave you alone to work." She stepped back after kissing him one last time. "I'm going to my bedroom to shower. How do I get out of here?" She looked around, not seeing an exit. There was only a door that led to a bathroom.

Daniel walked to his table and typed something on the keyboard which opened a secret sliding door.

Jade smirked. He liked concealed doors. "Paranoid much, are we?"

"I like my privacy, even inside my own house."

She blew him a kiss and disappeared into the corridor.

# CHAPTER THIRTEEN: STEVIE

**STEVIE LOVED PANCAKES**. It was her sibling's guilty pleasure. Jade normally made them in the morning before going to work. Since she was probably unemployed for missing work, and she hadn't made breakfast for Stevie for two days now, she was making up for the lost time.

While he was doing his homework on the kitchen counter, she was preparing pancakes and helping him with Calculus. He didn't really need help, but Jade liked to keep an eye on him.

With all the new technologies, kids were learning to read and write faster than in the past. In Stevie's case, he was gifted. Therefore, he had mastered writing and reading earlier than the rest of his classmates. He was already solving logical problems that were intended for older children and had a large vocabulary for a five-year-old. That didn't mean he didn't enjoy drawing and painting like any other kid his age would. But, he was a perfectionist, and his drawings of animals were remarkably accurate and creative. He also had an excellent memory.

Jade was humming as she cooked. She had missed their time together. She was also answering all of the questions her brother had about the new home and Daniel. He was astute and understood that something was going on. In turn, that made him worried about his sister. It was easier to soothe him when Jade told him they were going to spend time at the pool with Jenna and a new woman. He loved water, so he got excited.

After eating the pancakes, they changed into their swimsuits. Jade also wanted to know where he was sleeping. She was dumbfounded when she saw the spectacular room that Daniel had prepared for him. The number of toys and crafts Daniel had bought to please the kid was surprising. Jade felt perplexed and livid. It would be much harder for Stevie to want to go back home with a bedroom like that there. She didn't know what Daniel was thinking or even if he was thinking at all. Giving false hopes to kids should be a capital sin. They weren't rich. Stevie just had the essentials. Jade didn't have money to give him any of those amazing toys. She didn't want her brother to have a taste of what it was like to be rich only to lose everything when it was time for them to leave Daniel's place and get back to their normal lives. She had to talk to Daniel about that and put up some boundaries.

But first, she talked to Stevie, making him sit down on his bed next to her.

"Baby, you know that this is temporary, don't you?"

He stared at her with his big brown eyes. "What do you mean?"

"This bedroom where you are sleeping...it's temporary. By the end of this week, we'll return to our place and...you can't take anything with you."

"But the beautiful girl said that we were family now."

Jade stared at him, puzzled. "Yes, I know. But I also told you that we were staying for a week."

Stevie pouted and looked at his wiggling feet.

"What's wrong?"

"I like Sakura. She's nice. We became friends. She likes playing games, and she's smart. She knows a lot of things about animals. We drew a whale and the bottom of the ocean together."

"I like Sakura, too, but this is theirs, not ours."

"Can I still play with her once we leave?"

Jade blinked several times, unsure of what to tell him. Shrugging, she mumbled, "I guess; if she wants to visit us sometime."

Stevie's lips formed into a smile, and then he became serious. "And Daniel?"

Jade's stomach flipped at his question. She decided to give him an innocent answer. "If he desires, he can visit us, too." Biting her lip, she asked, "Do you know what they are?"

Stevie looked away. "I know they're vampires, but they seem nice. I like them even if you said we should fear vampires," he said in his sweet childlike voice, making her heart clench in her chest. "Jenna likes vampires. She had a vampire boyfriend. He was nice, too. They are a lot like me. They are vulnerable to the sun... I know that you don't like them, and I won't play with Sakura anymore if you don't want me to."

"That's okay, baby," she said, caressing his head. "I like her, too."

"Is Daniel your boyfriend?"

"I don't know. He... It's complicated. We'll need to stay in his mansion for a week. After that, we can go back home."

"And why did Sakura say that we are family now?"

"She likes us." She smiled softly. "And Daniel says—" Jade stopped what she was going to say because she didn't want grown up problems troubling him. "I guess, they feel lonely and want someone here to keep them company."

"I like having company, too. You work too much. We don't have a lot of time to be together. And, you're exhausted a lot of the time. You looked pretty last night in the new dress, just like a movie star."

Jade smiled, but her eyes were shining with unshed tears. "Honey, I wish I was rich enough to give you a room like this, but you know that we're poor. I work a lot to pay the rent and give you food and medicine. I'm not complaining about it because I love you to pieces." Getting up from the bed, she crouched in front of him, holding on to his hands. She wanted him to look at her and understand that he shouldn't get attached to that new bedroom. "It's you and me against the world," she whispered, leaning her forehead against his. "When I finish college, I can find a better job than being an office clerk and a part-time waitress. Then, I can give you a bedroom just like this one."

"I would rather choose the heroes I want."

She smiled and nodded. "Whatever you want."

"But can I take the train home when we leave? Daniel said it was mine."

Frowning, she asked, "What train?"

"We are going to build a train station, and we are already building the railway around the city. Daniel said he was going to give me a train like the old ones. You know, the steam locomotives? He explained to me how they worked, and I helped him paint the trees and build 3D puzzles of old western buildings."

"Where?" She blinked in surprise at the amount of time Daniel had spent with Stevie while she had been sleeping the previous day.

"In Daniel's playroom. Hasn't he shown it to you yet?"

Jade shook her head.

"He has several toys there. Even a big spaceship and lots of action figures of older cartoons and movies. We even played with heroes costumes."

"Oh!" She gasped, astonished. "Was it yesterday or did you also see him this morning?"

"I was with him after I came back from the hospital. He said you were getting dressed for a party."

"Yeah, we went to a party. Did you like Daniel?"

"He is cool. And he seems nice," Stevie said.

"Because he played with you and gave you stuff?"

"You always say to mistrust people who give us too many gifts," he retorted.

"Yes, I do. I've taught you well."

"Daniel is nice because he talks about you all the time. He asked me things about you, and he said you were the greatest sister in the world. I can't disagree with that."

"Oh!" Jade chuckled at his words. That clever vampire had played another card to win Stevie's affection, or he used the kid to get precious information about her. "What did you tell him about me?"

"I didn't tell him that you drink milk from the carton even if you tell me not to," he said. Jade giggled and ruffled his hair. Her little brother was adorable. "I told him that you work hard to raise me since our parents died. I said that you are funny, and you like to eat popcorn with me when we go to the movies, which we don't do often because you have double shifts, and I also get sick when I eat too much sugar."

"Okay." Jade rubbed her nose against his. Stevie chuckled as he pushed her away, playfully. "Did you tell him anything else about me?"

"I also told him that you make up a lot of funny stories when we are drawing together, even if you aren't good at drawing. But, you are incredible at taking care of sick people and that you want to be a doctor. You study really hard for that."

Jade probed further. "Did he ask anything about what happened to our parents?"

He shook his head. "Did I do something wrong?"

Getting up, she assured him, "No, baby. Let's get ready for the pool."

Jade didn't have to tell him twice. He got ready in no time, and they made their way to the pool.

When they arrived, Jenna and Emma were talking while the cameras recorded them. It seemed as if all eyes were on Emma like she was the most important person there.

Jade didn't care and was thankful that there were no cameras around her brother and her.

Upon arrival, Stevie ran over to kiss Jenna, and they chatted for a while. Emma was actually nice with the kid as she introduced herself to him. Stevie was polite to her and gave her a kiss. He had seen movies where she was the leading actress—at least, the ones that were age appropriate for him. He was a charming boy with his chocolate eyes and a cute dimpled smile, so it didn't surprise Jade when Emma gave him her attention.

Taking her place next to them, Jade took off her dress and showed her pink bikini. The cameras moved to film her. She felt uncomfortable, but she tried to act normal and lay down on the pool chair next to Jenna.

Meanwhile, Stevie helped her put on sun block, and she bathed him in it because she didn't want him to have sunburns and then get sick. The sun wasn't good for him. He got weak if he didn't have the right protection on, or his skin erupted into blisters. He was a sensitive kid with lots of allergies. His allergy shots helped minimize the problems and let him have a normal life. They still needed to take extra precautions when it came to his health.

Soon enough, Stevie was jumping and running around. He was excited to get in the water. Since he had eaten, he had to wait a bit longer. Besides, Jade wanted to let the sun touch her skin so Daniel could... Her stomach filled with crazy butterflies when she thought about it. Thinking about his kisses left her aroused.

The sexy vampire was destroying her defenses, and she hoped she wouldn't get hurt because of it. She should act smarter. Still, it had been a pleasant night after the party was over and the misunderstandings had been cleared up.

*Am I falling for his story about being his beloved?*

Was she ready to put her trust in him and fall for his charm? She had to proceed with caution. Vampires tended to be irrational when defied or when someone denied them what they obsessed about.

For the time being, she had to understand that she was trapped in a vampire's mansion and had to participate in some stupid reality show that was the symbol of everything that was wrong with their society. Her future was uncertain and her world had been turned upside down.

Jade sighed deeply and squealed when she felt the cold water hit her legs. Looking up, she saw Stevie with a wicked smile. He had his hand in the pool and was aiming a water splash at Jenna.

"Stevie!" Jade warned him before he would make Jenna jump from her chair.

"You're all lazy! I want someone to play with me!" he complained.

Jade sighed in defeat. She was going to get up to play with him, but Emma beat her to it.

"What do you want to do?" Emma asked, getting up and walking to his side.

"Swim and play with the ball," he replied.

Emma offered him a smile and patted his head.

"Do you know how to swim?" she asked in her sweet voice.

"Of course!"

"Does he?" Emma questioned Jade.

She nodded as she sat down and leaned forward to watch them interact. She didn't like the girl, but she wasn't going to forbid her from talking to her brother.

"So, let's swim," Emma proposed, stretching her arms and legs. "Let's see who gets in first!" she dared him and dove into the pool.

Stevie got up fast and jumped, splashing water all around them. Then he surfaced and swam next to Emma who started to throw water at him.

The two were playing and having fun. Jade was a bit taken aback because Emma was being nice to him and acting like a kid herself. Maybe she wasn't such a bad person, after all. Maybe she was just in love with Daniel and wanted him back. Or maybe she was trying to keep her career on solid ground. Jade didn't know. Daniel was the one who had dated the actress. One thing Jade was sure about, Emma would do everything to get things to go her way.

One hour later, Jenna had joined in on the fun. Jade stood nearby, watching them because she didn't want to get wet.

Jade had her reasons, and she let her brother have fun with the girls as they played with the ball and splashed water all around. Was Daniel watching them or if he was too busy with his work? Abruptly, she realized that the vampire was assaulting her thoughts more than she wished and was willing to admit.

The fun stopped when the director came out from somewhere unknown and urged everybody to go to their bedrooms. They had a contest coming up, and they needed to look pretty and elegant.

After drying Stevie off and getting him inside, Jade met Stevie's babysitter, Molly. Molly was young and friendly. Stevie seemed to like her and began chatting about his day at school with the girl. Jade questioned her about what their plans were for the evening and instructed her about his favorite cartoons on the TV and what he should eat for dinner. Also, she made sure that Stevie would be in bed at half past eight.

After kissing Stevie, Jade stopped in the corridor, deciding whether to go to Daniel's bedroom or not. She didn't want to seem too eager to see him and comply with his request. She decided to go back to her bedroom at around six in the evening and noticed the new green cocktail dress that was laid out on her bed.

As soon as the sun went down and the vampires could come out to play, the real circus would start again. Despite the beautiful dress on her bed, she had no idea what they had in store for that night.

The noise of her bedroom door opening and closing startled her. She spun around and relaxed when she saw it was Daniel. She should have locked the door behind her. But if she had, he wouldn't have been able to come in, and her heart wouldn't be skyrocketing as it was in that moment.

Jade nibbled on her lower lip, drinking in the sight of him. He was wearing a T-shirt and a pair of jeans. He was barefoot and looking sexy as hell with his messy, wet hair.

Silently, he shortened the distance between them.

Her heart was in her mouth. She was agitated and eager to have him even closer. But he was just staring at her with his mischievous smile that was making her body temperature rise to extremes.

*Isn't he going to say anything?*

He didn't. He motioned for her to come closer, and her feet moved of their own volition.

Jade parted her lips slightly to be able to breathe better. The vampire lowered his face, smirking before kissing her lips. It was a gentle touch, asking for her permission and her surrender.

On instinct, Jade closed her eyes, offering her mouth to him. A wave of passion hit her when he pulled her into a hug. Wrapping her arms around his neck, everything around them ceased to exist. She leaned into his body and let it happen. Fireworks, butterflies—nothing was accurate enough to describe the feelings that were taking over her body. He was just kissing her, his tongue touching her tongue, his lips brushing and caressing her lips, but it was enough to melt her to magma.

"Jade," he called huskily, trailing kisses down her throat. "I told you what I was going to do to you, didn't I?"

She sighed in reply.

"So, can I?"

Jade placed her hands on his face and made him raise it to stare at her. They shared a brief moment of untamed lust flickering in their eyes. She was finding him to be the sexiest guy ever, and she couldn't care less that he was a vampire. She should be more reasonable. Then again, she was pretty sure that Daniel didn't care about being reasonable, either.

"I thought you were good at keeping your promises," she whispered against his lips, smirking when the realization of her words hit him. "What do I smell like?"

"Like sunshine and heaven," he murmured, brushing the hair off her face and making her heart stop with the notion that she trusted him with her life, literally.

"No biting," Jade warned him before letting him continue.

"Promise, just licking and kissing," he assured her, his face betraying no humor.

It should have calmed down Jade's heart, but it made it beat even faster. Her cheeks became redder. Yet she was a big girl. It was about time to stop running from physical contact.

"I'll be careful, Jade," he added as if he was reading her mind. It made her feel better.

Jade nodded, losing her breath when he cupped her face and kissed her. Closing her eyes, she let it go.

# CHAPTER FOURTEEN: SWEET OBLIVION

**DANIEL'S BODY TENSED WITH** anticipation when he noticed Jade's lustful eyes. It warmed his heart, the fact that she trusted him enough to let him kiss her and show her pleasure. He could hear her erratic heartbeat and sense the remaining tension that she was trying to chase away. The sensation of each kiss he planted on her skin was enough to drive him insane.

She was beautiful, and her scent was like a drug. The perfume of the sun mixed with sun block and vanilla were enough to make him want to lick her and nibble on her softly until his lips went numb. He wanted to know how she tasted, and it didn't mean he wanted to taste her blood. No, he had done that already. It was enticing, mind-blowing. However, there was something he wanted to taste more than her blood. He wanted to taste her skin and the softness of her quivering body while she spasmed in pleasure.

Nonetheless, it was more than a taste experience. It was also an auditory experience. He wanted to listen to her moaning and gasping under his hands and lips. For the time being, he was kissing her tenderly, tracing his tongue along her lip until she parted her lips and let him slip his tongue in.

He sighed deeply, enjoying the slow and tender movement of their tongues against one another. His hands cupped her face as his fingers tangled in her hair and made her tilt her head slightly back, so he could explore every inch of her mouth. He wanted to melt into her and leave her panting for more.

Jade's fingers drew paths of fire down his chest. She hooked them in the sides of his T-shirt and slowly pulled it upward. With her open palms, she made his skin sizzle.

Stepping back, Daniel got rid of his T-shirt and registered her narrowed eyes, consumed by lust. She was flustered, and her breath was irregular. He said he was the one who was going to kiss her everywhere, but he didn't want to deny her anything. She could stare at him all she wanted. Also, he wanted to feel their skin touching.

He smiled, pleased, when her hands undid her summer dress. It fell down her body, caressing her curves in the process. She was gorgeous with flawless alabaster skin, long brown hair, and mouthwatering round breasts. Her nipples pebbled against the fabric of the bikini, showing her arousal. He could stare at her the entire day, but he had already had his share of staring at the TV screen in his bedroom while she was at the pool. In that moment, he wanted to take off all of her clothes and craved to touch every square inch of her body with his lips and hands.

JADE'S EYES WERE LOCKED on his perfectly ripped torso. She felt her heart ache with anticipation. They stood there for a moment in an awkward silence until Daniel offered his hands for her to take and come closer to him.

She moved to grab his hands, and he pulled her near, making her giggle. He dipped his mouth to the hollow of her neck. She could only smile, her insides dancing with happiness and her body melting under his touch. Grasping her hips, he took possession of her mouth, transforming the giggling into moans.

Jade's hands ran down his chest, and her body shivered in pleasure. Daniel's lips trailed little kisses across her cheeks, eyelids, forehead, and nose, making her exhale a deep sigh when he sucked on her earlobe.

"This may take some time," he said against her mouth, "but I will enjoy it immensely. So, let me do it without distractions."

"What distractions?"

"Your hands on my pants," he growled huskily when her finger ran along the waistband of his boxers. "Do you like what you see?"

"Yes."

In a swift movement, Daniel molded her against him and walked forward with her legs between his, making her tense with the realization that he was aroused. Then again, so was she. Her body was throbbing with desire, her stomach was swirling with excitement, and she was wet.

He made her sit on the bed. Jade wrapped her legs around his waist because she needed and wanted the contact of their bodies together. His head dipped toward her cleavage, and he licked and sucked while his hands cupped and massaged her breasts with tenderness.

DANIEL LEFT A TRAIL OF WET kisses on her chest. Shifting his hands to her back, so she wouldn't fall back on the bed, his lips sucked and nibbled on her skin. He focused on the moans coming out of her mouth to understand what she liked him to do to her. By the panting and the slow movement of her hips against him, she was enjoying everything.

He unclasped her bikini top and pulled it off slowly, observing her pink cheeks and shining eyes. Her heartbeat increased and her temperature rose slightly. She did nothing to stop him. He didn't even break a smile because he didn't want her to feel embarrassed. They were doing a serious thing. Besides, he was too mesmerized by her to smile. He wanted to keep kissing and tasting her. His own heart was beating erratically because he was aching with love and lust.

His love for her was a certainty. Love at first sight, which increased exponentially each day that he spent next to her. His love for her was the only thing that was helping him understand that their relationship had to be taken seriously. He couldn't mess that up. He couldn't break her heart. She would leave him and there was nothing else in the world to make him want to keep enduring eternity.

Daniel was tired of feeling lonely and misunderstood. He wanted someone to share all of his dreams with, his quirky hobbies, and his sexual fantasies. He wanted Jade. He didn't know why, but all his sharp senses were telling him that she was perfect. She was everything he had ever dreamed of finding in a woman. That captivating woman was his beloved, and he was set on making her surrender and fall in love with him. Above all, he was set on making her happy to fix the broken pieces of her soul and make him whole in the process.

"Are you sure you want to do this?" she asked.

"I told you this was going to take time."

"So why are you so serious? Did you change your mind?"

He kissed her deeply in response to her wary question. His tongue swirled inside her mouth, making it impossible for her to speak or even breathe properly. Her breasts were pressed hard against his chest. Her hands seized his head tighter, entangling her fingers in his soft hair.

Daniel broke the kiss, so they could both breathe. Then Jade placed small kisses on his face. He relaxed as his lips curled into a smile. He was enjoying the softness of her lips and the pressure of his erection against her core. She wasn't avoiding him. His beloved was pressing and rubbing it slowly, using her body to build up the tension in his muscles and to make him get even harder. She was hot between her legs. He could climax like that, and she could probably, too, by the way that her breathing was coming out in ragged gasps. Her heart was beating way too fast, but it only aroused him more. He was losing his ability to think straight because he was imagining how good it would be to slip his pants and boxers off, take off her panties, and make her straddle him as she moved her hips up and down his shaft. But then again, he didn't want to rush things.

Daniel ground their hips together to make Jade stop moving provocatively.

She obeyed, seemingly reluctant, her eyes showing how high on yearning she was. She whimpered when his hands grabbed her ass, and his tongue flickered over one of her hard nipples. Her whole body vibrated, and he rejoiced in it. Then he reached out and touched her breasts, molding and licking every inch of them.

Jade tipped her head back, offering herself to him. Moaning and biting her lip in response to each wave of pleasure that he offered her.

After a moment of licking and kissing her neck and breasts, Daniel laid her down on the bed, caressing her from her breasts to her stomach. He admired her beautiful legs and the shape of her sex against her panties. Kneeling on the bed, he could barely control his desire as he contemplated her ivory skin and perfect curves. He hoped she wouldn't look at him and see that he was in his vampire form. She didn't like vampires.

*What if she screams because she thinks I will harm her?*

"Daniel," she gasped, covering her breasts and looking at him.

Their eyes locked, and he noticed that she tensed at the sight of his dark eyes and scary face.

"It's okay, Jade. It's okay," he cooed, leaning over and reaching to touch her face. He placed his finger over her mouth and kissed her forehead.

She nodded, searching for his eyes and sucking on his finger.

He relaxed. "Aren't you scared of us anymore?"

"Not of you," she replied.

Daniel felt his heart exploding with happiness in his chest.

"That's good because I only want to give you pleasure, not pain," he whispered, taking his finger out of her mouth and placing his lips against hers.

Her hands touched his chest, tracing his hard muscles. Daniel's left hand trailed its way down her breasts and stomach before he placed it between her legs where she felt extremely hot and wet.

She squirmed and gasped under him with the contact. His fingers wanted to stay there, rubbing and fondling her intimately, but he had said that he would kiss and taste every part of her. It was not his fingers that he wanted there. It was his mouth. He was salivating at the thought of it, craving the softness of her pussy and her aroused clit against his tongue. His cock jolted inside his pants, begging for release. He had to keep ignoring it.

Daniel's tongue was inside Jade's mouth, sliding in and out in an imitation of what he wanted to do orally to her sex. He broke the kiss when her legs parted in a clear invitation to satisfy her there.

He trailed kisses down her chest and stomach, only to reach the limits of her panties. Then, he slowly pulled her panties down to give her time to complain and stop him. She didn't. Instead, she moved her hips and legs to let him do it.

# CHAPTER FIFTEEN: PROMISES

**JADE FISTED THE COMFORTER**, perfectly aware that she was naked under his eyes. She felt embarrassed, but his hands massaging her inner thighs and his lips softly kissing her legs were making things easier. Her pleasure was surpassing her shyness as she ached between her legs. She was so wet and needy that she was trying not to beg for him to go further up and give her the peace she needed.

"Do you like this?" he asked, putting her legs on his shoulders, spreading them even more and pulling her closer to his mouth.

She lost her breath and tensed. He was staring directly at her mound. She could feel his breath and his fingers gently stroking the soft skin of her crotch. His tongue flickered out, and he licked her labia, sending shockwaves through her whole body.

She panted and gasped, moving her upper body and her hips in the process.

"I'm going to take that as a yes," he teased, holding her hips tighter, so she stopped moving.

Daniel's dark head nestled between her open legs, his tongue started to roll around in small circles, making Jade moan and wriggle in pleasure. She had her eyes closed, enjoying the sensations that were floating around her. Every nerve ending in her body was on fire. She was moaning louder and louder, squirming at each stroke of his tongue, losing her breath every time he sucked on her clit. She felt like cursing and screaming out his name.

He skillfully moved his tongue to torment her ferocious desire. She was throbbing and trembling between her legs while her hips were moving out of control and her body was begging for release. All she wanted was his tongue devouring her, making her scream and laugh at the same time.

DANIEL'S TONGUE SWIRLED around her clit, trailed its way down to her labia, and gently stroked her entrance. He sensed her body shivering again. He wanted to suck on her harder, so she would release more of those amazing sounds that were making his body go crazy. The pain and need were excruciating in his pants, but it was all worth it. He had his woman gasping his name and biting her arm to mask her screams of pleasure. She moaned louder when he started to use his fingers to part her folds and play with her pink little clit. He just needed to keep stroking that bundle of nerves until she would lose it and come. But he was having too much fun prolonging her pleasure and delaying the orgasm. She smelled wonderful, and she tasted even better. He wanted his tongue licking her and pressing against her clit the moment her body gave in and burst into shivers of untamed pleasure.

JADE FONDLED HER BREASTS with one hand and stroked Daniel's hair with the other. She had no control over the movements of her hips against his mouth. She arched her back and panted when he speared his tongue into her opening and tension coiled in her stomach.

Daniel cupped her ass with his hands, pressed his mouth fully against her, and suckled. It was enough to make her body convulse as the bed started to spin and the contractions inside of her rippled like oncoming waves as she fought to breathe. The pleasure had shot through her, her defenses fell away, and she moaned until her body calmed down, and Daniel came up for air.

With the back of his hand, he cleaned his mouth and pressed his tongue against his lower lip. His eyes seemed to be adjusting to the light, resting on Jade's blissful face. She was chuckling as he smiled with a pleased expression.

"Kiss me," she said with a husky voice and erratic breathing.

He climbed back on the bed and kissed her forehead and nose before placing his lips over hers.

She didn't hold back in the kiss. She tasted him, engulfing his lower lip and pressing her fingers hard against his chest. Her right hand ran down his body and cupped his crotch, making him break the kiss and moan in pain for what Jade couldn't perceive.

"I'm sorry. I'm sorry," she gasped, horrified for hurting him.

"You didn't do anything wrong," he whispered, but she wasn't so sure. "And you don't need to do this. This is about me giving you pleasure."

He tried to take her hand away.

"I want to touch you, too," she complained, avoiding his hand and trying to open his pants.

"Have you ever done this before?" he asked, holding on to her hand again and entwining their fingers.

JADE SHOOK HER HEAD and bit her lower lip with an innocent face that made his stomach explode with anticipation. He gulped. Kissing and hugging her against him, he rolled on the bed and accommodated her body under his.

They would have other opportunities for her to touch him. At that moment, he just wanted to kiss her and hold her. She was desirable beyond words.

"Doesn't it hurt?" she asked with a troubled face.

"Oh yes," he confessed, fondling her breasts and bending down to suck one of her nipples into his mouth. His tongue swirled around her pink bud, making her close her eyes and gasp for air.

"So let me," she said between pants. "I want to, Daniel."

He sighed, finding her a total turn on. The simple sound of her voice saying his name was enough to make him get harder.

"Use your hand then. We can try something else another time."

She nodded, nestling her face against his neck and sliding her hand to his pants where she struggled with the buttons. He helped her with that and, soon enough, her fingers were slipping inside his boxers and grabbing hold of his shaft. Pumping her hand, she squeezed with caution.

His mouth sought hers. While her hand stroked his hard erection, he moaned and gasped, tensing and stiffening against the silkiness of her body.

HIS JAGGED MOANS WERE the only sign Jade needed to know that she was doing it right. Her heart was racing in her chest because of what she was doing. She found it incredible how hard he was and how thrilling it made her feel to offer him pleasure. She kept stroking him with care, using her thumb to gently rub the tip of his erection.

Unexpectedly, his hand fell over hers, making her stop. Holding her hand, he showed her how to rub it faster and grip tighter.

Jade's breath halted in her throat when she felt his cock tremble in her closed hand. Daniel kept on groaning her name with his head nestled between her breasts. It was deliciously decadent listening to him while he was drawing close to an orgasm. It aroused her even more.

His mouth moved to suck on her breast, making her core ache to also be touched. She wondered how it would feel if he was inside her, and they were wrapped in each other's arms.

Her voice came out sultry and needy. "Daniel."

He raised his gaze at her face. “Are you okay or is this making you feel uncomfortable?”

Jade shook her head with pursed lips. Mustering courage, she asked with a timid voice, “Do you still want to have sex with me?”

Daniel blinked several times before frowning. “No.” His arm pulled her near. “I want to make love to you,” he clarified before the negative answer made her feel uncomfortable.

“Do you want to do it now?”

He didn’t answer. As the silence stretched between them, he continued to look deep into her eyes.

Her voice shook as she asked, “Why not?”

His hand stroked her heated cheek. “I want to. Yet I don’t want to rush things between us. Your first time should be special. I know how to make it special and I don’t want to ruin it.”

“This is special.”

Daniel’s eyes sparkled as he smiled and pecked her lips. “Being with you is always special—”

A loud knock on the door of Jade’s room startled them and interrupted Daniel’s speech.

“ONE HOUR UNTIL THE CONTEST, Jade!” an unfamiliar voice warned and went away.

“It seems we’ve run out of time,” Daniel whispered. “When we make love, Jade, it will be even more special, okay? For now, let's take a bath." He kissed her forehead.

Sighing, she crossed her arms to cover her breasts and curled on the bed.

"Stop pouting," he demanded, sitting on the bed and taking his jeans and boxers off.

Jade's eyes widened, staring at his naked body. He knew that he was still hard for her and, by the look on her face, she wasn't used to seeing naked and aroused men. But, he didn't want her thinking that he didn't want her. He did. More than blood. More than breathing.

"Bath. Now," he ordered her, motioning to the bathroom.

She sat up on the bed, staring at the wrinkled dress on the floor that she was supposed to wear that night.

"I thought we weren't going to have sex," she muttered, defying his order.

"Do you say those things just to annoy me?"

"Yes," she confessed.

"Do you want me to punish you?"

"I don't know. What do you have in mind?" she retorted with a teasing grin.

He smirked. "We will talk about that some other day. Now, Jade," he said as he softened his voice, moving next to her and grabbing her by the hands so she stood up, "let's get you clean and ready, baby. We have some stupid contest to attend."

"Do you know what it is?"

"No. I can't have a favorite. Therefore, I can't know anything about the contest so everything is fair to the other two. I really don't care. Whatever it is, it won't change the fact that you are going to spend the night in my bed," he said, emphasizing each word as he whispered them into her ear.

"Only if I want to," she argued, walking to the bathroom and stopping at the door. She spun around. "Are you coming or what?"

He stared at her with dark eyes and a demonic face, totally aroused by her naked figure.

"I'll give you a damn good reason for you to want it," he retorted, speeding his way to her and grabbing her before she could evade him.

She screamed after he let her go inside the shower. The speedy ride could be scary. Her protests ended when he kissed her and let the water fall over them.

# CHAPTER SIXTEEN: A SPECIAL PRIZE

**THE CREW FROM THE SHOW** had erected a portable set in the backyard of Daniel's mansion. It resembled more a quiz show set than anything else, so Jade assumed that they would be asking them questions.

There were three seats in the center of the stage with touchscreen monitors directly facing each seat. The floor was made of Plexiglas, displaying the logo of the program underneath.

The host stood behind a single podium while the crew checked the sound and the cameras that cruised around, searching for the best angle to record. As his lines appeared on the teleprompter opposite his podium, the host cleared his throat and waited for the director to shout that they were recording.

"Welcome back to the '*Who Wants to Be a Vampire*' - *Special Edition!* The number one reality show in America. Tonight, we are recording at our bachelor's house, the rich and good-looking Daniel Wolfe," the host said with an excited voice.

He resumed his speech after a dramatic pause, "Yesterday, we've met his three beautiful choices of the week. Only one can be the lucky lady who is going to marry him and become his vampire companion for all eternity. But, to get Daniel's attention, these three young ladies need to fight among themselves for his affection."

He moved from behind his podium and walked to the seats where the light turned on to illuminate the contestants.

With a happy and casual voice, he stirred up the nonexistent audience around the set. "In tonight's contest, the three ladies are going to have to survive three rounds of questions. Whoever knows more intimate details about our bachelor wins a romantic dinner in a tent especially assembled in his garden for this special occasion. May the sound of violins awaken new feelings or...renew the old flame!"

The contestants waited in the seats where the touchscreens turned on. Jade's attention was on the host while Jenna's hand was grabbing hers. Her best friend was in the middle which prevented Jade from seeing Emma's two-faced expression. Even if she tried to stay relaxed and at peace with her soul, the fact was that the organization of the show was giving a head start to Daniel's ex. It couldn't be more obvious!

Jade tried to smile at the cameras that kept recording. With no idea where Daniel could be, Jenna's presence was a relief. He might be behind the set, listening to everything. Earlier, he had left her, so he could get dressed. Then she had to endure the makeup team and the hairdresser around her. The tension was taking over her body because she couldn't see him. What was he thinking about the contest? He had told her that he didn't know what the game rules would be, but the point of that contest seemed slanted in Emma's favor.

The host's rules were drifting inside her mind, and she only paid attention when the lighting system darkened the set and the spotlight was pointed at them.

"Are you ready, ladies?" the host asked. His sympathetic smile was aimed at the screen where the question was going to appear.

"Of course we're ready, Simon," Emma spoke with a beaming smile.

"Pay attention and look at the screen to see the four options for the correct answer. Press the letter to lock the answer of your choice. First question: What was Daniel's human mother's name? A: Evelyn, B: Sarah, C: Lindsey, or D: Felicity."

The ten seconds countdown was displayed on the monitor behind the host while the girls stared at their screens. It didn't take long for Jade to listen to the first sound of a locked answer and then the second. She was the only one who was taking longer since she had no idea about the right answer. She chose it randomly and stared at the host.

A new sound was heard and the host spoke again, "Some of you were fast at answering and others hesitated. The right answer was Evelyn! Jenna and Emma got it right. Better luck next time, Jade."

Applauding sounds and happy people cheered. Jade faked a smile and looked at Jenna. If she was going to lose, at least, Jenna should win. Even if she wasn't so sure that her best friend wouldn't hit on Daniel if she had the chance.

"For the next question, we are going to reveal something really personal about our bachelor. Something that only his closest friends know, or maybe one of the girls who knows a little bit more about our vampire's hobbies."

"Besides breaking women's hearts, you mean?" Emma teased.

The sound of laughter echoed in the studio.

Emma was either being provocative or following a script.

Jade clenched her teeth and gave her attention to the host, eager for him to reveal the next question and end the anxiety that was overtaking her.

"Daniel is known for his taste in beautiful women, fast cars, and eccentric houses. However, there's another means of transportation that he likes to build in the comfort of his home. Are we talking about: A: planes, B: spaceships, C: trains, or D: bikes?"

Jade was the first to answer that question. It helped that she had spent time with her brother that day. Then, her body broke out in a light sweat. She hoped that she had picked the right answer. She wanted at least one correct answer. It would be rather disheartening if she failed in all the questions about Daniel. She realized that she didn't know much about his life, his tastes, and his background. How old was he? Where did he grow up? How did he become a vampire?

Jenna and Emma locked their answers, and Jade waited for the host to end the suspense.

“We have two winners once again! Emma and Jade have the correct answer. Daniel likes to build small scale trains.”

Jade’s heart drummed, happy that she got it right.

Meanwhile, the host summed up what had happened. “Emma is in the lead with two correct answers while Jenna and Jade have one each. If Emma answers the next question correctly or if the other contestants choose the wrong answer, she’s the winner of the romantic dinner for two!”

Music played in the background, providing the drama and the tension while the host made a suspenseful pause.

Cold sweat dripped down Jade’s spine as her stomach twisted. She didn’t want Emma to go on a date with Daniel.

“Daniel is the CEO of several companies. One of his companies is the leader of what best-selling technology? A: a cell phone watch, B: interactive robots, C: glasses with integrated displays, or D: virtual reality headsets.”

Jade stared at her screen with puzzled eyes. She knew that Daniel liked games as any other guy, but she had no idea of what kind of technology his companies were selling. She chose the option D and hoped for the best. She heard a lock sound before she answered and, when she raised her head, Emma was still looking at her screen. Then the actress locked it before the time ran out. The contestants stared at the host who had his lips curled up.

If Emma got it right, she was the winner. If Jenna or Jade got it right, they would be tied up with Emma. Tying meant that they were going to sudden death, which meant that the host would ask several questions until the last girl with more correct answers remained. Jade was sure that Emma would win in a heartbeat. After all, she had dated Daniel.

The suspense ended when the host declared, "None of you got it right. Daniel is selling millions of glasses with integrated displays in all shapes and colors. It's been a huge hit in Japan and America. It's selling rather well to help other vampires like him to have a virtual experience of what it is to walk in the sun and have someone doing what they can't do during the day."

Jade wanted to face-palm herself for being such an idiot. Daniel had shown her that in his bedroom. She should have remembered it. Now Emma was the winner and was going on a date with Daniel. The actress had already left her seat and was hugging Jenna, expressing her happiness for winning.

Jade couldn't conceal the grumpy face and murderous eyes on Emma.

"Congratulations," Jade said to Emma, who gave her a fake smile and a kiss on the cheek.

"No hard feelings," Emma mumbled in Jade's ear after patting her back.

"Emma, come and let's take you on your date. Daniel is waiting for you outside where an exquisite dinner awaits. You two will have the privacy to talk and remember old times. After dinner, you will join him for a carriage ride in the park."

The host seemed excited with all the amazing prizes that Emma had won. Jade was not. A romantic dinner was already nerve-racking, but a romantic carriage ride in the park was a perk that Jade wasn't expecting. It hadn't been mentioned until then.

Jealousy was rising inside her chest, together with rage that she did her best to conceal. She couldn't believe that Daniel would have to spend his night with Emma. He could succumb to her charm. He could forget about the time he had with her. Jade didn't want Daniel and Emma back together. Not now that they had shared something that she was wishing she hadn't shared with him. She had been stupid and naive. That contest was rigged and the next ones would be, too. No one wanted her to be with Daniel. Including the viewers who loved Emma and were most likely rooting for her to get back together with him.

"Is everything okay, Jade?" Jenna asked, squeezing her hand. "We need to go back to the mansion. Dinner awaits us, and the director said we were free for the night while Daniel and Emma are spending time together. The cameras are going to follow them."

Jade blinked, sucking in her words. "I'm sorry. I'm not feeling well."

Jenna smirked. "Come on, silly. Don't be jealous. He will come back to you. It's just a stupid dinner and a... He will hate it and if he doesn't, then he's not worthy of you." She put her arm around her shoulders, trying to cheer Jade up while walking away from the set. "I bet they prepared us a lot of delicacies to eat. I'm starving, aren't you?"

"No. I'm good."

"Stop being so dramatic. It's not the end of the world. Besides, whatever happens in that dinner will be shown on TV. So you can kick him in the nuts if he falls for her again or does something stupid like kiss her."

Jade stared at her with wide eyes. "You are not helping! That doesn't cheer me up at all."

Guess their night together was out of the question now that Daniel had to entertain his ex. She was envious of Emma because she was going to go on a carriage ride with Daniel.

She balled her hands into fists. "They made it so that we would lose!"

With a shrug, Jenna said, "Yeah, I know."

Jade turned her head to look at her best friend with furrowed brows. "Why aren't you mad?"

Jenna paused in the garden and smirked. "I get to spend time with you!" Jade rolled her eyes as Jenna pouted. "Don't you want to have a girl's night? Or are you so infatuated by the hot vamp that you don't care about your bestie anymore?"

"It's not that." Jade sighed and held her left arm.

Carrying the wind because of her speed, Sakura appeared in front of them. "Why are you taking so long to come inside?"

"Jade is annoyed because Emma won the contest," Jenna explained.

Sakura smiled at Jade and held her hands. "There's a party going on inside. You aren't going to sulk around while Daniel is away. He doesn't care about her. You're special to him, Jade. Now stop brooding. We are going to get drunk!" Sakura squealed, throwing her arms in the air with excitement.

Jade probed, "Do you think that's wise?"

"It's more than wise. Tonight, we are going to play games and get drunk!" Sakura stated, grabbing Jade's arm and pulling her to the house.

"Girl's night, girl's night!" Jenna cheered behind them, marching as if she was in a cheerleading parade.

Jade smirked and decided that if she wasn't going to be with Daniel, at least, she wasn't going to sit around feeling sorry for herself. Having a couple of shots and partying with the girls was a great idea.

# CHAPTER SEVENTEEN: A TASTE OF POSSESSIVENESS

**IT WAS TWO O'CLOCK IN** the morning when Daniel arrived home. He was tired and all he wanted was to get rid of Emma, so he could spend some time with Jade. He hadn't stopped thinking about her. He didn't even try to conceal the boredom of having to endure Emma's presence and small talk. It had been five excruciating hours together.

However, as soon as he entered his front door, he knew that something was going on. The music was loud, the laughter was louder, and there were strange people inside his living room and hallway, partying and sharing drinks.

Daniel's bad mood increased exponentially when he saw Jade on the table dancing, clearly intoxicated, while Jenna, Seth, and Sakura were tapping their empty shot glasses against the table. They were encouraging her to take her dress off, and she was slipping down the sleeves slowly and teasingly. To makes matters worse, a recording crew was around her, filming the whole thing. Seth's recording crew, no doubt.

Daniel cursed under his breath and did what any jealous boyfriend would do. He sped his way to the table, grabbed Jade, put her over his shoulder, and bolted to her bedroom. In leaving them behind, all the fun ended, and the others were left complaining.

DROPPING JADE ON HER BED, he clenched his jaw at the sound of her laughter. Their eyes met and it was obvious to him that she wasn't even recognizing him. Her eyes were blank and spacing out.

"What the hell was happening downstairs?" Daniel asked, unable to conceal how angry he was with the situation.

"We were partying!" She waved her arms around to show her excitement.

"And did you have to take your clothes off?"

"We were playing drink or dare," she claimed.

He frowned. "First, it's truth or dare. Second, why would you be willing to take off your clothes like that?"

"No, it was drink or dare. We had to spin the bottle and whoever the bottle pointed at had to dare someone to do something. If we didn't want to do it, we had to drink a shot. I was dared to take my dress off," she explained, covering her mouth and holding still with wide eyes. "The bed is spinning..."

"You should have drunk the shot instead of doing the dare," Daniel snapped.

"I couldn't pass the dare. We can't refuse two times in a row... I'm not feeling so well."

"Whose clever idea was that?" Daniel asked, clenching his jaw and narrowing his eyes.

"Sakura!" Jade answered, laughing and then covering her mouth again. "I think I had too much to drink."

"Yes, it doesn't take a genius to see that," Daniel muttered, pacing around the bedroom. "Why would you do something like that?"

"What?" she questioned, following his movements as if she was watching a tennis match.

"Take off your dress." He stopped in front of her with his hands folded behind his back.

"I told you why. The last dare had been to kiss Seth. I refused to do that," she explained. Daniel squeezed his eyes as rage overtook him. "So, I had to take off my dress."

"You shouldn't have been playing in the first place!"

"Why not?" She frowned as she balled her hands into fists. "I'm allowed to have fun, too. And who are you to judge my actions? Weren't you out on a date, having fun with your ex?"

"No, not really." He tilted his head with curious eyes, trying to decipher the reasons behind her actions. "Were you jealous?"

"Of course not! I don't care about what you do in your spare time."

DANIEL'S QUESTIONS WERE upsetting her. Jade secured her hands to the mattress and focused on the wall, hoping that the bed stopped spinning.

"Nothing happened," he assured.

Daniel sat down next to her and Jade concentrated on his good-looking features. He had tempting lips, perfect blue eyes, and smooth skin. She leaned closer to his face, hitting him with her alcohol-laced breath.

"God, how much did you drink?"

"I don't know." She sighed, captivated by his mouth. "A lot, probably." She laughed, held her hands to his shoulders, and fell forward into his arms when she aimed at kissing him and missed.

DANIEL SECURED HER IN HIS ARMS. She hid her face against the hollow of his neck and kept giggling. He caressed her hair and let her calm down. He didn't want to be mad at her but seeing her taking off her clothes in front of other people and a camera crew wasn't his idea of entertainment. She was too drunk to know what she was doing, anyway.

"Daniel, make it stop," she pleaded.

"What baby?"

"The bedroom keeps spinning around!"

"I can't do anything about that. You should try to sleep."

"I don't want to sleep," she complained, her voice catching between sobs.

He cringed at the thought of having her crying because she was drunk. He was never good at babysitting drunken girls. But Jade wasn't just any girl, and he had no intention of leaving her alone. He wanted to take care of her and be with her.

"Then what do you want to do?"

Jade mumbled in a childlike voice, "I want to talk."

"About what?"

"About anything. I realized that I don't know anything about you, and that sucks!"

"Is that what's troubling you?" Daniel laid her head against his shoulder, bringing her into his lap. "Are you mad because you didn't win the contest?"

Jade muttered, "It was an unfair contest. The questions were planned to make Emma win."

He cuddled her hair. "True. But you did well."

"I only got one right!"

"And it was an important question," he praised her.

"I don't want you going out on any romantic dates with Emma," she grumbled, holding her hands to his shirt and sighing deeply. She groaned, tilting back her head to stare at his face with narrowed eyes. "Did you have fun?"

"Not really. I couldn't wait to get back home to see you," he whispered, brushing her cheek with his fingers. He smiled at her, pleased by the deep and sensible stare she was offering him. If only he could be so lucky as to have her falling for him already. "Did you miss me?"

"Of course not," she replied, pushing him away. He wrapped his arms around her waist, preventing her from leaving his embrace. "I was busy partying. I didn't even think about you."

"Oh really? Then can I go back downstairs and finish my date with Emma?"

"Do whatever the fuck you want," she snapped at him, getting up rather fast for her drunk state. She staggered from left to right while attempting to reach the bathroom.

His beloved was a feisty thing, and he was stupid to provoke her.

"Jade..." He went after her.

Daniel grabbed her inside the bathroom. Holding her by the waist, he turned her around to face him. He wanted to say something meaningful to ease her aggressive personality.

"Are you okay?" he asked instead since she looked rather pale and sick.

"Not really," she whispered, putting her hand in front of her mouth.

He immediately let her go, and she turned around to vomit in the bathroom sink.

"I think I'm going to die," she complained, after a moment of running water in the sink and splashing it against her face and mouth.

Daniel was next to her, holding on to her hair and drawing circles on her back to make her feel better.

"You'll feel better after you stop vomiting. I'll make you some strong coffee, okay?" he said sweetly.

She just nodded and vomited again.

"I'll be right back."

Daniel sped his way out of her bedroom and walked down the stairs to go to the kitchen. The party was still on. Seth was drinking shots, and Emma had joined in on the drinking game. She was giggling and throwing shots down her throat. There were couples making out on his leather couch and others playing his video games. His place was a mess—cans and bottles everywhere. The fridge had been raided and there were a lot of empty beer bottles on the counter.

He tried to act cool about having a rave party in his house. He just wanted to make coffee for Jade and then spend the rest of his night with her. He'd be happy to watch her sleep if that was all he was getting that night.

"Are you okay?" Seth asked, appearing behind him.

Daniel turned around to face him. His brother had a shot in his hand and a goofy look on his face.

"No. What are you doing here?"

"Mother invited me," he declared, pointing at Sakura, who was laughing and talking with Jenna.

Meanwhile, Emma was licking salt from her hand and slamming another shot down her throat. She wanted to get drunk, and he was almost appreciating the idea and thinking he might do the same. But he had Jade waiting for him. She was feeling sick and most likely still mad at him for going out with Emma. He had to play nice.

"Next time you dare my girlfriend to take off her dress, be prepared for the consequences," Daniel warned, grabbing the mug of coffee and glaring at his younger brother.

"We were having fun! Since when are you such a buzz kill?"

"You can go have fun with one of your groupie friends, with your choice of the week, but not with Jade," he said.

His cold eyes made Seth step back.

"Well, it wasn't me who dared her to take off her dress. It was Mom after she refused to kiss me," Seth explained as he smiled wickedly at Daniel. "You know, while you were out having fun with Emma."

Daniel wondered if he should punch him or ignore the obvious provocation. He'd had enough of fighting with his brother. Besides, he had hit Seth the other night and it wasn't even his fault, so he was going to let it slide tonight. Jade wouldn't like it, and she was all alone upstairs, feeling sick. He wanted to get back there and cuddle her to sleep.

"I wasn't having fun with Emma. I had to obey the stupid contract that Dominic forced me to sign," Daniel clarified.

"It's good publicity for your company and for our community."

"I don't see how it can be good publicity," Daniel retorted. "The only thing they want is a scandal and promoting Emma's acting career by using our former relationship."

"Stop complaining. You've found your beloved! Lucky bastard! You just need to endure this for a week. I have to endure it for six more months." He turned around to join the remaining party-goers.

Seth's words fell hard on Daniel. His brother was right. Their vampire father had been harsher on Seth. However, in Daniel's defense, he had a rather mundane and simple existence with the human community. He had played by the book, using his companies for the good of humans and vampires. He wasn't expecting to find his beloved the week he had to play the playboy role. But thinking about it, having Jade move into his house because of a signed contract was probably the best way to seduce the girl and make her his. She wouldn't give him the time of day in the nightclub. He wouldn't be in the nightclub if he hadn't had to go there and pick a random girl to have around the other two and pretend to fall in love with one of them. He was happy that he didn't need to pretend anymore.

Daniel walked calmly to Jade's bedroom, so he wouldn't spill the coffee. When he got in and closed the door behind him, she was sitting on the bed, out of her dress, wearing a T-shirt and shorts. She was staring at the wall with empty eyes and wild hair.

He smirked, finding her too damn sexy. She had amazing eyes, amazing lips, and attractive legs. It didn't help that he was thinking about their playful afternoon in that same bed.

"Are you feeling better?" he asked, sitting next to her and showing her the mug.

Jade made a weird sound of complaint and shook her head. She probably had an upset stomach. Vodka could do that to a person.

"Drink up." He handed her the mug.

She obeyed, cringing, and Daniel watched her. He could smell the toothpaste and the soap she had used to clean herself. It was a nice upgrade from the alcohol breath.

"You could have put sugar in it," she complained, putting down the mug and sighing deeply. She placed a hand over her forehead and slid her body down on the headboard, putting her chin on her knees. "I don't feel good."

"You shouldn't have had so much to drink," he said, touching her cheek.

She closed her eyes with the contact of his hand.

"I was bored." She sighed deeply and leaned forward to get closer to him.

He lifted her arms and grabbed her by the waist, so he could bring her into his embrace.

"I'm here now. No need to be bored," he whispered sweetly, kissing her closed eyes.

"Did you enjoy the carriage ride?"

"No, because you weren't there with me. It was tedious and I—I missed you."

“You’re just saying that to please me,” she muttered.

He smiled. Her crankiness was adorable. “Don’t you like it that I want to please you? Doesn’t that mean that I like you a lot?”

“We’ve just met.”

“Meaning?”

Jade pouted before she answered. “We barely know each other. I can’t have strong feelings for you.”

His breath feathered her mouth. “Why not?”

“You *are* annoying, and I don’t trust you.”

“Yet, you were jealous of Emma.”

Jade hid her face against his neck and sighed. “I’m stupid.”

Daniel kissed the top of her head. “You are as mine as I am yours. Nothing will change that. And I’m home now. We can talk about anything you’d like.” When he noticed, she was staring at him as her nail played with a button of his shirt. “Why the gloomy eyes?”

“Everybody wants you to get back with her.”

He cupped her cheek. “All I want is you. If you are willing to make love to me, then you should be willing to open up your heart to me.”

Jade pulled his hand away. “It’s not the same thing. Sex isn’t the same thing as making love. Don’t try to trick me. Just because I’m sexually attracted to you doesn’t mean that I’m going to fall for you.”

"But this between us isn't just about sex," he tried to explain. "You are my beloved."

"It's always about sex with you."

"What do you mean? Vampires? Guys?"

"Vampire guys," she stated. Daniel sighed with hurt. "And don't pretend like you don't know," she accused him with a shattered, sad voice.

"What do you think I know?" he asked, feeling vulnerable to her sadness.

"About what happened to me."

"I don't know. I'm waiting for you to tell me."

"The director knows. Didn't he tell you?"

"No. I want you to tell me when you're ready for that."

"You said you didn't care about my sappy sad story," she complained. He witnessed her tears falling down her cheeks, wetting his shirt.

He didn't want to be precipitate. She was drunk; the last thing she needed was to talk about the depressing events of her life. That night was about her knowing more about him.

"I was lying," he whispered, cleaning her tears with the palm of his hand and kissing the top of her head. "Let's talk about something else. I don't want you being upset tonight. You can tell me when you feel ready. Why don't you ask me what you want to know about my life? Anything you want to know," he said, and she opened her eyes to face him. "Ask me anything."

"Really? Anything? Even about...about your life before being a vampire?"

"Yes. Anything, darling," he confirmed, smiling as he kissed the tip of her nose.

# CHAPTER EIGHTEEN: HANGOVER

**JADE WOKE UP WITH A LOT** of noise clouding her mind. Memories of her dream were still obscuring her view and making her head hurt. She had been dreaming about Daniel and about them talking and kissing. But she wasn't completely sure of what they were telling each other. The pain clenching at her skull wasn't helping her remember.

She moved on the bed and felt a warm body next to her. She tried to focus her eyes, searching for memories of the events of what happened before she fell asleep. A lot of shots, loud music, laughing, there was joking around with Seth, Jenna, and Sakura. The alcohol left her loose and irrational. She danced, screamed, and applauded the wildness that took over the house. She drank too much. The effects were pressing against her temples, making her sick to her stomach and dizzy. On the top of that, she was feeling aroused. Her nipples were hard and her body was needy.

Staring at Daniel's body next to her, she moaned. He was dressed in his shirt and tuxedo pants. He was innocently asleep and all she wanted was to attack him, kiss him, and wake him up. He looked so edible that it was hard for her to breathe. Even with the hangover, she wanted to get closer to him and get his arms around her.

Jade leaned closer to his body and stroked his face, staring at his lips. She felt guilty for touching him while he was asleep. Not like she was doing anything wrong. She just wanted to stare at him, touch him, and feel his presence. She could get used to having him around.

The night before, Daniel had shared a lot of his private life with her. She remembered, even though she was drunk. They had also laughed and kissed. There were always fireworks inside her mouth when their lips locked, going down her throat and bursting in her stomach with lust and untamed pleasure. He was so gorgeous that it hurt her chest.

She was startled when his arm fell around her, and he brought her closer to his chest. He was warm, and she felt a wave of peace washing over her.

"Good morning, beautiful," Daniel whispered, hugging her tight.

"Good morning," she whispered back.

Daniel opened his eyes and smiled. "How do you feel?"

"Bad," she confessed.

Daniel touched her cheek with the tip of his nose. "Two aspirins and some food will make you feel better."

"I'll never drink that much again," she declared as he kissed her forehead and tangled his legs with hers. "What time do you think it is?"

"It's still day time. My body feels it. We slept late. We spent a lot of time talking, but there's still light outside. Do you remember what happened last night?"

"Not everything down to the finest detail. Did I do something I might regret?"

"Other than almost taking your clothes off so everybody could see your sexy lingerie, no, not that I know of. But I wasn't here when the party started. Do I need to know anything in particular?"

"I don't think so," she said timidly. She noted the amused tone in his voice. He wasn't censoring her, but she was feeling ashamed for acting like a reckless person.

"Oh, and you also told me you love me," he added.

"You are lying!"

"No, I'm not. You said it."

"You're such a liar!" she declared, sitting on the bed and staring at him with an annoyed expression.

He smirked and sat against the headboard.

"Well, it's about time you admit it."

She picked up a pillow and threw it at his face.

He chuckled and grabbed the pillow. "No need to get violent about it."

"Oh, I'm feeling sick," she complained, falling on the bed and curling her knees until they touched her belly.

"It's okay, darling," Daniel whispered, stroking her hair and kissing her eyelids. "Just take a bath, and I'll order some food. After eating, we can sleep a bit more."

Jade opened her eyes to stare at him and smiled.

Frowning at her, he asked, "What?"

"What are you doing in my bedroom?"

"Sleeping with you."

"So why are you dressed?"

"I didn't want to take advantage of your drunken state. Do you remember anything that happened last night?"

"Yes, I don't lose my memory from a couple of drinks. That's why I know you were lying when you said that I said that I love you."

"You could have said it," Daniel retorted.

"No, not really."

He pouted. "So, you don't like me a bit more than when we first met?"

"Maybe a little more. Doesn't mean that I love you."

"I need to try harder then," he said.

"Daniel," she sighed, stretching her hand to grab his shirt, "just shut up and kiss me."

He leaned down to kiss her lips. "You like to boss me around."

"And you talk too much," she complained, pulling him lower and wrapping her arms around his neck. "I'm not drunk now. You can take all the advantage you want."

Daniel laughed at her teasing suggestion and kissed her forehead. "No, you need to eat."

"And then you'll take advantage of me?" she questioned, batting her eyelashes.

"Then, I'll kiss you."

“Okay,” she agreed. “I’m going downstairs to take care of my breakfast, check the time, and I’ll be right back. Are you staying here?”

“I’ll wait for you,” he replied, laying down on his side of the bed and closing his eyes.

Jade got up and fixed her hair to go downstairs. When she was in the corridor, she was grateful for the quietness in the house, but when she arrived at the stairs, a door opened. Emma sneaked out of a bedroom, wrapped in a bed sheet and with her clothes and shoes in one of her hands.

There was an awkward moment of silence between the both of them. Then Emma continued her way to her bedroom, and Jade watched her disappear in the hallway. She was sleeping around with someone and it wasn’t Daniel. She didn’t like the smug smile on Emma’s face when she passed by her. If she was trying to imply that she had spent her night with Daniel, Emma was in for a rude awakening. He had spent the night with Jade, and they had talked until they fell asleep together. Now she just needed a nice breakfast and to get back to her bedroom to play with Daniel. Emma might have had fun that night, but Jade was going to have fun for the rest of the day. There was no way that she was going to miss spending time with Daniel.

Jade walked down the stairs and ran to the fridge. She opened it and started to prepare some scrambled eggs and black coffee. Then she noticed that there was someone else on the upper floor, sneaking away.

“Jenna,” she called.

Her best friend stared at her, startled. “Oh, it’s you! What are you doing down there?”

“Breakfast. And what are you doing up there?”

“Well, uh, wild night,” she explained with a goofy smile. “I’m starving. Can I join you?”

“Sure. I’ll make you some eggs, too.”

“What are you doing with the blood powder?” Jenna asked, sitting on a stool.

“Trying to figure out how to prepare this stuff.”

Jenna’s curiosity spiked as her eyes grew bigger. “For Daniel? You want to serve him breakfast, too. Did you guys sleep together?”

“He’s in my bedroom,” Jade stated mildly.

Jenna squealed with enthusiasm. “Holy shit! You both danced the horizontal mambo!”

“Calm down. Don’t get so excited. We just slept. I was drunk but... Well, we have been getting closer,” she confessed with a timid, dreamy smile.

“I’ll help you with that. I’ve plenty of experience,” Jenna said, helping Jade prepare the blood beverage.

Jade watched carefully how Jenna was doing it, so she could do it on some other occasion. Then she shared a plate of scrambled eggs and toasts with her best friend while drinking hot coffee. They talked about random stuff, and Jade was curious to know where Jenna slept and with whom.

“I saw Emma leaving a bedroom upstairs. And I know that Seth is just one, so umm... What the hell happened?” Jade asked, bursting with curiosity.

Jenna started coughing, choking on the eggs. After drinking her coffee, she stared at Jade with a guilty face.

"Well,...you can only imagine." Her best friend smiled wickedly.

"No!" Jade placed her hands on her face with her mouth agape.

"Oh yes! It was...wow, amazing! Seth talks a lot but when he actually shuts up, he's just...wow!"

"And Emma, too? Seriously?"

"You should try it. Do you want to share Daniel with me?"

"Hell no!"

Jenna laughed at her expression and stood up. "This was fun, but I need a bath and some rest before the new night starts. There will be another contest, and I want to look my best. Go have some fun with your vampire lover to see if he can loosen up your crankiness."

Jenna ran before Jade could complain about her mean words or throw something at her head.

Moments later, Jade entered her bedroom, and Daniel was leaving the bathroom with wet hair and a towel hugging his waist. Jade stood there, taking in his gorgeous figure. She was beginning to melt at the sight of him. It was a nice sensation but, at the same time, her brain was warning her about the danger of letting her guard down around a vampire.

"Is that for me?" he asked, going to get the glass of blood. "Thank you, I appreciate you taking care of me."

"Yes. Is it good?" She watched him drink it. It didn't repulse her like she thought it would. "Is it too hot?"

"No, it's perfect. Thank you."

Jade offered him a timid smile while staring at his abs and creamy skin. She needed to stop thinking of assaulting him with her mouth and hands every time she was in front of him.

"I'm going to take a bath," she said, walking to the bathroom.

She was a bit disappointed because she was hoping that they could take a bath together like the day before. It had been fun, exciting, sensual, and amazing.

Getting rid of her clothes, she entered the hot water. She washed her body, tensing under the sponge with the awareness of how aroused she was. Her breasts were hurting and she couldn't stop thinking about Daniel inside that tub with her.

Wrapping a towel around her body, she dried her hair as she walked to the mirror. She cleaned the fog with one hand and stared at the reflection of her pale expression. She didn't look well.

"Do you need some help?" Daniel asked, coming in.

Spinning around, she noticed that he was still wearing his towel around his waist. She bit her lower lip when her eyes landed on his ripped torso.

"I'm good," she stated, narrowing her eyes when he stood in front of her.

He caressed the hair away from her face. "Are you sure? I could help you get dry."

She smiled and leaned her face closer to his hand. He touched her cheek and placed a kiss on her lips. Heat coiled in her stomach as she placed her hands on his bare chest, molding his muscles and grabbing his neck. She pulled his head down to kiss him savagely, becoming lost in his mouth, tangling, and dueling with his tongue. The adrenaline rushed to her heart and she never felt so aroused by any other man. In that moment, she was craving his touch and his mouth on every square inch of her skin. It didn't help that she knew how much pleasure his mouth could give her. Her core was aching, and she was feeling breathless and stirred.

"I want you," she murmured against his lips, engulfing his lower lip and leaning her body against his. "And I really need you to—kiss me everywhere," she whispered, needy, taking one hand from his neck to untie her towel and let it fall at her feet.

DANIEL SHIVERED WHEN HE noticed her towel dropping on his feet and her skin touching his. Their legs became intertwined and her breasts were pressed against his chest. His erection was more than obvious against her lower stomach.

"Jade," he complained, sucking on air while her mouth trailed kisses down his neck and chest. The softness of her lips drove him insane. Her fingers explored his body, burning a trail of heat across every cell of his anatomy from her touch.

"Kiss me," she begged, offering her neck to him, pressing her breasts harder against him, and cupping his ass with urgency.

Daniel's hands trailed down her smooth skin as he gripped her ass and lifted it to sit her on the bathroom sink. Her legs wrapped around his waist, and he continued to kiss her mouth and massage her back and sides. He just needed to let his towel fall down, and they would be naked against one another. It was enticing to know that she simply needed to spread her legs, so he could press the head of his cock against her core and gently push it inside, making his whole body quiver and shatter in pleasure.

He wanted her badly. It was easy for him to fulfill his fantasies, but he didn't want her first time to be on a cold bathroom sink. He had to behave. She was so damn hot and spontaneous with him; it was unbelievable how a girl like her never had a guy to show her the pleasures of intercourse. Her innocence made him love her even more. She was his—just his—and he would make sure that she didn't want anyone else.

Drowning his head between her breasts, he used his hands to mold and tease them. She was offering herself to him, arching her chest and moving her hips against his waist. He could melt against the hotness of her core and her moans of pleasure. Her nipples hardened with his touch. She was squirming with pleasure under his mouth. He sucked and massaged her breasts, watching how her stomach was contracting and her sex was ready to be tasted. She smelled aroused. He definitely was. The towel didn't conceal it at all. It was sticking up, finding some comfort when she rubbed her stomach against it.

"We don't have condoms here," she whispered.

"Vampires can't give you babies or diseases. We don't need it," Daniel informed her.

"Then take me to bed and do it," she said, grabbing his neck and speaking huskily in his ear. "I'm burning up. I—can't understand, I just want you badly, right now, right here if you want."

"Yes, I do have that effect on women," Daniel teased her, massaging her back and controlling his own urges.

"Don't be the smart-ass, Daniel," she mumbled out of breath, grinding him tighter against her pussy and gasping when she felt once again how hard he was.

"I really, really want to make love to you right now, but, Jade–" He growled when she nibbled on his neck and kept moving against him. "Please, Jade. Let's—calm down a bit."

"I don't want to calm down," she complained, kissing his neck and moving her hands to loosen his towel and take it off.

HIS TOWEL WAS THE only thing that was preventing them from touching completely. She wanted the same experience that she had inside of the shower, with him touching her everywhere and kissing her while using his fingers to give her another orgasm. And, this time, she wanted him to finish the job and show her what all the fuss was about with having sex.

The orgasms he had given her were better than any she had done to herself. His tongue was skilled, and she would get wet every time she thought about his performance between her thighs. Now, she wanted to have the total package, the complete experience.

“Just do it,” she begged, high on lust, feeling insatiable. “You were desperate to do it the other night. So why don’t you do it now?” Her voice came out shaky and sad.

Daniel cupped her face and stopped kissing her. She opened her eyes to watch him.

“If you want me to do it, I’ll do it. But not here. I would hurt you unnecessarily. I’ll make love to you in the bed where’s more comfortable.”

“Okay,” she agreed, breathing deep to control her drumming heart.

DANIEL LOOKED INTO her eyes for a few seconds, trying to understand if this was what she really wanted or not. He knew he wanted it. He was aroused beyond words, and it couldn’t hurt more than it already did.

“Damn it,” he cursed. “I can’t do this to you.”

"Why not?" she complained. "I'm asking you to. Don't you like me?"

"I like you too much, that is the problem! Jade, you aren't thinking straight."

"Maybe not, but, Daniel, I don't need to think straight. I need to feel you. And I want to feel you right now. All of you," she whispered huskily.

His body became even more tense. He clenched his jaw and had a hard time breathing. Her argument was compelling.

"I trust you." She kissed his lips softly. "I know you will be careful and this is going to be special for me. I know that it'll be perfect."

"We won't have enough time," he said

"It's one o'clock. We have plenty of time."

"Trust me, we don't. I might not want to leave this bedroom for a couple of days."

Jade giggled and leaned her forehead against his. "Come on, Daniel, make love to me."

"What made you change your mind?"

"I realized that you aren't evil. Not evil at all. You are different when you are with me. You are gentle and sweet to me. I like you, and we are kind of great together." She offered her face for him to kiss. His stomach swirled with anticipation. "And you make me happy. When we touch, I'm happy."

"You also make me happy," he said as he ran his fingers down her chest and pressed them inside the folds of her pussy. She was wet and hot. He made her move against his hand, moaning with the contact. "I can make you come. And then we'll try tonight."

"No," she protested. "I want everything now."

"You aren't ready yet. You are too tight," he claimed, slipping his finger to her entrance and gently rubbing around it.

"Then make me ready." She sighed, close to his ear. She moved her hips to fully take advantage of his fingers. "I know you want to do it. I know—please, just do it with me. I want to make love to you. I want you so bad."

"Damn it! You are such a tease," he cursed, fully aroused by how she asked him to take her between deep and husky moans of lust.

She kept moving against his hand, letting him go deeper and deeper. Jade offering her body for him to take was all he had ever dreamed of when he first saw her. He wanted to take her right there in the nightclub against the wall. He wanted to take her home and keep her there with him forever.

"Jade," he moaned, feeling his body shiver in pleasure.

She was nibbling and sucking on his neck while gripping his back tight and digging her nails into his skin. She was out of control, and he was barely hanging on by a thread.

In a moment of clarity, he grabbed her under her butt and walked with her to the bedroom.

# CHAPTER NINETEEN: ONE AND ONLY

**DANIEL KNEELED ON THE** king-sized bed and placed Jade, naked, on the sheets. His towel fell away when they both lay down. She was distracted, nibbling his shoulder. He caressed her thighs and moved his head to kiss her neck and shoulders.

She tilted her head back, gasping when he trailed his mouth to her breasts. His hands held her under her armpits, bringing her closer to his mouth and body.

Daniel was on top of her, kissing her exposed flesh and tasting the waves of heat leaving her skin. She was hot everywhere. Her breath was erratic as delicious moans left her throat. He loved the way she let herself go when they were touching and kissing. He could only imagine how good it would be when he finally pushed inside of her and felt her whole body tremble and shake with pleasure. His shaft was aching and, every time it touched her skin, shuddered with impatience.

Daniel kissed her thoroughly on her breasts, his tongue swirling around her areola as her nipples grew stiffer. Then he engulfed one and sucked on it until she quivered under his mouth. Giving the same attention to the other breast, his hand softly caressed her navel. She squirmed under him as her hands gripped his hair.

Swallowing and wetting his lips, Daniel parted her legs gently to nestle his head between her thighs. He relished the feeling of her soft waves of muscles as they tensed and softened with every lick of his tongue circling the soft spots of her pussy. She gasped and swayed her hips, opening herself up to him and encouraging him to keep stroking and lapping his tongue from her core to her clit. He pushed one finger inside to test the moisture of her entrance. Her inner thighs pressed against his face, and he stroked them, spreading them gently and trailing kisses back up her stomach until he reached her throat.

JADE OPENED HER EYES, breathless and aroused beyond words. She almost came before he stopped kissing her and trailed kisses up to her neck. She felt unsatisfied. She wanted more. Yearning swirled around her body as she gasped and shivered under his lips. She needed him to keep touching her where she ached the most. Her clit was swollen and her insides were burning. Daniel's skilled tongue felt like a cool breeze in the desert.

His kisses trailed their way to her throat as his body fell over hers, and they molded together. She could feel the hardness of his shaft pressing against her mound. He pulled back to rub his length against her labia, and she tensed, pulling his head toward her to kiss him on his mouth. She needed more; her body needed more contact and more of him.

His hand parted her lower lips, teasing her entrance, rubbing her, and tracing circles around her clit. Then she felt the head of his cock pressing against her entrance. His fingers were softly teasing her pussy, encouraging her to relax and yearn for his touch. She arched her chest, needing him inside. He obeyed her demands, entering gently and pressing against her walls. The pressure caused her to bite her lower lip hard as she tried to relax and let him in. Gasping, she squeezed her eyes shut and sank her nails into his back.

Daniel trailed kisses down her face, tasting her lips and lifting her under her buttocks to position her more comfortably. When she opened her eyes, he was staring at her face, and she gulped with the realization that he was filling her up. She dug her teeth into her lower lip, unsure if she was experiencing pain or pleasure. Maybe a mixture of both.

Daniel looked worried. He stopped moving while she arched her back and laced her legs around his waist, pulling herself up with her arms around his neck. She kissed him and smiled because she could feel her walls relaxing and adjusting to him, so he could sink deeper inside.

“Why the serious face?” Jade asked Daniel.

“I’m not serious. I’m just paying attention to what you need from me, so I don’t hurt you.”

Jade kissed him voraciously before she gasped, “I’m okay. It doesn’t hurt now.”

“That’s because I haven’t moved yet.” Breathing deep, he added, “It may hurt in the beginning.”

Jade covered his mouth with hers.

“How does it feel to finally be inside of me?” she asked.

"It feels so good to be inside you, baby," he mumbled, breathless and hugging her tightly. "You're so tight and hot."

"It feels nice to have you inside me, too," she breathed, arching her back again when a wave of lust swept over her. "My skin tingles and shivers every time you touch me and I...have this crazy desire... I want you to touch me everywhere."

"I want that, too," he said, slowly drawing out and then moving in again.

She clenched her teeth. Despite her efforts to endure the sharp pain, she groaned.

Daniel spoke softly against her mouth as he said, "Just relax. It'll be good. I promise."

"It's already good," she told him to ease his fears.

Daniel's heart pounded against her palms. A concerned look swept across his face. He was gorgeous and caring. Her lips searched for his, prolonging the sensation of their bodies touching as she closed her eyes and relaxed, glad that Daniel was her first. She liked how patient he was. It was refreshing to have someone who worried about her well-being and feelings.

Jade tightened her hug and softly nibbled on his neck as he rotated his hips and thrust into her slowly, sparking fire between her legs.

DANIEL SEARCHED FOR HER mouth and kissed her plump lips. He kept kissing her while cautiously moving inside her. Pressing himself against her softly, he slid up and down slowly enough to give her time to adjust to each stroke of his shaft buried inside her virgin walls. He didn't want to hurt her. He felt pleased when he realized that she was getting wet, allowing him to slide more deeply and easily. She was so tight that it was difficult not to come involuntarily. He could also smell the blood. It wasn't much, but he was a vampire. It would be impossible for him not to smell it.

Jade's sighs of pleasure encouraged Daniel to plunge deeper, using his hand to stroke her clit to increase her pleasure. Then, he started moving to her rhythm, concentrating on her breathing, and her panting cries of pleasure. He smiled in delight every time she tensed and gasped for more. His body was begging for release, but it would also get more aroused with each gasp and thrust of Jade against him. He could stay buried inside her forever. It was a magical experience, and he was amazed how she seemed to be custom-made for him. She was sexy, funny, blatantly honest, and reacted to him sexually in a way he had only dreamed of being possible. It wasn't a momentary whim of pleasure. He could see himself dedicating his existence to making her happy—to please her and give her anything she longed for.

JADE FELT A WAVE OF yearning swirl between her legs, and her hips lost control. Her body started to push forward to meet each of his thrusts. She breathed out in frantic pants, feeling everything around her spinning. Her hands kept gripping him hard, wanting him to be closer, to go deeper.

Making love to Daniel seemed to defy the fabric of time and reality. Her consciousness was trapped in a spiral of pleasure, numbing her ability to connect with reality. She could feel every single inch of him moving inside her, rubbing and tensing her muscles until they spasmed and rippled sparks of bliss up her stomach.

Jade felt the pressure inside her building from deep down. Her core was burning up for more pressure and more contact. Daniel increased the pace, and Jade's eyes rolled in their orbits as her toes curled on the bed. She was tense and in desperate need of release, but the tension kept building until it finally burst in an earthquake of pleasure.

JADE THRUST DANIEL deep inside her, and he groaned and gasped his bliss. She was milking him with her spasms, pushing him to come. Pleasure shot up his spine at the way she was saying his name repeatedly and in rhythm with each quivering orgasm. It made him groan louder and whimper her name back at her like a boy experiencing his first orgasm.

"Jade, I love you so much," he moaned against her lips, kissing her savagely and becoming hard again.

He didn't want to get off her. He wanted to keep thrusting and make her pant and whimper against his mouth all over again.

She stopped moving under him, and he opened his eyes to understand what was going on.

*Why had she stopped replying to my kisses?*

Daniel got worried. "Am I hurting you? Do you want me to stop?"

"What did you just say?" she asked, pulling him back and trying to get out from under him.

"I asked if you were hurt."

"No, before that."

"That I...uh...l-love you," he stuttered uncomfortably. He sat on the bed and stared at her reddened face and parted lips.

His beloved was gorgeous. He wanted her back in his arms and kiss her until they were both out of breath. He gulped, staring at her pink nipples and luscious curves. Her wet and wild hair fell down her shoulders, framing her pretty face when she sat on the bed and looked for something to cover herself with.

"You don't need to say that to make me feel better."

"I'm not," he stated, feeling hurt by her words.

"We barely know each other, Daniel."

"Look at me." He leaned forward and brought her back into his arms.

Jade stared at him with her shining eyes and erratic breathing.

“We’ve just made love. You let me be your first. I want to be your one and only. So, I expect you to believe me when I say that I love you.”

“Daniel, you’re hot. We have lots of fun together. We clearly have chemistry in bed, but...you’re a vampire.”

“And why does that keep being a problem for you? What have I said to you about being biased?”

She evaded his eyes. “You’ll live forever or, at least, for a long time. I will not. You won’t get old. I will.”

“I’m entitled to change my beloved into a vampire. We can be together.”

Jade raised her eyes to meet his. With a trembling voice, she asked, “And if I don’t want to be a vampire?”

“I won’t force you to be something that you don’t want to be,” he asserted. “I won’t lie and tell you that I don’t want you to accept because I do. Now that I’ve found you, I don’t want to lose you. I want to keep you with me, locked inside this house, and never let you go.”

“That doesn’t help make me feel better around you.”

“I know,” he declared, brushing his lips softly against hers. “But I know that you wouldn’t have come with me if you weren’t forced by a contract.”

“You bet I wouldn’t!”

“And then we couldn’t be together, kissing, making love,” he reasoned, molding her breast against his hand and licking her earlobe.

“You could have…” She lost her voice when his hand slid between her legs.

She was wet and hot. His hardness was constricted against her thigh.

“What?” He urged her to speak. He enjoyed feeling how much she was sexually attracted to him.

“You could do what normal guys do. They invite me out before trying to take me to bed.”

“That didn’t work since apparently none of them had taken you to bed before. So maybe my way was a better method of convincing you to spend time with me.”

“You were kind of a jerk when we first met.”

“Yes, I know.”

Jade devoured his lower lip and moaned, moving her hips to meet his fingers.

“But I’m not used to having girls decline my offers.”

“Cocky much?” she complained.

“I was possessed by lust,” he murmured, swiping his tongue across her lower lip.

“Lust is not love, Daniel.” She exhaled as her body quivered. She pushed him away and removed his hand. Breathing deep, she resumed her speech. “You may use making love as a euphemism for having sex but that doesn’t give you the right to keep manipulating me with words. I gave you what you wanted, there’s no need to keep…”

"Keep what?" He encouraged her to share her thoughts even if his heart was hurting with her lack of trust and reciprocated feelings. "Do you believe that just because we've slept together, my obsession with you is cured?"

"Am I an obsession?" she mumbled with a shattered voice. Her eyes blinked with what appeared to be pain.

"No. You are more than an obsession, honey. I want you in my life, not just in my bed."

"Why should I believe you?"

Daniel moved her, so she was strapped around his waist and his cock was pressed against her navel and lower stomach.

He nibbled on her lower lip as he spoke huskily against her mouth. "Do you want me to stay away from your bed to prove my love to you?"

"No."

"Then how can I prove myself to you?" Daniel asked as his heart clenched inside his chest.

"Stop talking about feelings," she whispered, kissing his mouth and his cheeks.

Jade moved softly against his cock, rubbing and almost making him lose his line of thought. Her hands were gripping his shoulders tightly, helping her move up and down against his length. She seemed to like that position.

"Make love to me like this," she moaned, her body quivering under his hands.

"I don't think I will," he said, eyes closed and body surrendered. But his words came out shaky and his body had other intentions. “Jade...” He concentrated on her pressing her flesh against his cock. It was a sweet torment. It would feel better if he was inside her.

He fought back the pleasure and opened his eyes. “What the hell do you want me to tell you? Why can’t I say that I love you when we’re making love?”

Her eyes were shining when she opened her eyelids. “Because I don’t want this to be some sappy love session. I want you to teach me to please you and, damn it, Daniel, we are not going to argue now, are we?”

“Honey,” he pleaded against her mouth as his eyes became lost in hers. “You need to stop pushing me away. If you are willing to share a bed with me, you need to be willing to share your heart. Do you understand me?” He secured her face between his fingers, but her hands pressed against his chest and pushed him away.

“I don’t want to do this anymore.” She pouted.

Daniel sighed in defeat as she released herself from his arms and turned her back to him.

# CHAPTER TWENTY: TELL ME YOU LOVE ME

**DANIEL LET HER GET AWAY** from him. Jade lay down on her stomach, hiding her head in the pillow. He was lying down beside her, caressing her hair and rubbing her back.

"Stop being like this," he begged, pulling her close and nestling her back against his chest. "Damn it, Jade! It's not my fault that I'm a vampire. I didn't ask for it. But, I can't be mad at it either. Do I like being a vampire? There were moments when I did and others when I didn't. It has allowed me to live longer. It has given me the opportunity to do a lot of good for the world and to find you. But if what made me be able to do all those things is what makes you reject me, how can I be happy?"

"This has nothing to do with the fact that you're a vampire. I've already accepted that. It's about the fact that you think that saying you love me is enough to make me your property. I'm not a thing. My brother isn't a thing. You can't buy us with money or empty promises of love."

Daniel turned her to face him. "They aren't empty promises."

"They are. You have a freaking circus around us. I'm bound to you by a contract. I have to stay locked up in your house. I can't go out and resume my normal life. I need to endure those stupid cameras and the stupid contests. I don't want to live like this. I don't like to share you with that bitch!"

Daniel lowered his head to the crook of her neck. “You don’t have to share me with anyone. I’m yours.”

“No, you aren’t. Yesterday, you went on a date with Emma. A romantic date! Tonight, they will make sure she wins so you go out with her again.”

Daniel understood that Jade was still jealous. That was why she was rejecting his declarations of love. He didn’t like her feeling unhappy about the contest or Emma. He especially didn’t want her to feel threatened by his ex.

“I’ve told you that I don’t want her back. If you must know, the whole date was boring as hell.”

“Even so, you went.”

He raised his head to watch her. “I have a contract. I couldn’t say no.”

“Why not?”

“I would lose money and, well, my vampire dad would be mad at me. There are certain laws among vampires.”

Jade pushed him back. “If this is a contest so you can find your soulmate and if I’m her, then why is the contest still on? Why can’t you just say to everybody that we’re together?” she reasoned with him, her eyes shining with unshed tears.

Daniel placed his hands on her waist so she wouldn’t escape the contact between them. “It’s just three more days and then I will.”

“She doesn’t even love you. She went and slept with Seth. I saw her coming out of his bedroom when I went downstairs to eat breakfast. She’s a liar and a fake. Why is she even here?" Her hands clenched around his shoulders while her voice trembled with emotion.

"What are you talking about?" Daniel blinked at her words.

"Emma. She's a liar. She slept with Seth and Jenna."

"I couldn't care less about her. Besides, it's not the first time she has slept with Seth. They were having an affair behind my back."

"Really?" Jade tilted her head to stare at him. "That isn't very nice of her."

His arm laced around her waist and he pushed her closer until her breasts were pressed against his chest. "She doesn't care who she hurts."

"So why is she here?"

Brushing the hair away from her face, he explained, "I've told you. She's here because she wants to have more publicity for her acting career and thinks that the public's pressure will force me to get back with her. She's a selfish bitch. I'm not in love with her. I'm in love with you. I care about you. No one else."

Jade went quiet for a few seconds. "Well, I can't accept this situation. You've kept me here against my will, kissed me against my will, and keep on making me have these stupid feelings towards you. I'm smarter than this. I'm not going to fall for your charming talk and lies."

Daniel was going to protest when her words resonated in his mind. "Feelings?" Smirking, his heart fluttered with hope as he mumbled, “Honey, you need to understand.”

She muttered, “Yes, the contract.”

“At first, you only stayed because of the contract,” he reasoned. “You are here because of the same contract.”

“Yes, so why would you assume that I love you?”

“That’s cold, Jade. I understand your reasons for being annoyed. I would be extremely upset if you went on a date with another guy. Nevertheless, do you realize the fact that you being upset about this means that you like me?”

Jade rolled her eyes.

“You may even love me,” he teased further as she turned her head to avoid his gaze. “Just like I love you.”

“You don’t love me. You just believe that I’m your beloved, so you think you’re forced to love me.”

Daniel frowned. “How do you explain liking me, then? Do you think it’s an involuntary sexual reaction?”

“What?” Jade frowned. “Like pheromones? That may explain a lot.”

“Whatever it is, we were drawn to each other. We are meant to be. I may have been driven by lust at first—and bloodlust—but now that I got to know you…and spend time with you, I’m pretty sure that I’m falling in love with you to the point that I don’t want to live without you anymore.”

Jade gulped as her eyes gleamed with hope. “Do you promise?”

Daniel nodded and aimed his gaze at her plump lips. “What do you want me to promise? That I love you?”

“Promise that you aren’t saying all those things because you are bored with your immortality.”

“I’m not. I’m not bored with anything. I love you with all my heart. I want you to be my girlfriend. I want you to date me. We are dating.”

“No, we are not. You’re going out with other girls and the next games will be rigged again, so you keep going out with Emma.”

“It’s not my fault, baby.”

“I know,” she mumbled with trembling lips.

Daniel touched her lower lip with his thumb and raised her chin to get her attention.

He spoke softly. “Promise me that you won’t forfeit and do something silly out of jealousy. I can’t let you go, Jade. If you leave, I’ll be forced to choose another girl to replace you. And if I don’t find anyone to date until the end of the week, they are entitled to start this charade all over again until my dad gets enough of this bullshit and cancels the show.”

Her eyes snapped open. “Really?”

“Do you want me to keep dating other girls instead of you?”

Jade shook her head. “No.” She was clearly annoyed by his explanation. “Your dad sucks.”

Daniel nodded and brushed her lips with his. “I love you. Stop pouting and don’t mistrust my feelings for you.”

Jade moaned against his mouth. “I’m sorry.”

Leaning back, he noticed the tears falling from her closed eyes. He kissed her eyelids. “Why are you sorry?”

“For saying all those mean things to you.”

“I forgive you. Just don’t do that again.”

Jade nodded with her lips pressing against his. “I ruined everything.”

Daniel drew circles on her back while Jade quietly sobbed. “Don’t cry.”

Trailing kisses on her face, Daniel was able to calm her down as his fingers wiped away her tears. Then he pressed soft kisses along her collarbone and shoulders, placing her under him as his hands left a trail of caresses down her body. Her sobs changed to long, profound sighs. He rose above her and rolled her over. Moving her hair away from her back, he trailed kisses down her spine and touched her buttocks to help relieve the tension from her body.

Daniel’s chest collided against her back, and he spoke in her ear. “Are you sore?”

Jade didn’t answer.

He nibbled her neck before he said, “Baby, I’m going to make love to you again. But I need to know if you are feeling sore or needy. What is it?”

“I’m burning up,” Jade whispered, turning her head and searching for his lips.

They kissed, tongues entwining and stroking until she tried to turn around to hug him.

Daniel stopped her. “Stay like this. We’re going to try something different.”

Jade nodded.

“You have no idea the effect that your touch and your skin has on me,” he mumbled in a husky voice. “Let me see how wet you are for me.” He brushed her breasts and slid his hand to her crotch to pull her closer. He pressed his hardness against her butt, longing for release.

“You feel ready against my hand. Now, be a good girl and do what I ask.”

Jade gasped as she said, “What do you want?”

“Spread your legs a bit more,” he instructed against her ear while touching her sex and breasts with his hands, making her squirm with pleasure. “Press your butt against my lower stomach and hold still. I’ll be gentle. I promise.” He moved her and placed his cock between the folds of her pussy, gently pressing against her entrance.

RED, HOT FLAMES OF NEED licked through Jade’s body. She shivered and panted as he pushed inside her. Slowly thrusting, he moved in and out, bending her for more contact.

“Do you like this?”

“It’s really good.” She used her hips to help him get deeper and felt her insides burn each time his cock pushed its way down her tunnel.

“You’re so tight and hot. I could be inside you all night long,” he said, gasping between the thrusts.

“We don’t have a night, not even an entire afternoon.”

“We will. I promise you. Now tell me how much you love me.”

“Oh my God! You’re insufferable,” she complained, barely able to speak but having a sudden urge to laugh. “Oh God!” she said for an entirely different reason.

“Say it like this: Oh Daniel!” He was teasing her as he caressed the bud of nerves that was tense and hard.

“Oh Daniel,” she indulged him, going up and down on him. “That feels great.”

She was enjoying it even more than the first time. He was consuming her everywhere. Her nipples were hard as her insides were filled by him and were contracting, helped by his hand on her labia and clit. The pleasure was almost unbearable. She was trying to control her breathing and her moans, but they were leaving her throat anyway.

DANIEL HAD HIS TEETH biting into her shoulder, but he wasn’t drawing blood. Drawing blood would bring her to orgasm faster. Yet he didn't want to rush things. He wanted her to have a full human experience, and enjoy herself while discovering all the pleasures of sex.

Moments later, she climaxed against his hand and milked his shaft with her inner spasms, making him pant and push himself deeper and faster. When he came inside her, she was still peaking, releasing soft and deep moans.

Daniel stopped moving, satisfied. He kept hugging her, sighing against her hair and feeling peace rushing down on him. It was the perfect place to be and the perfect way to hold her tight.

"Promise you'll never leave me," Jade said in a shattered voice that made Daniel open his eyes to analyze her request.

"I'll never leave you. I won't, I promise you. You'll never be left alone, and I'll take care of you."

She nodded, and he knew that she was listening. Her heartbeat was slowing down and her body was relaxed against his. She was tired and sleepy—he could sense it.

Daniel hugged her closer, overwhelmed by his need to protect her. He knew how hard it could be to feel alone. Jade had experienced loss and hurt when her parents were stripped from her and left her to take care of a baby. She could have refused the responsibilities. She didn't, and he admired her for being a strong and brave woman. His woman.

"We'll be a family. Sakura, Stevie, you, and I. We are a family now," he whispered, kissing her cheek and noticing that his words were pointless because she was sleeping.

He could tell her that when she woke up. In that moment, he needed to rest. It was still day time and vampires had to sleep to keep their energy up. He was weaker during the day.

Daniel did his best not to wake her. He moved his arms and got up. Then he took her in his arms and placed her under the covers. He lay down next to her and hugged her against him. He could get used to sleeping with her like that.

Since he had found her, sleeping alone or being away from her was excruciating. There was always a void inside his heart and soul when they were apart.

“Jade, tell me you love me,” he requested, next to her mouth, watching her peaceful sleeping face.

“I love you, Daniel.”

He smiled, pleased. When sleeping, she wouldn’t keep her feelings to herself. It was adorable to watch her sleep talking.

“I love you too, baby,” he whispered, finding it cathartic to tell her that.

He kissed her forehead and then closed his eyes to sleep.

# CHAPTER TWENTY-ONE: A NEW CHALLENGE

**THE DIM LIGHTS AND THE** diminutive space she was in made Jade's heart beat faster. Standing up also increased the tension surrounding what was going to happen next. There was a force field around her, soundproofed. Only she and the computer would be able to listen to the questions and her own answers. The rest of the studio around her was watching as she had been when Emma and Jenna were in the same place as her, answering the questions she had to answer in a few seconds.

Rubbing her hands down the skirt of her dress, Jade gulped and reminded herself of the rules. She tried to ignore the soreness in her muscles and the smile that tugged at her lips when she remembered what had happened that afternoon between Daniel and her. She had to stay focused. She couldn't lose the opportunity to spend time with him. Most importantly, she couldn't let Emma win again.

A twenty questions questionnaire about Daniel's life and random culture was the challenge for that night. The winner was whoever got more correct answers, of course.

The sound of drums suggested that it was time for her questionnaire to start. Jade braced herself to the fast and deadly quiz.

She heard the bell, and the questions began.

"Where was Daniel born?" a female voice inquired.

"Arizona."

"What did he want to be when he was a child?"

"An astronaut."

"What's his master's real name?"

"Hmm… Kim!"

"How old was he when he was turned into a vampire?"

"27."

"How old is he in human time?"

"87."

"What disease did he have that would kill him if he hadn't been turned into a vampire?"

Barely able to breathe between the questions, Jade answered, "Leukemia."

"When was the cure for cancer discovered?"

"2025."

"What's the name of the pharmaceutical company that first sold medicine to prevent cancer?"

"Uroboros."

"What was Daniel's favorite food when he was human?"

"Hmm, I don't know."

"What's Daniel's favorite color?"

"Uhh…blue!"

"What's Daniel's favorite sport?"

"Ice hockey," Jade blurted out.

“How many times did he get married?”

“Once.”

“Did he have any children when he was human?”

“None.”

“What’s Daniel’s favorite charity?”

“I don’t know.”

“Where did Daniel live after being turned?”

“Japan.”

“What college did he attend when he studied to be a lawyer?”

“I don’t know.”

“How many people has he turned into a vampire?”

“None.”

“Who does he love the most in the world?”

“His mom?”

“How can we kill a vampire?”

“By decapitation.”

“What year did vampires let humans know of their existence?”

“2030.”

The buzzer signifying that the round was over echoed and the transparent shield disappeared as the voice of the host warned the audience. “And that’s the end! Thank you for your answers, Jade. We are going to compare the number of correct answers with the other contestants and find out the winner after the break."

It was time for the commercials. Jade breathed deep, briefly closing her eyes as her lips curled into a smile. The questions weren't that bad. Luckily, she recalled their conversation during the previous night. It would be difficult to answer most of the questions if Daniel hadn't shared with her some private information.

Hoping that she received more correct answers than Emma, her heart drummed fast and her palms were sweating. She couldn't lose again. Still, she was aware that Emma had the advantage of having known Daniel for longer.

How much had he shared with Emma while they were together? Daniel wanted her to think that she was special to him, but he was older and had had a lot of lovers. Maybe she was his new obsession. Even if she was falling hard for him, she wasn't foolish enough to think that she had become his entire world in a matter of days.

Jade joined the other two contestants on a circle podium with no chairs. The assistant had instructed her to wait there. After the commercial, the winner would be announced.

"How did you do?" Jenna asked her with an excited smile on her lips.

"Fine. And you?" Jade asked, displeased by the smug smirk on Emma's lips.

"I didn't know many of the answers. It sucked," Jenna confided.

Her best friend's words made Jade think that Daniel's private life wasn't scattered around the gossip magazines. Maybe he shared things about himself with her that no one else knew. It gave her hope that she might be able to compete against Emma's score.

Her stomach dropped, aware of how pathetically fast she was falling for him. He had said that he loved her. She wanted to believe that. Cold shivers ran down her spine, and she felt flustered by how excited her body reacted to their memories together, to his promises of love. Fear and happiness ached inside her heart and soul.

"You look happy," Jenna mumbled as her eyes roamed up and down Jade. "There's something different about you."

Jade bit her lower lip. That was not the time or the place to talk about what happened. Plus, they had microphones on, and the staff could hear everything they said.

"Ten seconds," a voice shouted as the lights got brighter, ending their chat.

The host reappeared from the corner of the studio. Shining in his black suit, he spoke to the cameras. "Before we announce the results, we are going to reveal the prize for tonight's challenge." He made a suspenseful pause as he flashed a white smile. "By request of our charming bachelor, the winner and he will have an unforgettable night at the glamorous Fundraising Ball at the Splendor Hotel in Miami. Our brilliant businessman has kindly offered his valuable 19th-century paintings collection to the auction taking place tonight. The money raised will be used to build new schools for the poor and finance scholarships to high-achieving youth with financial need. You can also join this cause by transferring credits to the bank account number appearing on your screen."

The applause sound played as the contestants clapped their hands. Jade felt her heart sinking even more in her chest. She wanted—needed—to win that date with Daniel. It would be excruciating if Emma won again and completely unfair.

"And the winner is..."

The drum roll suspense played as Jade held her breath.

"Jade!"

Jade didn't realize that she had won until Jenna screamed hysterically in her ear and hugged her effusively while shouting, "You won! You won!"

"Congratulations, Jade! Daniel is waiting for you to join him in the mansion," the host said, heading to Jade and giving her his hand.

He escorted her to the exit of the set. An assistant came to take her away as the host returned to the set and continued to chat. The rest was all a blur since her heart was beating deafeningly loud and all she cared was that she was going to see Daniel again.

APPROACHING THE HOTEL, the limo pulled up out front. The valet helped Jade get out and Daniel offered her his arm as they moved forward to the grand hall. Immediately, people spotted them, cameras flashed as other guests rushed to shake Daniel's hand. He mumbled compliments but strode toward the elevator.

Jade sped up to keep up with him. Moments later, the elevator opened in front of the doors leading to the ballroom. Daniel's hand brushed her lower back as he wrapped his arm around Jade's waist. He led them into the crowded hall without saying a word. His body told her everything she needed to know.

All eyes fell on the billionaire as they made their way towards the table that a helpful waiter had prepared for them.

The vampire pulled out a chair for Jade to sit on, kissed her cheeks, and whispered, "I'll be right back, honey. I'll greet the most important guests and then we can watch the auction together, dance, and talk for a while."

"Okay."

"After an hour or two, I'll make up an excuse and we'll go upstairs. I booked us a suite." Jade's body shivered at his words. "It will be our romantic date for tonight."

"We're not returning home?"

"Only after my romantic surprise. We'll have more privacy here than at home."

"Okay."

Daniel's lips curled up. "I'll try not to take long. In the meantime, Sam will keep you company. She's my most trustworthy assistant."

Sam showed up from among the crowd of rich people, chatting about their lives.

"Hi. Nice to meet you," Sam said with a wave. Turning a chair, she sat next to Jade while Daniel began charming the guests.

Waiters cruised by and offered Jade food and drink. She accepted them gladly but stayed away from alcohol.

"Jade!" Seth greeted with a boyish grin. "You look so pretty tonight. I understand that you won tonight's challenge?"

"Good evening, Seth," Jade said, smiling.

"Would you give me the pleasure of a dance?" Seth asked, taking her hand and slightly stroking her palm with his thumb.

"I don't think that's wise. Daniel is still upset about what happened the other night."

He released a small chuckle. "It seems my brother loses his mind when it comes to you. I won't insist."

"Thank you. I hope you have fun."

Seth left and, moments later, another familiar face hovered over Jade's table.

"Hello, Jade," Dominic said with a glint of danger in his blue eyes. "Please join me for a dance."

It wasn't a request but an order because he pulled her from the chair with one swift tug and took her hip within his grip. "We didn't have the opportunity to properly meet each other the other night. I'm..."

"I know who you are," Jade interrupted him.

"Good." He moved to the center of the room where other couples danced to the soft sound of classical jazz.

Despite the physical contact, Dominic kept a friendly distance between their bodies. "It seems my son has taken quite an interest in you. It's preventing him from keeping his head in the game."

"What game?"

Curling lips and serene expression alerted Jade that Dominic was playing nice.

"We are facing dangerous times. Vampires are losing points. People are beginning to be afraid of us and want to control our number even further. We need the good publicity. I needed Daniel to get back with Emma."

"He clearly doesn't want to." Jade glared at him. "We are in love."

Dominic grinned, and Jade swirled in his arms, unaware of her surroundings.

"Yes, it seems that he's under the impression that you are his."

Jade arched an eyebrow, waiting for the snarky remark.

"I can respect that," Dominic added. "As long as it's good publicity. I guess what I'm trying to say is that your union is being well-accepted by the viewers. So, I'm not against it anymore."

"Really?" Jade's eyes widened in surprise.

"Well, don't look so shocked. We had some backlash when you were taken against your will. A few activists signed a petition to release you from your contract."

Jade's stomach dropped. "Are you serious?"

"I am. You have been all over the news."

"I hope I didn't cause Daniel any trouble."

"You did, but nothing we can't fix now that your animosity toward him is gone."

Jade looked at the couples around them and wished that Dominic would stop spinning around.

"Of course, there are still people who want Daniel to get back together with Emma," Dominic continued. "However, it's clear that you're his favorite. After all, you are his beloved."

"Yes," she mumbled.

"I'm glad you agree. You should know that by law, you are allowed to be turned into a vampire. Therefore, it's in my best interest that you allow Daniel to date you."

"Hmm." Jade frowned deeply. "What do you really want from me?"

Dominic smirked. " The director warned me that tomorrow, we will have a special edition of the show. Just remember this, Jade. If you truly love Daniel, save him the trouble of having to participate in this show once again because you were too proud to tell him yes."

"Say yes to what?"

Dominic turned Jade around and she stumbled against a man behind her. Strong and warm hands secured her on her feet.

"She's all yours, Son," Dominic said.

Jade realized when she looked up that she had bumped into Daniel.

"Are you all right?" he asked with caring eyes.

She nodded.

"What did he want?"

"He wanted to give us his blessing, I think."

Daniel's brows furrowed as his lips pursed. "The auction is starting. Let's sit down."

He led her to their designated seats, and more appetizers were served.

The auction went by without Jade realizing since her attention was on the beautiful paintings and Daniel's explanations about who the painters were and what era they were from. Nevertheless, once everything was sold, her date was once again shadowed by guests wanting to talk to him.

Jade made her way to the balcony and watched the city below. Minutes later, Sam showed up beside her, carrying a glass of orange juice which she offered to Jade.

"Thank you."

"Are you bored?" Sam asked.

Jade nodded.

"It's always like this. You will need to get used to it."

"At least the auction was a success."

"Yes. Daniel is pleased. He sent me here to take you upstairs."

"To the suite?"

"Yes. He will be joining you soon enough."

Jade nibbled on her lower lip. "Does Daniel bring a lot of girls to attend his parties?"

"No. Not really. He dated Miss Emma for a while, but she was always too busy to come with him. Mr. Wolfe is...a remarkable man. His life isn't how it's portrayed by the press. The majority of gossip items are made up to sell magazines. My boss is a philanthropist and not a womanizer."

Jade took in her words with an elevated heartbeat. She needed the confirmation that Daniel was a good guy.

"Shall we go?" Sam asked.

Jade gave her another nod.

Shortly after, they were exiting through a safety door and entering an elevator that would take them to the room Daniel had booked for them. She wasn't going to pretend that she didn't want to be with him. Her body missed him. She was going to wait for him and enjoy their time alone—away from other people and the cameras.

# CHAPTER TWENTY-TWO: IMPORTANT PLANS

**DANIEL TAPPED HIS FINGERS** on his desk as he looked at the screen of his computer. Leaning back in his seat, he instructed his virtual assistant, "Jaz, could you call my father?"

Jaz was Daniel's artificial intelligence software that ran all aspects of his business and his home.

"It's ringing, sir," the virtual assistant warned.

Dominic's hologram showed up from across the desk. "What can I do for you, Daniel?"

Daniel sat straight and fixed his jacket. "Good afternoon, Father. I'm calling to make sure that Jack warned you about the modifications that were made to tonight's contest."

"I knew about this since yesterday. He just called me to confirm that everything was ready," Dominic informed with a serious face.

"And?" Daniel crossed his arms. "What do you think? Are you going to talk me out of it?"

Dominic fixed his cuffs before smirking. "No. I believe it will be beneficial for the ratings. I'm just worried that you'll make a fool of yourself. After all, you are going live and there's no way we can edit it after or remove it completely."

Daniel opened his arms and gestured Dominic to calm down. "Let me worry about that. I just want to make sure that you'll not boycott my intentions."

Frowning, Dominic assured, “I would never do that, Son.”

Daniel arched an eyebrow. “Last time we’ve talked about Jade being my beloved, you didn’t seem that excited.”

“How did your night go? Did you have fun? You left the party early.”

Daniel pursed his lips, aware that his father was changing the subject. “It was good. I spent the night getting to know Jade.”

“I heard that you went for a helicopter ride with her.”

“Yes. I showed her the city before we returned home.”

“That’s nice. I’m glad you are happy. It’s been a while since I’ve seen you this happy.”

Daniel’s lips curved into a smile. “Thank you. I’ll call you to tell you how it goes.”

“Don’t bother. I’ll see it live tonight. I’ll talk to you tomorrow,” Dominic said, waving his hand and disconnecting the call.

Daniel placed his hands on his desk as his eyes focused on the painting on the other side of this office. Seconds later, someone knocked on the door.

“Sam is outside,” Jaz warned.

“Let her in,” Daniel ordered.

“Good afternoon, sir.” His personal assistant entered with a reader in her hand. “I hope you had a good rest. There’s a lot of paperwork to be done, and I have a few documents that require your signature."

Daniel leaned back in his chair, a sigh leaving his chest. "Hi, Sam. How are you?"

The young woman smiled. "I'm great, sir. Only a bit busy with all the preparation for tonight."

"Did you find what I asked you to?"

Sam sat in front of his desk. "Jaz, please show Mr. Wolfe the contracts that need to be signed right away." She tapped on her reader and swapped the documents to upload them to the computer's main system. "And yes, sir. I have your order."

"Great." Daniel looked at his desk that lit up and showed a document. "I'll take care of business and sign all you want. Yet I need you to tell me when Stevie arrives from school. I want to spend some time with the kid."

"Okay," Sam replied.

Daniel looked up. "Jaz, is Jade still sleeping?"

"Yes. Do you want me to open the shades?"

"No. Let her rest. She'll have a stressful contest tonight. Where's Jenna and Emma?"

"By the pool."

"Could you tell one of the servants to pack Emma's belongings? She won't stay here for much longer."

"I'll take care of that, sir."

"Mr. Wolfe, do you think that's wise?" Sam asked with an apprehensive expression.

"After tonight, her presence here won't be required."

Sam hugged her reader against her chest. "I'm happy for you. I am. But I still believe we should investigate the girl and her brother, further. There's a lot of things we don't know. The whole incident in the club wasn't favorable for your image. She didn't want to come..."

Daniel raised his hand to stop her from talking. "We are over that. Jade is happy with me here. She understands what she means to me and that she's safe."

Sam bit her lower lip. "Still..."

Daniel folded his hands over his desk. His voice was calm when he spoke. "Sam, Jade is my beloved. I'm happier than I've ever been. I don't care about what is being said on the news or tabloids."

"It can damage the company's value."

Daniel shrugged as he rested his back in his chair and folded his arms on the back of his head. "I have more money than I need."

"And if... I don't want to see you have your heart broken, sir."

"I appreciate your concern. But everything will be fine."

Sam half-smiled and nodded.

# CHAPTER TWENTY-THREE: SPEED DATING

**"WELCOME TO 'WHO WANTS TO BE A VAMPIRE?'"** the host of the show announced, gesticulating as if he was conducting an orchestra. "In tonight's show, our bachelor has prepared a five-questions quiz for a speed date contest. According to their answers, our bachelor will choose a date for tonight. The chosen one will have the opportunity of dining and going on a boat ride with Daniel."

Daniel fixed his collar before stepping into the set and grinning at the host.

"Welcome, Daniel. Yesterday, you had a date with Jade. How did it go?"

"It was wonderful. We danced and talked. I had the opportunity of getting to know her a lot better."

The host opened his arms in a theatrical gesture. "And that's the point of tonight's contest. You'll have three speed dates with them in which you will ask them five questions. In the end, you'll choose who you want to have a date with. Do you think you'll have a hard time choosing?"

The host grinned at Daniel who smirked in return. "Not at all. But I hope that this contest proves me right."

"Then you have a favorite, already?" the host's voice hit a high pitch note that made Daniel cringe.

"That's a secret," he whispered as he leaned forward. "Let's say that I'll surprise everybody before the night ends."

The host's eyes widened. "Oh! Now, I'm curious."

Daniel's eyes lowered to his shoes and a smile tugged at his lips. "Shall we begin?"

"Who will be the first?" the host questioned, looking at the inexistent crowd that had previously clapped. "Our random choice generator will decide."

Daniel and the host looked at the screen where Jade, Jenna, and Emma's pictures were flashing in turns. It finally showed Jenna's picture as the first one to go on the speed date.

The girls weren't far from the main set. They were all dressed up and looking nervous.

Daniel flashed a smile at Jade when their eyes met, and he noticed that her face lit up. She looked stunning in a golden short dress with high heels and loose hair that fell in waves of curls down her back and about her face. His mouth became dry and his heart pounded. The nerves were taking the best of him, but he hasn't going to give up on the surprise he had prepared for that night.

JADE WAITED IMPATIENTLY as Daniel and Jenna had a private conversation that no one could hear because of the soundproofed force field. It was a speed date contest. She only had to endure a bit more before spending time with Daniel. If he chose her. She would feel a lot more confident if they hadn't spent the day apart.

The buzzing sound announced that Jenna's speed date was over. Startled, Jade returned to reality and bit her bottom lip as she witnessed the computer picking Daniel's next date. Her picture remained on the screen. For a few moments, she didn't know what to do.

"Jade, it's your turn," the host informed.

Her legs obeyed, and she walked to Daniel. Jenna passed by her and returned to the podium where Emma awaited.

Daniel's hand reached for hers and it gave her a sense of calm and relief. Breathing deep, she sat opposite him and the sounds around them disappeared. The camera filming them hovered above their heads, searching for the best angle. Jade focused on her vampire lover as he leaned back in his seat and smiled at her.

IT WAS AS IF THAT NIGHT'S contest never ended. Time passed terribly slow when Emma was on her speed date with Daniel. With squinted eyes, Jade could almost swear that Daniel was smirking at his ex while having a pleasant chat with her. She thought jealousy wouldn't take over her emotions, but she was wrong. Daniel was her boyfriend, and she didn't want him near Emma.

"Calm down or they will use your angry face to create more drama." Jenna held Jade's hand that was closed into a fist.

Jade looked at her friend and nodded. “I was just...”

Jenna’s hand covered her microphone and she whispered, “Thinking of different ways to murder Emma if she touches Daniel?”

Widening her eyes, Jade shook her head. “No. Of course not.”

“Then breathe in and smile,” Jenna advised as she removed her hand and smoothed her dress down.

A few more minutes were gone before the buzzing sound was heard. Emma returned to her seat, and the host kept doing his job. Jade tuned him out, aware that Daniel was gone and that the host was just creating suspense before the winner was announced.

They stopped recording for a few minutes, and Daniel was nowhere to be found. Jade did her best to be still in her seat. Jenna kept talking about how her day had been.

“Then, one of Emma’s agent came here to visit her. He brought a photographer and they shot some pictures. Emma was looking gorgeous in the new bikini line. They asked me to join her and I did. I had to sign a non-disclosure agreement and give the rights for them to use my image. It was fun. The guy said I was a natural.”

“I’m glad that you enjoyed your afternoon,” Jade said, looking at her bouncing feet.

“Where were you? Were you really sleeping or having fun with Daniel?”

"Are the mics off?" Jade put her hand over her mic and looked at Jenna.

Her friend shrugged but covered hers. "They said you were sleeping and didn't want to be disturbed."

"I was sleeping. I spent the night with Daniel, but I spent the day sleeping."

Jenna smirked. "Did he exhaust you?" Wiggling her eyes, she added, "You know."

"No. We just talked after leaving the reception. We went to a charity auction and danced. It was…nice."

"Just nice?"

"I got to know a side of him that's a bit scary. He's beyond rich and important. Yet he has a good heart. Our lives couldn't be more different."

"Do you think we'll be famous after the show is over?"

"I have no idea, but I hope not. I can't deal with the media following my every move and talking about my private life."

"He'll—"

"Everybody return to your places. We are going to record again," a voice announced.

People rushed to the set and prepared everything.

Jade and Jenna focused their attention on the host while Emma returned to her place.

"Three beautiful women. One bachelor handsome vampire. Who will the billionaire Daniel

Wolfe choose to be his beloved?" the host began his speech. "On tonight's show, our bachelor had three speed dates with these gorgeous beauties. One conquered his heart for the night and is going on a date. Who will it be? The answer is in this envelope." He showed the golden envelope. "The lucky winner will have dinner with him, followed by a boat ride on his private yacht. Under the stars, they will share a drink and get to know each other even better. It's a unique opportunity to conquer our bachelor's heart and become his chosen one."

The suspense sound effect echoed in the background. The host smiled as he began to shred the envelope. His eyes focused on the paper when he screamed and showed it to the cameras, "Jade!"

Jade's heart leaped in her chest, and she looked at the paper with her written name on it. She had been holding her breath, her hands squeezing her dress. Getting up, she walked to the host who was waving for her to join him.

"How do you feel?" his arm circled her shoulders as he spoke closer to her.

"I'm happy for being chosen," she managed to say.

"Do you think that because you won two times in a row you are his favorite so far?"

Jade blinked several times, unsure what to reply to the host.

The vampire reformulated his question, "Did you want to win, Jade?"

"Yes."

"Are you eager to go to Daniel?"

"Yes."

"He's waiting for you upstairs. We are going to escort you to him." The host let go of Jade and redirected his attention to the camera hovering in front of them. "And you are going to join us in a few minutes, after the commercials, to watch all the best parts of their date. Don't miss out on the most important moment of this show."

"Cut," the director shouted.

The host's shoulders slumped, and he lost his smile. "Someone bring me a glass of blood. The heat in here is killing me."

Loosening his tie, he strolled away and left Jade behind without even looking back.

"Jade," someone called her name.

She looked across the set and saw Daniel's assistant waving at her. Smiling, she walked to her.

"Hi!" the young woman said with a happy smile. "I'm here to take you to Daniel. He's waiting upstairs in his bedroom to talk to you before they start recording again."

"Okay."

"Are you okay? You look pale."

"I'm feeling a lot better now."

"Let's go, then. Daniel is eager to see you."

MOMENTS LATER, JADE ENTERED Daniel's bedroom and smiled at the sight of him.

Walking to her, Daniel wrapped his arms around her and hugged her tight.

"Did you miss me?" he asked.

"Yes," she whispered, smiling and hiding her face against his neck. "Why didn't you come to see me this afternoon?"

"I had contracts to sign. Sam kept me busy. But we have the whole night to be together."

Jade nodded, raising her head to look at him.

"What's wrong?" He tucked her hair behind her ear.

"I don't feel like facing the cameras again. I like the idea of dining with you, but with the cameras, we can't say everything we want to say."

"What do you want to tell me that the others can't know?" he asked her sweetly as he caressed her cheek with his thumb.

Jade scratched her nail on his coat. "You know what I mean."

"I do. That's why I wanted this moment alone with you."

Her heart raced and her lips curled into a smile.

Daniel added, "There's plenty of things we can do once the dinner is over and the cameras are off."

"And the boat ride?"

"I made a few modifications to tonight's plans. Don't worry about it," he whispered against her ear, making her giggle when he feather-kissed her neck. “Are you happy with a romantic dinner in the dining room’s balcony or do you wish for something else?”

“It’s fine like this.”

“In a few moments, they are going to take you to the balcony. The recording crew is there. I’m going to be there, too. Just smile and play along. After they record what they want, they will leave us alone until we go live in my brother’s reality show.”

“What do you mean?”

“It’s part of the plan to increase the ratings. Don’t worry about it.”

“Okay,” she agreed.

“I’ll be there with you, honey.” Daniel cupped her face and kissed her lips.

“Your hands feel cold,” Jade noticed. “Are you trembling?”

“I’m a bit nervous.”

“Why?”

“We don’t have enough time to talk now.” Before she could protest, Daniel kissed her deeply, making her lose her breath. “See you in a bit,” he said before exiting his bedroom.

A girl came in to fix Jade’s makeup, and another instructed her on how to make her grand entrance to the balcony. She schooled her on where to stand and which camera would be capturing her interview.

Jade nodded to everything. She was nervous and

excited at the same time. She would gladly skip dinner if they could be left alone. She was happy the crew members weren't around her twenty-four seven, recording and following her and Daniel everywhere.

JADE THOUGHT THAT she had an idea of what was waiting for her outside on the balcony, but she didn't. The moon was huge in the black sky and the dinner table was breathtaking. There were candles and flowers, and the table was set for three. That intrigued her. Daniel was gorgeous in his tuxedo, looking like Prince Charming. Next to him was a violin player, who began playing the moment Daniel walked his way to get Jade and take her to the table.

"You look gorgeous," Daniel said, grabbing her hand and kissing it. "Do you like my choice of restaurants?" he asked, grinning wide.

Jade laughed and nodded. "It's perfect! But why three seats? Who is going to join us?"

"Well, I have another surprise for you," he announced. "We have a guest."

Jade narrowed her eyes. She wasn't fond of surprises. "Who?"

"Him," Daniel motioned to the balcony door.

Jade turned to look where he was pointing. "Oh!"

She couldn't believe her eyes. Her little brother

was there, dressed in a tuxedo like the one that Daniel wore, looking like a mini-adult and smiling cheekily at her.

“He looks so cute!”

“We'll have our first family dinner,” Daniel said.

Jade didn't respond to Daniel because she was too mesmerized by her brother coming her way. Her baby brother, walking proudly, trying to be an adult in his mannerisms. The thought brought tears to her eyes. The fact Daniel arranged this touched her deeply.

“You look so damn cute!” She squealed at her brother, kissing him on his cheeks and squeezing him tight.

“Come on, Sis, I know I'm adorable. Now, let me breathe,” Stevie said, making everybody laugh at his words.

“I've missed you,” she said sweetly and released her hold on him.

Stevie kissed her cheek and hugged her around the neck.

“I've missed you, too. I don't like to eat alone.”

“It's only for a few more days.”

Daniel cleared his throat, demanding attention. “Don't I have the right to a kiss, too? I'm also quite adorable.”

Jade straightened up and stared at him, smiling. “I'll have to think about that.”

“We have matching tuxedos,” Stevie said proudly.

Pleased, Jade admired them. “You both look gorgeous.”

“He’s going to break some hearts tonight,” Daniel claimed, looking at the cameras.

“You don’t mind having him with us tonight?” she asked.

Daniel shook his head. “He’s just dining with us. Afterwards, he will go to bed. Besides, this little fellow helped me with this romantic dinner and even chose the menu.”

“Yes, we are eating mac and cheese,” Steve said, jumping in the conversation and smiling proudly.

“Mac and cheese,” Jade repeated, incredulous about the choice of food. “Seriously?”

“He said it was your favorite,” Daniel explained. “Isn’t it?”

“Well...hmm, that’s our comfort food. But it’s Stevie’s favorite. It’s fine.”

“Jade says that it reminds her of Mom,” Stevie explained.

Jade nodded. “It’s true, little Taz. Mom would make me mac and cheese when I was sad. For a long time, it was the only thing I knew how to cook.”

“I can order something else if you want,” Daniel said.

“No, it’s fine. Let’s sit down and talk because this little fellow has a lot of explaining to do. I went to his bedroom to tuck him in, and he didn’t tell me a thing about this surprise. He kept this secret really tight,” Jade said, tickling Stevie’s belly.

Her brother giggled and tried to run away, hiding behind Daniel's legs.

"He had orders not to tell anyone," Daniel explained, protecting Stevie.

"I told you that she doesn't like surprises," Stevie said to Daniel.

"She liked this one," Daniel argued.

"Yes, I did," Jade confirmed. "Let's sit down and eat."

Stevie ran to the table and sat with a grin on his face.

"I guess he's hungry," Jade said.

"Let me accompany you to your seat and pull out your chair," Daniel said, giving her his arm and escorting her to the table.

# CHAPTER TWENTY-FOUR: FAMILY DINNER

**THE FACT THAT DANIEL** was taking his time to get to know her and her brother made Jade extremely happy. Stevie seemed to get along with Daniel and that was crucial if Daniel was going to be in her life. Though, she shouldn't be that surprised about their bonding since Daniel also acted like a kid. Not that she didn't like the fact that he was playful and witty. She loved that about him. She loved how relaxed he was and how everything looked less stressful when she was around him.

Jade was having a great time. She had laughed and joked. She had even blushed intensely every time Daniel would tease Stevie by saying that his sister was now his. Stevie was territorial about her. She was territorial about him, too. However, she was letting Daniel become part of their family, their secrets, and private jokes.

She almost forgot that they were being harassed by cameras and, soon enough, it would be the time to do a special appearance on TV. Their private dinner would be broadcast across the nation to millions of people, mainly women, who would give an arm and a leg to be in her shoes.

Jade couldn't find any more faults in her situation. She had complained and bitched about it, but she was glad that Daniel had chosen her. Jade wouldn't have gotten to know him if he didn't bring her to his home. Instead, she would have run away and hidden from him.

She hated vampires. Maybe they weren't all the same. Daniel was, without a doubt, special. He was also different from what she had to endure before. Having a vampire stalker was anything but fun. Her family paid a high price for it. But with Daniel, it was different. She liked him, she was completely enchanted by him and dying to be alone with him again.

"After dinner, we will play with Stevie in his new fortress of solitude," Daniel said, waking Jade from her thoughts.

"What?" she asked, pausing the fork in the air to talk.

"Daniel and I made a fortress with sheets," Stevie explained, clearly excited by it.

Jade blinked several times.

"Stevie doesn't like the dark. So, I built him an enchanted fortress to keep the monsters away," Daniel clarified.

Jade's eyes shone as tears rushed to them. She knew why Stevie didn't like the dark. Although he was just a baby, she was pretty sure that the nightmares he'd had about that awful night when their parents were killed were the reason for his fear of the dark. His mind must have kept the memories buried deep inside to torment him during the night.

"Daniel says that no one can harm me when I'm there. We even put some stars to keep me company and they'll be my light in the dark. I can let you sleep there if you want, Sis," Stevie whispered.

"That's okay, little man, I'll keep Jade safe,"

Daniel assured and ruffled the little boy's hair in a paternal way that made Jade smile at him. "No one will ever harm her. I promise you."

"So, when will you ask her?" Stevie blurted out, jumping on the chair and making Daniel become pale and Jade curious.

"Ask me what?" She finished drinking from the glass and stared at their guilty expression.

"Two minutes to go live," a voice shouted to warn them that the live broadcast was close.

"It's a secret," Daniel teased, smirking mischievously.

Jade knew that they were up to something.

"Makeup," another voice shouted.

A wave of people came to interrupt their dinner and spread makeup powder on their faces.

Jade giggled when Stevie coughed and grimaced because of the makeup powder they were putting on him. She shouldn't laugh because it wasn't fun to have so many people around them, trying to make them look perfect for the cameras. But, it was hilarious to watch the makeup artists annoying her little brother.

She let the girls fix her eyeliner and put on more lipstick. Moments later, they all disappeared, and Daniel was staring at her passionately.

"What?" Jade asked, finding him weirder than usual.

"Nothing, you just look gorgeous," he stated.

Staring at the waiter, he made a movement with

his hand. The waiter left, and the director approached them as all the cameras pointed at them.

“Look happy, people! And you are on air,” the director warned.

“Are you happy for winning the game tonight?” Daniel asked on cue to add to the conversation between them.

Jade knew that it wouldn’t look good if they were silenced once the cameras were rolling.

“Yes, you know I am,” she answered with a sweet smile. “I am happy for spending time with Stevie and you.”

“Good because Stevie and I have something to ask you,” Daniel declared.

“Yes, we have,” Stevie confirmed.

Jade stared at him with suspicious eyes. They were definitely up to something.

“What do you want to ask?” she demanded, noticing the movements around them.

A couple of violinists were coming their way. They started to play and, by the look on everybody’s faces, she was the only one who had no clue about what was going to happen. People were smiling oddly around them.

“Jade, look at me,” Daniel requested, putting one hand over hers.

She obeyed.

“This contest is for us to find our perfect match. I must confess that I didn’t think it would happen to me. Even if I was tired of being alone."

Jade curled back in her seat as her cheeks burned and her body trembled.

"I've always wanted to have a family. I didn't have the opportunity to have one when I was a human. I know that there are so many things that we still need to work out and find out about each other. Still, I'm certain about something. You are my beloved. That means that we are meant to be...and..."

Daniel got up. Stevie took a box from his pocket and gave it to Daniel. Kneeling in front of Jade's chair, Daniel cleared his throat before speaking again. "Will you marry me?"

The moment she saw the box, she knew he was going to propose. It was so cliché and romantic that she freaked out and panicked. Her breath was narrowed and heavy. Her hands started to shake. Her mind went totally blank and her eyes were frozen on the amazing diamond ring that was inside that little black box.

"What do you say? Do you want to spend the rest of your life with me?" he asked, caressing her hand.

"The rest of my life," she repeated, unsure if she was hearing him correctly.

He nodded. "I love you and you love me, too. I want to marry you. I don't want another week of searching for a soul-mate that I already know I've found. I don't want to play any more games. We are meant to be, you just need to say yes. Please, say yes."

His voice trembled when he spoke. Jade knew he was afraid she was going to say no. Why did he even ask then? He should have prepared her for it. He caught her off guard. It wasn't nice of him to do that to her. She was on national television, with millions of women envying her right then. Millions of women wanting Daniel for themselves.

Jade focused on his eyes and face. Then she focused on what her heart wanted. Her heart wanted Daniel for herself. Saying yes would end that freak show, and it would send the competition away.

She stared at Stevie. He was quiet, waiting for her to give Daniel an answer.

"What do you say, little brother, do you approve of Daniel or not?" she asked him, trying to be cheerful about it.

"He's okay for a vampire," the kid replied.

Jade chuckled and placed her hand against her mouth to muffle the sound. Her brother was right. Daniel was nice for a vampire. If her brother approved of him, then she didn't have anything to worry about. The most important person to her, before she found Daniel, was approving Daniel. If Stevie was happy, she was happy, too.

"We can be a family, Jade," Daniel whispered as his eyes became darker.

"Okay," she whispered almost inaudibly.

Daniel frowned. "Did you say okay?" he questioned as if making sure she was agreeing to marry him or not.

"Okay. I'll marry you," she said with a nod and a smile. "I'll marry you," she repeated, leaning closer to his face and kissing him. She almost fell on the floor when he grabbed her to kiss her deeper.

A wave of applauses echoed around them.

Daniel released her mouth, and Jade watched as he removed the ring from the box and his hands shook nervously. Placing the ring on her finger, it got stuck and she had to help him finish the job. After, she kissed him again.

Knowing that he was nervous only made her feel happier. It meant he cared for her as much as she wanted him to. She touched his face, trying to make him understand that everything was fine, and he didn't need to be worried and anxious. She wanted him and was happy he wanted her, too. Her heart was beating fast and there were no words that could describe what she was feeling. She could almost cry from happiness. She was trying not to. Not while live on national television.

"I love you," he whispered only for her to hear. He kissed her still on his knees in front of her.

"And we are off the air," a voice shouted and the wave of applause stopped.

Daniel kept kissing her until he got up with her in his arms and broke their kiss.

"I could swear you were going to say no," he confessed.

Jade smirked, caressing the tension on his furrowed eyebrows. "So why did you ask me?"

"I love you. I want to marry you. And I'm tired of

this freak show. I want them to leave us alone."

"I want them to leave us alone, too."

"Could you please stop the kissing? I'm trying to eat here," Stevie complained.

Jade and Daniel laughed.

"Congratulations." Some guy came to Daniel's side and reached to shake his hand.

A lot more of the crew came to congratulate them on their engagement. Jade stood there, next to Daniel, thanking them and smiling like a fool. She was a happy fool, though.

Then, it was the director's turn to approach them. The guy rubbed his neck and looked at Daniel uncomfortably.

"The audience ratings went through the roof with this marriage proposal," the guy said. "It was a smart move. Now you have to keep your part of the deal. We are going to leave tonight. The other contestants will also leave."

"Can Jenna stay?" Jade asked, jumping into the conversation. "She's my best friend. I want her to be here with me."

"She can," Daniel said, holding her closer to him.

"Remember that you agreed to broadcast the wedding, and you've sold the rights to us. It's a good publicity for vampires all over the world, a real fairytale. It's been a year since the show first broadcast, and there weren't any couples coming out of it. Your dad will be pleased," the director added.

Jade noticed how Daniel's face became dark.

"The details can be shared in private with me. Jade doesn't need to listen to this," Daniel said with an unfriendly tone. "I want you and your crew out of my home. Take Emma with you. Her bags are already packed. Next time you come to my house, it will be the last. I don't want anyone else meddling in our private life."

"It's a shame that you didn't pick Emma, but...well, I'm sure she'll find a more suitable mate," the guy said before leaving.

Jade was certain he was trying to provoke Daniel.

"I'm sure she will," Daniel retorted as his lips curled into a smile and his hand tensed against her hip.

Jade felt like slapping the guy for being such a prick. He was being stupid on purpose because he didn't approve of Daniel's choice. He didn't approve of her. She couldn't care less.

"What a jerk," she whispered when the director disappeared.

"He should marry her if he is that keen on defending the witch," Daniel said only to smile wickedly as he faced her.

Jade got worried. "What?"

"We got rid of all of them, and we have the house to ourselves," he reminded her.

"What was he saying about the wedding?" Jade questioned.

"We'll talk about that in the morning. Now," he

said, staring at Stevie who was finishing his dessert. Raising his arms above his head, he shouted, "Fortress fight! Let's show Jade our lasers and our fortress."

"Yay!" Stevie screamed in excitement, pushing the plate aside and jumping on his feet to follow Daniel into the house.

"What?" Jade had no idea of what they were talking about.

Daniel picked her up, bridal style, and rushed inside the house. They ended up in Daniel's playroom, where a huge tent made of sheets was displayed.

"Welcome to your castle, Milady. We need to get in before the enemy arrives. Battle stations, Stevie! We have trolls to defeat!" Daniel yelled orders, making Stevie run inside the fortress and pick up laser beam swords.

Jade joined the fun, fighting against the invisible enemy. Then, they laid down on the mattress, under the starry sky of the fake stars glued to the sheets. Daniel told Stevie a crazy story about astronauts and evil extraterrestrial beings that wanted to conquer the universe. Stevie fell asleep, tired and happy. Daniel took him to bed and helped Jade change him into his pajamas and tuck him in.

"WHY DID YOU SAY YES?" Daniel asked when Jade kissed Stevie good night and turned to join him outside of her brother's bedroom.

"Why do you think I said yes?"

Daniel smirked, not letting on that he didn't like it when she tried to avoid his questions.

"You love me," he stated, kissing her before she could protest.

"I love you," she confirmed, evading his mouth.

Arching an eyebrow, Daniel wondered about how easy it was to tell her those words. He felt his chest growing heavy and his breathing narrowing. For some moments, he stared at her in silence as her eyes shone like they always did when they were together. Yet he was unsure if she meant those words.

"Do you really love me, Jade?"

Nodding with red cheeks, she said, "I said yes because you asked me to marry you. You said it would be for the rest of my life."

"I can't live without you anymore."

Jade nibbled on her lower lip with a lopsided smile. "I love how you treat my brother. He trusts you. I like that you care about him."

"He's your family and a great kid. We'll be best friends."

Her hand touched his face. "Daniel, saying that you'll love me for the rest of my life, does that mean that you are giving me the choice to want to be a vampire or not?"

"Yes, I am. That doesn't mean I would like to live anymore once you are dead," he replied, voice laced with emotion. "I can't...fully explain to you, Jade, but, without you, my life looks dull and pointless.

I've lived more than I was expected to, and I'll be more than grateful for the years that I'll have with you."

Jade stared at the buttons of his shirt and played with one of them. "I have time to decide whether I want to be a vampire or not. I'm only twenty-one. You were twenty-seven when you were turned."

"Yes, you have a lot of time to decide. I'll love you even when you are old and wrinkly," he said in a playful tone.

"You better or I'll chase you down and stake you!" she warned, trying to make a serious face.

"I'm so scared right now that I don't know how I'll be able to sleep!" he joked. "Wait, it's night. I don't need to sleep. We don't need to sleep. The night is still young, and I have a fiancée to play with tonight," he teased. "Do you want to try on the wedding gift I bought for you?" he asked huskily, playing with a strand of her hair.

"What wedding gift?"

He smirked, and she rolled her eyes at him.

"It's something naughty, isn't it? Your face gives you away."

"French maid costume," he answered as he wiggled his eyebrows.

Jade slapped him on the shoulder as her eyes went wide. "You better be joking!"

"No, I'm dead serious. Now, come on, it's time for the grown-ups to play," he said, slapping her butt as he escorted her to the corridor.

Jade shrieked at his action. He grabbed her by her waist and threw her over his shoulder to carry her to his bedroom.

# CHAPTER TWENTY-FIVE: THE DRESS

**WEDDING ARRANGEMENTS.** Who knew it was so hard to plan a wedding in a week? Jade was glad Daniel had hired help to speed things up. There were the flowers to choose, the cake—not that vampires eat cake—, and the dress. Oh, the dress! She thought it would be easier to choose the right one. It wasn't. There were many types of dresses. Should she choose a more fashionable look or a more old-fashioned one? Jade loved the princess ones with a lot of lace and silk. Daniel wanted it to be white. She would rather have it golden. They decided to go for pearly-white.

She was thrilled that Jenna was there to help her choose and handle her meltdowns. After all, she was the maid of honor and best friend. She had to be there. Daniel was helping, too. He was being supportive about the flash-wedding ceremony. He had to be helpful if he was planning to marry on such a short notice. Jade was just happy for marrying him and for him to be joyful about it. Her happiness was beyond explanation, and it warmed her soul.

Despite the stress, it had been several truly steamy nights. The sex was out of this world kind of amazing. They also talked, it wasn't just about sex, even if she couldn't take her hands off him.

Daniel was attentive to all her needs. They would spend time with Stevie in his enchanted fortress before her brother would go to bed. Jade was glad the competition was over, and she had Daniel all for herself. The cameras weren't gone, though. He had sold their wedding rights to the television network for them to leave them alone for eternity after it. Therefore, she was fine with them recording the moments where she would be trying on some dresses and choosing the cake. It was essential for the show.

Yet Jade didn't know what to think about the big change that was going to happen in her life. She was going to get married to a vampire...and live in that gigantic house with Daniel and Stevie. They were going to be a family—a real family. It had been so long since she knew what a family was... It'd been longer since she let someone win her trust. Daniel melted down all her defenses. He made her believe in love again. Love at first sight.

That day, Jade was in her bedroom trying wedding dresses on with Jenna. She would move to Daniel's master bedroom once they got officially married.

"I don't like that one. It makes you look like a scary porcelain doll," Jenna stated, disqualifying the dress.

When it came to finding flaws in wedding dresses, Jenna was worse than her. There was only one day left before the wedding, and Jade hadn't found the perfect one yet. She was getting desperate.

"So, have you decided where you are going to spend the honeymoon?" Jenna asked as she checked a new ruffled white dress.

"Not yet," she answered, trying to open the

zipper. "I think the zipper is stuck, can you help me get out of this?"

"Sure, stay still." Putting the dress down, Jenna came to her aid. "The wedding is tomorrow. You don't have your wedding dress, and you don't know where you are going to spend your honeymoon. Is anything else going wrong in all of this?" she queried with a hint of sarcasm.

Jade knew that Jenna was happy for her. Still, Jade couldn't blame her for being dazed by how fast everything was happening. One of Jenna's biggest problems was that there wasn't going to be a bachelorette party. If this was Jenna's wedding, she'd want male strippers and a lot of drunkenness to fully commemorate her departure from the single status.

"Do you even know who is coming to the wedding?" Jenna asked, unzipping the dress after fixing the wrinkles.

Jade bit her lip nervously. "Well, Stevie, you, and your parents. I don't know who Daniel has invited."

Jenna frowned as she walked to find a new dress. "Aren't you going to invite any more of your friends?"

"Not really. You are my closest friend. The others...they would come just to appear on TV. I could invite my former boss and his wife, though."

"Or your uncle from Connecticut."

"No, he didn't want to know about us when my parents died. He doesn't need to care about us now that I'm getting married to Daniel. You have no idea about the amount of phone calls and messages that people I know make just to ask if they can come to my wedding or to ask me how it is to get married to Daniel. People are such…"

"Leeches?" Jenna tried to guess.

"Girls that never wanted to be friends with me, now all of the sudden, want to know how I am and if I want to hang out with them."

"Glad I kept being your friend, then. I'm lucky to be in the first row to witness all this madness."

Jade didn't know if Jenna was kidding or not. She sounded serious when she said that. She stared at Jenna in the mirror, watching how concentrated her friend was about choosing a new dress from the many that were hung next to the door.

As she picked a dress and showed it to Jade, Jenna asked, "I hope you are happy. I don't want this marriage to be some rushed decision because you had sex with a guy and now you think you should marry him."

She shook her head at the dress. "Of course not, I love Daniel. Besides, I'm not that old-fashioned."

Jenna smiled wickedly. "For what it's worth, Daniel is head over heels about you. He loves you and seems on cloud nine."

Jade's heart tugged at her chest at her friend's words. She placed her hands against her heart. "Yes, I know. I'm just worried about Stevie."

"He loves Daniel."

"I'm still worried. He says he's okay with us

getting married. I don't know what this will do to him. He's used to having me all to himself."

"He's no longer a baby, Jade. Besides, you have to live your own life."

"Can I come in?" It was Daniel at the door, but instead of waiting, he simply entered.

"No!" Jenna and Jade screamed hysterically with his arrival.

His fiancée looked around for a place to hide but there was none.

"You can't see the bride in her wedding dress!" Jenna exclaimed as she rushed to put herself in front of him.

Daniel smiled and peeked from behind Jenna. "Is that the wedding dress she chose?"

"No." Jade slapped her hands to her hips. "But it could have been. It's bad luck for you to see me in the wedding dress before the wedding, don't you know that?"

"Yes, baby. But what I have to tell you can't wait," he said promptly.

Her arms lowered. "What's wrong?"

"Dad wants to talk to you."

"When?" she asked, conflicted about the news.

His famous dad, the guy who was behind the bachelor show and the one trying to make vampires look good to the world, wanted to talk to her. What if he didn't approve of Daniel's choice? The pressure was getting to her. She was paranoid.

"Now. He's in his office, waiting for us," he

warned.

Her heart sunk in her chest. "But...but I'm...not ready."

"Change into something else and meet us there. I'll entertain him until you arrive."

Jade nodded as she fisted her hands in the dress.

Daniel stepped forward since Jenna had resumed her quest to find the perfect dress.

"Don't look so worried. Everything will be okay, babe," he assured with a honeyed voice. He stepped closer and kissed her lips. "I'll be there with you." He smiled and brushed her cheek.

Jade nodded as she curled her lips into a smile.

SEEING DANIEL'S DAD left Jade more anxious than she wanted to be. Sakura was adorable, and they were becoming good friends. As for his dad, she honestly had no clue if he approved of her marriage to Daniel or not. What if he didn't? He didn't have the nicest words to tell her when they danced at the party.

Her stress seemed to be in vain. Daniel was a big boy and old enough to make his own decisions. They were getting married, period.

When she entered Daniel's office, she saw the gorgeous, tall, blond guy who had saved her from drowning in the pool on the first night. She stood at the door, shaking, with her hand on the doorknob.

"Dad, this is Jade, as you know," Daniel said.

Frowning at his bride, Daniel paced to reach her and guided her into his office. He placed an arm around her waist in a more possessive way than protective.

Jade swallowed hard.

"Good evening, Jade. I'm pleased to see you again," his dad said, stepping closer and taking her hand in his. He placed a light kiss atop her fingers.

Jade noticed the amused glint in his eyes as if finding Daniel's possessiveness humorous.

"How have you been since we last met?" Dominic asked.

"Good," she whispered hoarsely. The stress of the whole situation made her feel shy. "And you?"

"I could be better. It seems that we have a lot to talk about, don't we?"

Jade frowned at him, clueless about what he meant by that.

"Let's sit down," Daniel proposed, indicating to the couches in the corner of his office.

Guiding Jade to a seat, Daniel sat on the couch with her as his dad sat in front of them on an armchair.

Fixing his coat, Dominic cleared his throat and resumed his speech. "We seem to have a problem."

"What is so important that you came here to see me in plain daylight?" Daniel's hand reached for Jade's.

"Your publicity stunt created ripples. Some

good. Some bad," Dominic said with a serious face.

"It wasn't a publicity stunt. Jade is my beloved, and we are in love," Daniel clarified.

Jade rubbed her thumb against his palm, so he would calm down.

Dominic fixed his hair and relaxed his left arm. With a smirk, he said, "Son, you above all people know that when we are famous, other people want to piggyback on our fame."

"What does that have to do with anything? Has Emma done something stupid?"

Dominic waved in dismissal. "Emma has moved on to boost her acting career with someone else."

Daniel arched an eyebrow. "Someone else?"

"You'll know all about this on the news. They are going to announce it after your wedding, since it's the hottest thing going around now, and it would overshadow her news."

"We haven't been following the news. I've been busy with work and the wedding," Daniel explained.

He was right, Jade had no idea of what was being said about their marriage or how people were reacting to Daniel choosing her.

"You have nothing to worry about with Emma. But, I thought I should bring this to your attention," Dominic informed. "Many people go out of their way to make vampires look bad and sell magazines. It was fortunate that the director of this particular magazine is one of our own, or we wouldn't have stopped this article in time."

"I don't understand." Daniel voiced Jade's

thoughts.

Dominic leaned forward with a digital reader. “Here is the article for you to read, Jade. Later, you should explain to Daniel what is going on. You shouldn’t have secrets, and Daniel must understand the cost of getting married to you.”

Jade accepted the reader with a blank expression since she had no idea what her soon-to-be father-in-law was talking about.

“I don’t understand.” Jade stared at the black title of the story that some magazine was going to publish. The title read: ‘The vampires’ black widow’.

“Jade should read it alone and decide if she wants to tell you or not. You already know my opinion about this wedding, Daniel. Let’s wait outside.” Dominic grabbed Daniel by the arm and pulled him outside against his will. He protested, but his dad continued shoving him out the door.

They left Jade alone as she began reading the vicious, mean, and far-fetched story that was twisting every single bad thing that happened to her when she was younger.

Jade felt breathless and outraged. People were hateful and evil. They would tell the events in a way that would sell magazines and make her look like the perpetrator and not the victim. The person who had written that was a liar—a pathetic jealous being that should be sued for defamation. She shouldn’t call herself a reporter. Even if it was signed, Jade had no idea who that woman was and what she had against her.

Kneeling on the floor, tears fell down her cheeks.

Her stomach ached and her throat went dry.

Jade heard the door opening. Suddenly, Daniel was beside her.

His hand touched her shoulder. “What is wrong?”

“You should know that the magazine isn’t going to publish that. I paid a lot of money to prevent that,” Dominic said.

His shadow towered over her, but she didn’t look back.

*Does he want me to thank him?*

She didn’t want Daniel to believe those lies. Yet, she had no idea if Dominic did. She had to talk to her fiancé.

Clearing his throat, Dominique said, “I’ll leave you alone. But Jade, you better tell Daniel what happened to you. If you want to marry him, you should tell him the whole truth.”

His words enraged her because the coldness in his voice made her believe that she was guilty as if she was a problem he had to fix. Someone he would rather not allow into his family.

“You should tell me what is in that news article,” Daniel said, crouching down and rubbing her back.

Jade heard the door close. Daniel’s dad had left, giving them space to talk.

Facing Daniel, she uttered, “This isn’t a news article. It’s a bunch of lies. Hurtful lies. Did you read it?”

Daniel helped her get back into her seat. Sitting

opposite to her, he rubbed his hands, looking at her with gloomy eyes. “No. I didn’t want to read it. I want you to tell me your version of the events. I’m old enough to know that some journalists manipulate the truth to sell magazines.”

Jade couldn’t help clenching her teeth before she muttered, “The title is quite explicit, isn’t it?”

“It’s rather stupid and sensationalist,” he retorted. Getting up, he sat next to her and placed an arm around her waist. “Stop crying, darling. Whatever happened to you, I’m on your side. I know you were the victim. Jade, look at me,” he requested, using his fingers to raise her chin. “We haven’t known each other long, but I’m good at reading people. You aren’t a bad person and your hate for vampires tells me that someone hurt you badly. We had decided that you would tell me when you were ready. Are you ready now?”

“Yes,” she mumbled, trying to control the sobs. “I’m going to tell you everything that happened to me.”

“Good. Now calm down, take a deep breath and relax.”

Jade nodded, cleaned her tears, and tried to calm down. She had a lot to tell Daniel. It was a long and painful story. She shouldn’t be sobbing when telling him since she needed him to fully understand the facts and know how everything began and ended.

# CHAPTER TWENTY-SIX: CREEPY OBSESSION

**"ALL OF THIS STARTED WHEN I** was fifteen. My dad worked for a big pharmaceutical company. My family wasn't rich, but we had a good life since he was a famous and important genetic researcher. We were happy. I was happy. At that time, I was an only child and a normal teenager. I had good grades, I had a gorgeous and caring boyfriend, and I thought the world was perfect."

Daniel caressed her cheek and nodded.

Sucking in a breath, she continued, "Everything changed when we went to a Christmas party, and I was introduced to my father's boss. He was a vampire, an old one. It was the first time I was seeing a real vampire. He didn't look young, he was older, at least, old enough to make a teenager see him as someone as old as her dad and not dating material. The problem was that the vampire started to come to our home often. He began by giving me expensive gifts and asking me a lot of questions. Then, he stalked me. He tried to grab me and kiss me. I didn't like him. I didn't want his romantic declarations, but he was obsessed. Even with my rejection, he kept insisting until he tried to buy me from my dad. It was then that my life became a nightmare."

"He tried to buy you? As if you were a thing?" Daniel's voice came out hard as his eye-color changed to black.

Jade nodded. "I'll go back to that. But, first, you

need to understand that things didn't happen fast. It was a slow process. First, he tried to charm me with the expensive gifts and the rich life he could give me. At the time, I didn't think he saw me as someone he could date. I thought he was just being nice. He wasn't. He had sexual intentions. Since I didn't reply to his ministrations and told my family about it, he got mad."

"What did he do? Did he hurt your parents?"

"My dad tried to fix the problem. We went to the police. We reported the stalking and the attempt of buying me. Apparently, we weren't rich enough to have the police's attention. The vampire must have had important friends and the case was dismissed. My dad lost his job and was disgraced. The company lied about his work. They said he'd tampered with his samples. Dad wasn't able to find another job after that. He was doing an important work to understand why vampires were vulnerable to the sun. Since he wasn't willing to give me to his disgustful and crazy vampire boss, he was no longer allowed to pursue his research. Nevertheless, he continued to work at home and spent all his money in trying to keep the vampire away from me. He sued him. He contacted groups that were supposed to help vampire victims. Some actually helped us. Yet the guy would always find a way to scare our helpers away."

"It sounds terrible."

Gulping as she fought the tears that prickled her eyes, she said, "It was. We decided to change our names and move to another town. Our home was taken by the bank. My dad had to take out a mortgage to pay the bills, and then he couldn't afford the mortgage. We had nowhere to live, and Mom, by then, was pregnant with Stevie. It was hard to live with the guilt. Sometimes, I wanted to give up and just go to the guy and let him have me if that was what it would take to make him stop ruining my life and hurting my family. But, my dad and mom weren't going to be bullied and give up. It cost them their lives, though."

Daniel stroked her hair as his other hand held hers tight.

Jade swallowed her pain. "Once Stevie was born, we were on the run again. We had found a group that was willing to give us shelter, a new identity, and move us to another continent. It was a more reliable group. Its leader was fearless. He had a daughter of my age. We became friends. Life seemed to get back on track. I went back to school and made new friends. Then, I was attacked. My new friends were killed, I was taken hostage. Before they could deliver me to their master, I was saved, and we had to move."

"He killed your friends? Why didn't the police do anything?"

"We were on the run. He had high-placed friends. We had no proof that he was the one behind the attacks. It seemed like a random act of violence."

Daniel nodded. "Then what happened?"

"My family and I weren't able to leave town. He tracked us down. The car he was in pushed us off the road. My dad died in the crash. A branch pierced his chest. My mom, I thought she was dead, too. Stevie was crying out with fear. I was scared, too. I could see my stalker walking to our car with a distasteful smile on his face. He was coming for me. I had no idea what he was going to do to me. I tried to push him away when he ripped the door away to pull me out. He entered, mumbling my name while smiling wickedly, showing his fangs and his dark eyes."

Daniel's hand held hers tightly and his hand rubbed her back.

Jade cleaned the tears from her eyes. "He had killed my parents, and I knew he was going to kill my brother. He was saying that I was an ungrateful whore and that I was going to pay for my rejection. He wanted to reach Stevie and kill him. I wasn't going to let him touch my little brother. I kicked and punched him, but he was stronger. He grabbed my arm and pulled me out. When I thought he was going to kill me, his eyes opened wide in shock as my mom had rammed a stake into his back. He turned around and slapped my mom's face so hard, he broke her neck. I screamed louder than ever. Then I did what I had been taught to do. I grabbed the gun that Dad had put in the car and shot him in the middle of his forehead. He fell backward."

"Was he dead?"

"I believe so. I wasn't sure about what I was doing. I was acting out of instinct. I grabbed my brother and ran to the road. I saw the police lights coming our way. There were other cars stopped, people staring, others on the phone, but no one wanted to help us. We were covered in blood and crying. Only when the ambulance arrived someone gave us assistance. The people who were helping us intervened, and we were taken somewhere else. We changed our surnames again. I found a job, I raised Stevie and…then you found me."

Daniel's hands trembled when Jade finished her story. He looked shocked.

"I'm sorry. I can understand if you don't want to…"

"To what?" he asked, frowning.

"To marry me."

"The only thing I want to do is kill the vampire who hurt you over and over again. It was not your fault. Why wouldn't I want to marry you, darling?"

"The person who wrote the article made it seem as if I had seduced the guy and was the one to blame."

"That person is a fool and should be sued. No one will publish anything about your tragedy. I'll make sure of that. I'll protect you and Stevie. I found you and won't let anything ever hurt you, Jade."

She nodded as tears fell down her cheeks.

His thumbs pressed against the tears and he leaned his forehead against hers. "This doesn't change anything. We are getting married, and we'll continue to be happy."

"I wanted to tell you sooner. But…I didn't know how to tell you. It would have only cast a shadow on our happiness."

"I understand."

"I'm glad I told you everything," she said.

"You are a strong woman, babe."

"Bad things happen to people all the time. We just need to move on and leave the past behind," she whispered. She was the one crying, but she didn't want him to feel bad for all that happened to her. He couldn't do anything about it.

"Does anyone else know what happened to you?"

"Jenna knows. She is the only one. Her and her parents. They are members of the group who protect humans who were victims of vampires."

"She seems to like vampires a bit too much for someone who was born in a family that is against the existence of vampires," he claimed.

"They don't hate vampires. They just think humans should be able to protect themselves from vampires when they are attacked by them."

"What do they teach there? How to use a stake or a gun?"

"Personal defense, how to use a gun, a stake, and who to call in case of an attack," she explained. "I won't be using any of that against you," she added, trying to be funny about it.

"I'm a good vampire," he said with his wicked smile.

Smiling, Jade nodded.

"And you love me. I'm not some creepy stalker."

She stared at him with a pensive grimace on her face. "Are you sure about that? If I recall it properly, you took me here against my will."

"You had signed a contract."

"That I had no clue was a contract when I signed

it."

"I didn't hurt you and... I didn't, did I?"

"No," she reassured him, touched by his concern. "You can be a bit rough around the edges, but you are sweet on the inside."

"You are my beloved. I love you."

"I love you, too."

"And...I look quite young for my age," he retorted.

Jade laughed while wiping her new tears away.

"I'm not a disturbed man with an infatuation for young girls. You were too young. He was a deranged person. He was a powerful vampire and that gave him the wrong idea that he could have you against your will. Still, you are mine, and if something had happened to you, and I had found you in his possession, we would have big problems. Beloveds are sacred."

"Please, let's stop talking about it." She didn't want to listen to any plans or crazy revenge plots against a bad excuse of a person that had killed her parents and ruined her life. "I told you so you'd understand my past and wouldn't believe all the lies people want to tell you."

"I know, but I can't help feeling protective of you and pissed with that vampire who tried to make you his."

"I know, I understand," she declared, putting her hands on his face and staring into his eyes. "Now, calm down and relax."

"I should be calming you down."

"You should," she agreed with a smile. "I love you, and we are going to get married. The past isn't going to haunt us in our happiest days, is it?"

He shook his head. "So, have you decided on the dress, yet?"

"I've been here since the last dress I tried. How do you want me to decide on anything?"

"I wanted you to think about something else. The florist is arriving for you to choose the bouquet and the flower arrangements."

After sighing deeply, she requested, "Can't you help me with that? I have no idea of what I want. What do you think?"

"White roses with lilies."

"That's nice."

"Stevie and I are going to try our wedding outfits on in a moment. He asked if he could take the wedding rings."

"Do we have wedding rings?" she asked, reminding herself about that important piece of the wedding ceremony.

"I have that covered," he said with a smile. "Do you want him to walk you down the aisle or would you rather have Jenna's dad doing that?"

"I would like Stevie to walk me down the aisle," she whispered.

He nodded. "All that's left is for you to choose the dress."

"No pressure then," she joked.

Daniel held her in his arms and kissed the top of

her head. “No one will ever harm you again. I promise.”

“I’m a big girl. I can take care of myself.”

“I want to take care of you.”

“I guess I can live with that,” she agreed, feeling her stomach clench with happiness.

“I’m a nice vampire, and I would never hurt you.”

“I know, I know.” She raised her head to look at him. “Hush, don’t worry about me. I’m okay.” She kissed him to prove that.

Jade didn’t want anything about her past to ruin her happiness. She was ready to start a new life. Even if her parents weren’t there to see how happy she was, the fact was that everything was possible because of them.

# CHAPTER TWENTY-SEVEN: THE WEDDING

**THE NIGHT WAS BEAUTIFUL**, full of stars and without a single cloud. The garden looked glamorous. The flowers were glowing under the lights. From the balcony, Jade watched the waiters finishing the last details on the tables and the orchestra tuning their instruments.

The wedding would take place at 9 p.m., and the party would happen shortly after. The newlyweds would leave for their honeymoon destination at four o'clock in the morning. Daniel had planned something special for them, a whole week away by themselves. He would have planned for longer, but Jade didn't want to stay away from her brother for too long. She had no idea where they would spend their honeymoon, yet she was certain that it wasn't going to be on an island in the Pacific Ocean.

She was excited about the surprise. It had been a long time since that kind of emotion filled her body. Yet, there was also a cold sensation in the pit of her stomach and crazy butterflies were threatening to come out from her mouth. Going to her bedroom, she ignored the anxiety and focused on getting dressed and having the perfect hairstyle. She wanted Daniel to be wowed by her dress. It had taken her a lot of time to choose it, and she was sure she had found the perfect one.

Jenna was also looking stunning in her pink silky mermaid dress. She was a real beauty, a perfect doll. Jade always thought that Jenna was a gorgeous woman, but she needed to value herself a bit more. She was too reckless about whom she dated, disregarding gentlemen for idiots that were only interested in having a good time. Regardless, it was Jenna's life. Jade had no right to tell Jenna how to live her life.

Her best friend seemed nervous while being a perfectionist with Jade's hair and makeup. She wanted everything to be perfect. Being the maid of honor was an important task. And Jenna wasn't just doing the part of the maid and the best friend, she was acting like Jade's mom. Jade was finding that to be quite funny. Jenna was taking her job seriously and wasn't chasing some hot guy around. Well, she was chasing guys, but only the ones that were preparing the party. She didn't want things to go wrong, and she could be a bit bossy when she was in charge of something.

“You are the prettiest bride ever,” Jenna said, clapping her hands.

Jade looked in the mirror for the hundredth time. She caressed her dress, then turned around to see the back. The dress was fashionable and simple. It was strapless and the bodice was embossed with pearls and crystals. The sheer tulle bottom—short in the front but long in the back—had a small swish of a train that trailed for a half foot behind her.

“Do you really like my dress?”

“It's stunning. Your hair is perfectly styled. It won't fall to pieces, I promise. Your makeup is waterproof since I don't want all your crying ruining the pictures,” Jenna explained.

"I'm sure I'll cry a lot. I'm almost crying right now," Jade whispered, moving her hands and trying to cool down. "Do you think I'm ready?"

"I'm sure you are. A bride always arrives late, and it's too soon to go downstairs. Daniel is still getting dressed."

"How do you know?" Jade asked.

Jenna motioned to her ear, where she had an earpiece. "I've been monitoring everything. They will tell me when Daniel gets downstairs."

"Peekaboo," Stevie said, giggling, after opening the door and peeking in.

"Baby! Are you ready? Let me look at you!" Jade yelped, excited to see her brother.

"No hugging, no jumping, no touching," Jenna warned the kid, who pouted and walked like a grown up in his white suit.

"You look so cute!" Jade exclaimed.

"I look sharp," he argued with a proud face.

Jade leaned down and teased his cheeks. Pinching them and landing a kiss on his forehead, she left a red lipstick imprint. He protested wildly, only to smile at her words. "You look adorable!"

"You should wait for your sister downstairs," Jenna said to him.

"I came here to see if she didn't run away." He stared at Jenna proudly.

"Why would she run away?" Jenna asked.

Stevie shrugged. "I told him that she wouldn't, but he was nervous and wanted me to check on her."

Jade giggled.

"You can tell Daniel that I won't let her run away," Jenna assured, wiping the lipstick from his forehead, fixing his bowtie, and sending him away.

"Weren't you too hard on him?" Jade asked.

"I want Daniel to be wowed so sending Stevie to spy is against the rules."

"Okay, calm down, maidzilla. I'm ready, you're ready. I'm not going to run away. All we need is Daniel downstairs, and we can start the marriage ceremony."

"Aren't you nervous?" Jenna asked.

"Of course, I'm nervous!"

"But you don't look nervous."

Jade placed her hands on her hips. "Should I be running around hysterically?"

"No. I guess you are actually sure that you want to marry Daniel."

"I am. He makes me happy." Jade smiled. "And, we are meant to be."

"Yet that story about you being his beloved..."

Jade stared at Jenna. "Don't you believe it?"

"I don't know," Jenna confessed. "We've all heard rumors. But, it seems to be something uncommon among vampires, or they don't advertise it that often. Do you feel it?"

"What?"

"That he is *the one.*"

"I can't explain it, but I do. Since the first time we met. Although he was rude, there was something about him. Every time we kiss, it feels perfect and right as if...we belong together."

"I'm so jealous." Jenna pouted. "I want a vampire lover to make me his beloved."

"I don't care if he is a vampire or not. We are meant to be. He can sense it because he is a vampire, but I'm sure we would still be in love if he wasn't a vampire. It's hard to explain."

"Okay, you don't need to. You need to pinch your cheeks and prepare yourself for your vows. Daniel is downstairs waiting for you," Jenna announced happily. "I'm going to scream so loud when you say yes that everybody will think I'm crazy."

"You will do no such thing. You will behave and stop me if I try to run."

Jenna laughed while helping her fix the dress and setting the veil on her head. It was a simple tulle veil adorned with a princess tiara.

"You are the prettiest thing. You look stunning, don't doubt yourself. Now, let's go," she ordered, giving Jade the round bouquet of white roses. Jade liked simple and chic. She didn't want to overdo it with the flowers and the colors.

DANIEL WAITED PATIENTLY next to the priest who

would perform the ceremony. He was nervous, he couldn't deny that. A lot more nervous than when he got married the first time. He didn't take it seriously back then.

At the time, it was necessary to have a wife and a family. He had married because he liked the girl and wanted to be a respectable businessman. They divorced shortly after. His wife couldn't handle his busy life, and they weren't able to conceive a child.

Soon after the divorce, he found out that he had a terminal disease. He fell into a spiral of depression, wild parties, and drugs. It was then that he met Sakura and Dominic. They were a couple back then. They fancied him and decided to give him eternal life. He had taken it willingly and never regretted his decision. Sakura saw to it that he changed his ways. She made sure he became a good vampire—one that cared for others and respected human lives. With her guidance, he studied and worked harder. He partied, had fun, and enjoyed life, but he was driven by the wish to find the cure for cancer.

It'd been a long time ago. He had become a solitary rich man, unsatisfied with eternity. Loneliness was the worst for vampires. He wasn't an exception. He had girlfriends, some crazy passions, but nothing like the overwhelming passion and feeling of belonging that he felt for Jade.

His quest to find a companion was only shadowed by his love for inventions. In the end, it was his father's outrageous plan to make money with reality shows where vampires were the stars that gave him Jade. His sweet and innocent Jade.

His gorgeous and sexy bride who was coming down the aisle with her brother, in her strapless dress and tulle layered train.

His future wife was a vision. He wouldn't change anything about her. Happiness reached its peak when he noticed the beautiful smile she had on her lips as joy glinted in her eyes. It was going to be the perfect wedding because they were in love and their vows would last forever, even after death.

Yet he felt restless. The need to walk to her and the thought to bring her closer taunted him. He wanted to hold her hands and feel that she was real and not a product of his imagination.

Dominic's hand on his shoulder stopped him. His dad was stern, but he knew that he wasn't against his marriage. He simply didn't like rushed decisions. Nevertheless, Dominic knew about the existence of beloveds. He hadn't found his yet. Still, he couldn't deny Daniel the happiness of finding Jade. Dominic had been with Sakura for a long time. They loved each other until they eventually grew apart. Sakura left him to pursue her own dreams and interests. She was too young when he found and turned her. Once she experienced freedom, no one was ever able to tame her and make her stay in the same place for long. Sakura wasn't Dominic's beloved, therefore, he didn't understand what Daniel was experiencing.

Daniel turned his thoughts to the boy walking with his bride.

Stevie looked cute in his tuxedo, wearing the white rose in the lapel. He was taking his job seriously and gave Jade's hand to Daniel with solemnity. Many were affected by how adorable he looked, and they were smiling widely at the boy. He was the center of attention. Daniel didn't mind. He liked having Jade's attention to himself.

Holding his bride's hand, he escorted her to the altar. It was decorated with white roses and small lilies. Their eyes locked and even when the priest began his speech, they stood there, hand in hand, smiling at each other and barely listening to what the priest was saying about the happy occasion.

Several minutes later, they were exchanging the vows, putting on the rings, and Daniel was kissing his bride. He brought her closer, holding on to her waist and sealing their lips together. He gave her a tender but passionate kiss. The cameras were recording everything, the photographers were immortalizing the moment. Daniel didn't care because that was their moment and nothing could ruin it.

JADE HAD SPENT the night greeting the wedding guests. She hardly knew anyone. Some guests were famous and others were Daniel's business partners or old friends. She only had Jenna, Jenna's parents, and Stevie that she knew.

Daniel wanted to introduce her to everybody. She didn't mind because she wanted to be a part of his life and that meant being introduced to everybody he knew and considered to be his friend.

She barely had time to eat. Not that she was hungry. Yet she enjoyed herself when it was time to dance. They waltzed and swayed to the rhythm of modern songs. They danced with Stevie, shared glasses of champagne, kissed, and whispered romantic words to each other.

Before she collapsed of fatigue, Daniel took her to their bedroom where she changed clothes and left for their honeymoon destination before the sun was up.

Daniel told her to dress in warm clothes and get ready to fly. His airplane was waiting for them, and they were going to leave the country. Somewhere where they could be together, alone.

The limousine parked next to the airplane, and Daniel helped Jade out of the car. She was exhausted, but she could rest on the plane.

“Where’s Arthur?” Daniel asked the captain that was coming outside the plane to greet them.

There was a hostess outside and another big man that went to get the luggage.

“He is sick, I’m going to replace him for today,” the captain said, touching the lapel of his hat and smiling at Daniel.

“That’s strange, I talked to him today and he said nothing about it,” Daniel declared, looking at the man and then at his driver.

Before Jade could understand what was going on, the captain was holding a gun and shooting Daniel three times in the chest.

She screamed, horrified.

The captain pointed at her and shot, but instead of her being the target, the bullets hit the glass of the limousine that was bulletproof and didn't harm the driver. The driver ducked instinctively and reached for his gun.

Jade kneeled in front of Daniel, panicking at the sight of blood. Vampires weren't that easy to kill, but Daniel wasn't moving. Did the man use some kind of gun that killed vampires? Why didn't he kill her?

The answer came shortly after. The hostess grabbed Jade and forced her to enter the plane. The man that had the luggage shot at the limousine, stopping the driver from exiting.

The captain rushed everybody to enter the plane. Jade tried to get free, but the hostess was strong, abnormally strong. She easily restrained Jade and forced her to sit and buckle her seatbelt.

"Play nice or I'll have to hurt you," the hostess hissed as she handcuffed Jade's hands.

"Daniel," Jade screamed out loud, afraid he might be dead.

The hostess slapped her hard, and Jade lost consciousness.

# CHAPTER TWENTY-EIGHT: ALEXANDER

**JADE SLOWLY WOKE UP**, growing aware of her throbbing headache and parched mouth as she drifted back towards consciousness. She realized her limbs had gone numb from the uncomfortable chair she was positioned in and tried to adjust herself, only to find that her arms and legs were tied up. The darkness around her remained oppressive due to the dark hood over her head. Her thoughts became a blur of panic as the desperation of her situation set in. She didn't know if it was day or night and where she was. She couldn't imagine why they had kidnapped her. Jade didn't even know who *they* were or what they wanted from her.

Worse of all, she didn't know if Daniel was dead or alive. With the saddening memory, she began to cry as her heart shattered into tiny little pieces. They shoot Daniel three times and he didn't move. They must have aimed at his heart. There was a lot of blood.

"I'm glad you are awake," a husky voice said as Jade listened to footsteps closing in on her.

Large, masculine hands uncovered her head, allowing her disheveled chestnut hair to fall around her shoulders. She blinked rapidly to adjust to the bright lights.

"Hi! How are you feeling?"

Jade turned her head slightly to the right and frowned at the source of the voice.

*Is he joking?*

Even through her outrage, however, she couldn't help but notice that he was quite an attractive man, especially when he displayed his perfect teeth like an actor in a toothpaste commercial.

"Hi, I'm Alexander. Nice to meet you!" Again, he flashed her that smile, which reached all the way to his eyes.

"I'm sorry but are you insane?" Jade asked bluntly. She didn't wait for an answer. Instead, she rapid-fired the rest of the questions that had been plaguing her since she'd woken up. "Who are you? And why am I tied up in here? Why did you kidnap me? I'm rather poor. And if you wanted to blackmail my husband, why did you tell your men to shoot him!" She yelled the last part, feeling the tears rushing back to her eyes. Verbalizing that Daniel could be dead was excruciating. They had just got married.

"Hmm." Alexander kept smiling while checking out Jade from head to toe. "You are quite beautiful. Much better looking than on TV."

"Go die in a hole!" she growled. "What do you want from me?"

"I want to ask you a few questions," he answered smoothly, his smile never wavering.

"You didn't need to kidnap me for that," her voice shook but grew louder. "You didn't need to shoot Daniel either."

"I think I did. You see, I've been looking for you for a while now. Then I got lucky and saw you on

TV. But there were a lot of vampires around you. Hell, you married one! I had to take you out of there to protect you."

"What are you talking about?" Jade asked, confused by his reasoning. "Protect me? You killed my husband, and your thugs hurt me!"

"Kierra shouldn't have hurt you. She can be a bit temperamental sometimes."

"Why did you kill Daniel?" she asked on the verge of crying.

"We shot him, that doesn't mean he is dead."

"He isn't?" Her eyes widened and her face showed sparks of hope.

"I don't know. He is a vampire and isn't easily killed. Besides, it wasn't my intention to start a war because I had killed the vampire prince. I just wanted to get to you."

"Why?"

"I'm an old friend of your father's. Since he died, we've been looking for you and your brother."

"That's bullshit. I know all of my dad's friends. You weren't his friend."

"I was. We were working partners. You were quite young when I traveled abroad to pursue my research elsewhere."

"You are too young to be dad's co-worker. Unless... Are you a vampire?"

Alexander blanched. "God no! I wouldn't like to be one of those nasty beings. I'm a werewolf."

Jade frowned, unimpressed.

"Your dad asked me for my help when...well, Octavio tried to kidnap you, but I was out of reach. I was in a faraway part of the world, questing for a plant that would help me speed up my research. I had just found out that you and your family were in danger when I returned to America. By then, your parents were dead, and you and your brother had disappeared." His tone dropped in seemingly genuine sadness at the end of his story, and Jade almost wanted to believe him. If she hadn't been kidnapped, tied to a chair, and held hostage, she might have, but she couldn't bring herself to trust a word this man said.

"That's a nice story." Jade spat. "But if you were my dad's friend, you wouldn't kidnap me and hold me here against my will."

"Oh, I'm sorry about the ropes. I didn't want you to run away before I could explain everything to you," he said, leaning down and starting to untie Jade's bonds. "By the way, it's useless trying to run. We are inside of a secret facility in the middle of nowhere."

"Great," Jade said, rubbing her sore wrists as the last of the rope fell away into a pile around her. "Is Daniel alive?"

"You shouldn't worry about him."

"He's my husband," she reminded him.

"An unfortunate mistake." He sighed deeply.

"If Daniel isn't dead, you will be sorry. He will find me," Jade warned, hoping that her threat scared him and he didn't hear her voice shake.

"Yes, I'm aware of that. Aren't you glad that he can't find us underwater?"

"No, not really," she answered. Then, curious about his words, she asked, "Underwater?"

"Yes. Do you want to see? We are in a secret lab to study marine life. We are almost one kilometer deep."

"Wouldn't the pressure kill us?" Despite herself, Jade's interest was piqued. "How would a lab even be constructed so deep in the ocean?"

Alexander's voice had a hint of amusement when he answered her. "One kilometer isn't that deep. A new transparent material was developed that can support the pressure of the water. We are in a quite extraordinary underwater maze."

Jade stared at the guy, confused by his behavior. "What do you want from me? I'm not in danger anymore. Octavio is dead, and I was happy with my vampire husband, for your information."

"Do you love him?" he probed. "Wasn't it just a show to please the audience?"

"Of course not. Daniel and I are in love."

Alexanders handsome face contorted in bewilderment. "This changes things," he mused to himself. "He won your trust and made you fall for him. You would do anything for him, wouldn't you?"

Jade pondered his words for a second and nodded.

"Even let them kill your little brother for researching purposes?"

Jade's stomach dropped and an icy prickle crawled up her spine. "What the hell are you talking about? Who would kill Stevie?"

"Vampires."

Jade frowned. "Why?"

"To get to your father's research. Can you imagine how the world would change if vampires could come out in the sun?"

Her dad was researching about vampire vulnerability to light when Octavio fired him. But his research was not finished. Jade remembered him complaining about how hard and complicated it was to study vampires and find something that could make them invulnerable to the sun.

"What does Stevie have to do with Dad's research?"

"Stevie was born shortly after your father completed his research. He claimed to have found out how to fix vampire's DNA. Your mother's pregnancy wasn't unexpected. He planned it, inseminating her with human and supernatural genes to give birth to the first hybrid."

"You are saying nonsense. Dad wouldn't do experiments on his own son."

"He was trying to create a cure."

Jade blurted out, "But he hated vampires by then. Why would he want to fix them?"

"To have leverage. If he could find the cure, Octavio would have to give up on you and pay your dad a lot of money."

"Dad wouldn't do that to one of his children.

Stevie... He loved him. He wouldn't make mom give birth to him to prove a theory. Dad wasn't like that."

"Are you sure?"

Jade objected, "He had principles!"

"Maybe, but he was also desperate."

"You are lying," Jade accused him, annoyed and revolted by his attempt of tainting her father's memory.

"I can prove it. All we need to do is get your brother, and I can test him to see if Frederic had found the cure or not," Alexander said with a serious face.

"Who else knows about this?"

"Just me, but I think others may suspect. Octavio was insane. He had a crazy fixation on you. Many weren't happy about him firing Frederic. He was the most talented one."

"So why did no one help him? Why didn't they force Octavio to stop stalking me and my family?"

"Because they were afraid of Octavio. He was an important vampire. They have ranks and degrees of importance in their community. Octavio had power, money, and means to chase you. He could buy-off judges and kill other vampires that could help your dad."

"If what you are saying is true, then why didn't you kidnap my brother? Why did you take me instead?"

"We need you to gain Stevie's trust. You are his sister, the person he loves the most. We don't want to harm him. We want to help him hide. I have no intention of letting the cure fall into vampires' hands. I brought you first because we saw a unique opportunity to rescue you from their domains."

Jade sucked in a breath. "Daniel knows nothing about what you are saying. He didn't even know about my past. I'm his beloved. Do you know what that is?"

"Yes, it means that he would do anything to get you back. Even trade you for your brother, don't you think?"

Jade ground her teeth. "So, I'm here for you to trade me for my brother?"

"If it comes to that. I want Stevie and you to be safe. Still, if you think that the vampire cares about you, then I'm not discarding the possibility of using you to get Stevie."

Jade balled her hands. "Stevie is my brother, I won't let anyone take him away from me."

Alexander waved his hands for her to sit back and calm down. "He isn't safe among the vampires. Do you think they don't know who you really are? And if they don't, they will figure it out. You've fallen right into the snake's nest. Daniel's family was Octavio's lackeys. It's the same as descendants. Octavio turned Dominic. They have blood ties."

"Does Daniel know about that?" Jade asked breathlessly as her stomach dropped.

"I don't know, but I'm sure that once Dominic recognizes you, you are doomed to suffer in his hands."

"He knows who I am," she mumbled. Facing her kidnapper's eyes, she claimed, "They...know, and they didn't do anything."

"They married you to one of them, didn't they? They tricked you to trust them. You can't deny that. Dominic's son made you fall in love with him and you let your brother into their house. What do you think they will do to him once they find out that Frederic's research is, in fact, your brother and that the cure for their vulnerability can lay inside his DNA?"

"They will try to study him and do anything in their power to have the cure," Jade replied as her hands shook. She fisted them over her legs.

"Even if it means they might kill the kid," Alexander added.

"Daniel knows nothing about it! He didn't trick me."

"It was a rather fast marriage and a far away honeymoon. You were going to Scotland. His excuse was to watch the Auroras, but I'm guessing that he wanted you to be far away from your brother, so they could test the boy. They are taking him a lot of times to the hospital."

"He is sick. He needs treatment," Jade explained.

"He isn't sick. He simply reacts differently to what surrounds him and is building up defenses. Stevie is going to be one of a kind."

"How could you possibly know that?"

"Your dad left me a detailed message of how I

could help your brother in case something bad would happen to him. I'm planning to help Stevie. What I want to know is if you are planning to help him or would you rather choose your vampire lover and let your brother die?"

# CHAPTER TWENTY-NINE: FINDING JADE

**VAMPIRES HEALED FASTER THAN** humans, especially if they had extra help. Daniel was submerged in light blue liquid that was pulling out the bullets and closing his wounds. When he was completely cured, he opened his eyes, coming to life and remembering Jade.

"Where is she?" he asked, sitting down and looking around. Men in white coats were there, writing on their LCD tablets. They stopped what they were doing to look at him.

"Where is she?" he asked again, making the movement to get up.

"Calm down," Dominic ordered him, appearing from a secret door that opened. "We're looking for her. Just calm down. There is nothing you can do now."

Daniel aimed his attention at his maker. "Who took her and why?"

"We don't know yet. Someone went to a lot of trouble to take your wife and erase their tracks."

Getting up, he exited the healing tube. Dominic offered him a towel.

After wiping his face and hair, Daniel threw the towel to the floor. "I want her back. I don't care how much they want me to pay them, but I want her back, unharmed. If they hurt her, I'll hunt them to hell and back."

"I don't think this was a kidnapping," Dominic stated. Approaching a desk, he grabbed a reader and tapped his fingers on the screen. "The bullets almost hit your heart. You were lucky. If they tried to kill you, I don't think they were expecting to ask a ransom for her."

"Then what do they want with her?" Daniel asked.

Placing the reader on the desk, Dominic shrugged and put his hands in his pockets. "We don't have a clue. We are as baffled as you are."

"Who else knows about what happened? Did they report it in the news?"

"It hasn't reached the news. I was able to contain it. For all the world knows, you and Jade are on your honeymoon in Scotland, happily married."

Daniel rubbed his chin, lost in thought. "They didn't contact you, they tried to kill me, and they took Jade. Is there something in her past that can explain this? The vampire that had a fixation for Jade, is he really dead?"

"You don't need to worry about him. I'm certain it wasn't him."

Daniel cocked an eyebrow. "How can you know for sure?"

"I know. Octavio couldn't have done this."

"Uncle Octavio?" Daniel frowned. "He was the one stalking Jade?"

"Yes. I didn't put it in the report that I gave you... I didn't want to taint his memory."

"I didn't read the report. Everything I know is what Jade has told me. And I believe her. If you have a report about it, explaining things from your perspective and exonerating Uncle Octavio, then I don't want to hear about it. All I want is to get out of here and look for Jade. I'm going to find her," Daniel stated, grabbing the robe that one of the medics offered him to wear.

"Uncle Octavio may have exaggerated with his fixation for the girl," his dad said, following Daniel around the compound. "However, you know that he wasn't a bad vampire. He...just liked younger girls."

Daniel lashed out. "Jade is *my beloved*. He had no reason to stalk the girl if she wasn't interested in him. He terrorized her, and you and the others let him. How is that right? How does that go according to the vampire code you like to recite and obey?"

"Things aren't so black and white. Uncle Octavio was sure he was in love with her. Of course, it was a fixation. You know there was nothing we could deny him," Dominic made up excuses as he followed Daniel down the corridor.

"I'm glad he is dead then," Daniel growled. "Or I would kill him myself."

"Don't talk nonsense. Octavio was the strongest of us all. He was stronger than you, and he would have easily killed you."

"Fuck!" Daniel punched the wall in the corridor, leaving a hole behind. "They can be hurting her. We need to find Jade. I don't care what you want, Dad, but I'm not going to sit here, doing nothing, while they harm my wife."

"We don't even know who they are," Dominic explained.

"I want a sketch artist. I'll describe the three people that were waiting for us at the airport. I'm sure that they are criminals and there are some mug shots of them and some known liaisons to follow as a clue. I don't care how much it'll cost me, but get me the best detectives and call the federal police. They have my plane, they must be far away by now, and we need to track the signal."

"They disconnected the GPS on the plane. For now, we've put an alert in several international airports to be on the lookout for your plane."

"Good. Now, where is Stevie? Did anyone tell him what happened?"

"He is in your home with his babysitter. She is taking good care of him. Sakura is also with him. Why? Do you believe they want to get to him, too?"

"I don't know. I'm just worried about the boy. I don't want anyone to upset him, but he will be suspicious if Jade doesn't contact him soon. She promised she would call."

"Maybe we should tell him. He may know something that can help us find her. Some old boyfriend..."

"Jade didn't have boyfriends. She didn't have time for that," Daniel explained. "What about the terrorist organizations that are against humans being married to vampires and turned? Did they make any threats to us?"

"Just the usual ones." Dominic shrugged.

"You should investigate them."

"I am. I'm doing everything to find the girl. I know she is important to you."

"How long was I out for?"

"Three hours. We had to restart your heart. The bullets were stuck close to it. They used wood," Dominic clarified.

Daniel fisted his hands and clenched his teeth. His fangs wanted to come out, but he had to be rational.

Looking at his dad, he analyzed, "To plan something like this, they had to have access to my schedule. Find out who in my organization sold the information. If we can track the payment, we may find the people behind this, and I can go get Jade and make them pay."

"We are interrogating all your personal assistants and the glass bearers. We are scanning our servers for Trojan horses and going through the recordings to look for any suspicious people observing your house and your company."

"Good," Daniel said, relieved by his father's actions. "I'm going to talk to Jenna. She might know something we don't. After all, she is Jade's best friend."

JADE HAD BEEN KIDNAPPED, and she should be freaking out, but she couldn't deny that being underwater, watching the fish, and hearing the whales singing was somehow relaxing. It was also beautiful and a unique opportunity for her.

Alexander had taken her on the tour of the underwater compound since there was nowhere she could escape to, in his own words. The corridors were made of a glass-like material, and she felt that she was swimming under water, surrounded by enchanted creatures. The fish were colorful and exotic. They were drawn by the light to approach the glass. She felt like a fish in an aquarium and the fish were the humans that were usually on the outside looking in with droopy eyes.

After the guided tour, her kidnapper left her in her bedroom. It had a white king-size bed, a closet, two comfy couches, and her luggage was waiting for her on the bed. It was a nice room for a prisoner.

"You can rest here and change clothes. Breakfast will be served in one hour. I'll come to get you, and we can eat while we talk."

"I think you should let me call Daniel and clarify this mess," Jade said, looking back in time to see Alexander close the door behind him and ignore her request once again. She heard the key turn in the lock and sighed. It was the second time in that month that she was trapped in a bedroom. It was getting repetitive.

She walked to the windows where she could see the laboratory's structure. The lab looked like small igloos with different corridors connecting them. It seemed a small town underwater. And the fish and the whales were the ones that were promenading outside, slowly and lazily. It was beautiful to watch. It was like a child's dream come true, like when she believed in mermaids and underwater towns. But, in that moment, she felt no happiness. Despite the beauty of her surroundings, she would give anything to be with her husband and to know that he was alive and okay.

She was tired and hungry, but, above all, she was worried. If she knew that Daniel was alive, she could relax and rest in the hopes that he would find her, even if she was underwater and it would be hard to get there without a submarine.

Jade had no idea how she had gotten there. She was knocked out. Where did they hide the plane? How did Alexander have access to that expensive lab, and who was he? She didn't want to believe his story. There was more to it than what he was telling her. He wanted to win her trust. He had appealed to what she loved the most, Stevie, and gave her nice accommodation, so she wouldn't think she was a prisoner. But she was. Running away was impossible since there was nothing but water around them. She didn't know if they had submarines that went to the surface or how to pilot one.

Her eyelids were heavy. Yawning, she looked at the inviting bed and rubbed her sore arms. Wanting to rest, she laid down on the bed and looked at the ceiling before closing her eyes and giving in to sleep.

DANIEL HAD ARRIVED HOME and went looking for Jenna. Sakura was right behind him since she had been worried sick about him and wanted to help.

"Are you sure Jenna is home?" Daniel asked his vampire mother, noticing that the bedroom where she'd been staying was empty. The closet was opened and some clothes were missing. It seemed like she left her bedroom in a hurry. "This is problematic. Where is Stevie?"

"In his bedroom. It was extremely late when he went to bed. Last time I checked, he was sleeping," Sakura informed.

"I'll check on him, and we need to find Jenna. Something isn't right," Daniel said, speeding to Stevie's bedroom.

He stopped in front of the door. Sakura stopped, too; her hair flowing back with the halt. Stevie's door was partially opened and, inside, Daniel heard noises. Jenna was hurrying Stevie to get his things, so they could leave.

"What the hell is going on in here?" Daniel asked, his eyes turning dark when he stepped inside the bedroom.

Jenna stopped packing Stevie's clothes and looked at him. Walking to Stevie, she put her hands on his shoulders and secured him against her.

"We are leaving, and you have no right to stop us," she informed.

"It's my brother-in-law that you are kidnapping."

"Where is Jade?" Stevie asked, looking at Daniel. He was sleepy, still in his pajamas, with a confused gaze and ruffled hair. "What's going on? Why is Aunt Jenna saying that we need to leave?"

"I don't know. Care to explain, Jenna?" Daniel asked her.

"Stevie is going to stay with me until Jade gets back," Jenna said, walking to Daniel. "Daniel just forgot his toothbrush and came back to get it," she explained, turning her face and smiling at the boy.

"I bet it was Jade who told you that you had to get it. She was always annoying about brushing my teeth. You need to get used to that," Stevie said, sitting on the bed and fighting to keep his eyes open. "I'm tired."

"Go back to sleep, baby," Sakura whispered, passing by Jenna and holding Stevie to put him back to bed.

The boy obeyed, letting Sakura cover him with a comforter.

"Good boy, have nice dreams. When you wake up, I'll make you some pancakes and we can watch some cartoons after. Would you like that?" Sakura kissed his cheek.

The kid nodded and smiled.

Daniel motioned his finger for Jenna to hush. She looked upset.

"I think we need to talk," he muttered, signaling her to follow him to the end of the corridor.

Jenna walked behind him, her boots echoing loudly against the marble floor.

Sauntering down the corridor, Daniel stopped in the living room.

"What the hell is going on? Were you trying to kidnap the kid?" he confronted Jenna as he turned around to face her.

“I heard them on the phone,” she muttered, folding her arms with an upset expression.

“Who?”

“Your vampire parents. You let Jade be kidnapped. I’m taking the kid away from here before something happens to him, too. After, I’m going to get my best friend.”

Daniel stared at her, perplexed by her words, especially her last words.

Raking his fingers through his black hair, he assured her, “No one will harm him. No one will harm Jade. I’m doing everything I can to find out who did this to her. I want her back as badly as you do. There is no need to scare Stevie.”

“If you are doing everything you can, then why are you here?”

“I came to talk to you. I want to know if you know of someone that would want to kidnap Jade.”

“I don’t know anything. Besides, they kidnapped her because of your money. You just need to pay, and I’ll take care of the rest.”

Daniel signaled for her to relax. “Calm down, Jenna. You are just one person, there isn’t much you can do. And they haven’t asked for a ransom yet. I’m hoping that this is all about money. I’ll give any amount to get her back. But are you sure that you don’t know anything?”

“All I know is that she had a stalker, but he is dead. That leaves your fortune as the only reason for Jade to be kidnapped. Why don’t you ask

Emma? She might know something about this. She wasn't happy with your wedding."

Daniel rubbed his chin. She had a point there. Emma could be behind all that was happening. However, she didn't have the capacity or the brains to pull something like that.

"I'm assembling a rescue team. As soon as I know her location, I'll send the team to track down the kidnappers. There isn't much more that I can do. Unless you have another idea. I brought sketches of the people who kidnapped Jade. I want you to look at them and see if you recognize anyone."

"You are wasting my time," Jenna complained, staring at her phone.

"Do you have somewhere else to be?" Daniel asked. She should be freaking out with what happened to her best friend. Instead, she was taking everything rather lightly and seemed impatient in a suspicious way.

Jenna raised her eyes from the screen and huffed. "As a matter of fact, I have somewhere to be. And I don't know if I can trust you or not because you let them take her away."

"They tried to kill me. They shot me three times. I could have died," Daniel defended himself.

Jenna narrowed her eyes and squeezed her phone. "Why would they try to kill you if they needed you to pay the ransom? Unless they aren't planning to ask for a ransom. What if the old creep isn't dead? Maybe he saw her on TV and now he wants her back."

"Octavio is dead," Daniel said. "It wasn't him. I don't have a clue who kidnapped Jade, but it couldn't be him."

"Jade came to live with us after what happened to her parents. When she got a job, she found a place for her and Stevie. She's like a sister to me. My parents help vampire victims. I'm trained, despite what you might think about me. You are not going to stop me from looking for Jade."

"Yes, Jade told me about that. Yet you are still human, Jenna. I have a lot of resources. If it's about money, I'll pay whatever it takes to get Jade back."

Nibbling her nail, she added, "I didn't know she told you about Octavio. Are you sure he isn't alive?"

"Jade and I don't have any secrets. I can assure you that Octavio didn't do this. Now, can you help me and look at the sketches?"

Jenna leaned forward. "I don't care about the sketches. I'm trying to decide whether I trust you or not."

"You can trust me." Narrowing his eyes, Daniel added, "What aren't you telling me? I want to find her as much as you or more. She can be in real danger, Jenna."

"Do you trust Sakura?"

"With my own life."

"Can you tell her to run and hide with Stevie? Somewhere secure where only you and she know about."

"Why?"

"He can be in danger. If we are going to get Jade, I need to know that he will be safe and that no other vampire will know where he is."

"Why?"

"You ask too many questions," Jenna complained and stepped back with a huffed sigh.

"And you are questioning the safety of my home."

"Can we talk somewhere private? Somewhere you are sure no one can listen to us," Jenna requested in a lower voice.

Daniel sighed with impatience. "I don't have time to handle your craziness. I need to find my wife." He pinched the bridge of his nose. He wanted Jenna's help, but it was becoming pointless since she was clearly delusional and wasting his time.

"I would help you if we could talk privately. I don't want anyone else to hear what I'm about to tell you," she muttered, folding her arms.

"Let's go to my office downstairs, and I'll show you the sketches," Daniel said, walking away and hoping that prolonging their conversation wasn't a waste of time.

Soon, they were entering his office and closing the door.

# CHAPTER THIRTY: IN THE MIDDLE OF NOWHERE

**AS DANIEL SAT ON HIS DESK**, staring at Jenna's sparkling eyes, he realized how he had underestimated that girl. He was baffled beyond words. He could almost grab her and kiss her cheek for being such a crazy friend and obsessive bodyguard. Jade had told him that she was kept safe by a private organization that helped vampire victims. Yet Daniel had no idea that they took their job so seriously. Jenna was not only Jade's best friend, she had been her bodyguard.

Her family had received Jade and Stevie when Jade's parents died. Jenna had entered the contest to protect Jade. She told him a crazy story about how she had convinced the director to get her on the show, so she could keep an eye on Jade and keep her safe from Daniel; due to Jade's past with vampires. Jenna felt guilty when Jade was chosen by him. She knew how much Jade didn't want to go to that event. Jenna had pushed her to go without the intention of ruining her life.

Daniel was still dumbfounded how Jenna could be a personal bodyguard for vampire victims and love vampires so much. It was a damn puzzle that he was in no mood to unravel. Jenna was too complex for her own good. Looking harmless, she seemed useless and the last one that someone would believe to be able to protect Jade.

The most important thing about what Jenna had to tell him was Jade's salvation. Jenna had put a tracking device in one of his wife's molars. She had a damn tracking device that could pinpoint his beloved's location. Jenna was awesome.

For a moment there, he was afraid that she had gone mad or that she was behind the whole thing. But she only wanted to protect Stevie before going to find Jade by herself—which was not a good idea. She could be some sort of bad-ass girl, what was quite intriguing for her slim figure and harmless appearance, but there was no way she could handle Jade's kidnappers alone. The fact that all vampire victims had a tracking device for their own safety was an unforeseen luck. Jade's sad past had a positive outcome in her recent future.

They had compromised. He would let her tag along with his rescue team, and she would share Jade's location. Nevertheless, Jenna was stubborn. She wanted him to sign a contract, so he didn't fool her. She was paranoid. Daniel was a man of his word. She had to take his word for granted.

"I understand your reasons. I won't trick you. You will come with me. Now, please show me your device, so I can pinpoint the GPS coordinates on a map," he tried to reason with her for the twentieth time.

"If you trick me, I swear to God, Daniel Wolfe, I'll track you down and make Jade a widow. I don't care if you are her soul-mate. I'll have your balls in a jar."

"For the love of God, woman, stop doubting me. All I want is to get my wife back. Just put your damn phone on my desk and let my A.I. access the data."

She held the phone tighter to her chest. “I know the coordinates. I’m just not sure if they are right, or if they found out about the tracker and removed it.”

“Why? What’s wrong with the coordinates?” He could go insane if what Jenna claimed to have was a dead end.

“It doesn’t make any sense. The coordinates are in the middle of the Atlantic Ocean. There isn’t any island on the map. My guess is that they may have her on a ship in international waters.”

Daniel leaned forward in his seat and motioned for her to put her phone down. “Just show me.”

The girl placed the phone on the glass desk. Pressing a button, Daniel turned on his computer and displayed Jenna’s screen on the wide screen behind him. Once she typed her password, she allowed his main computer access to withdraw the GPS information.

Daniel mused at the red point on the map. She was right. The beacon was shining in the middle of nowhere.

Jenna leaned back in her seat. “If she was on a ship, the beacon would move. But it hasn’t moved at all. Maybe they dropped the device over the ocean.” She rubbed her chin. “It would be easier to destroy it than drop it.” Sighing, she crossed her legs. “Maybe they are on a ship, but they aren’t moving. I hope she’s okay.”

“I think I may know where they are,” Daniel stated, searching his brain for the information. That particular place in the map sounded familiar.

"Jaz," he called his virtual assistant. "Please access the information regarding New Atlantis and match its location with the coordinates of the GPS tracker."

In seconds, Jaz found the connection that Daniel was looking for.

"What does it mean? Do you know where she is?" Jenna asked, leaning forward and resting her arms on the desk.

Daniel's fingers drummed on the desk as he clenched his teeth. "Yes, I know. I'm the one who paid for those underwater facilities. It was supposed to be a vampire underwater village. However, because of the reclusive conditions, it became a secret laboratory. Dad wanted to use the laboratory for one of his foolish reality shows about a vampire community living in a place where the sun wouldn't be a deterrent. He is trying to convince me to stop the research they are doing there with exotic plants to cure new types of cancer so he can pitch the new show."

"Why would scientists kidnap your wife?" Jenna probed.

"That's a good question. It would also explain why they didn't find my plane. It's a hybrid plane and can go underwater."

Jenna stood up. "We are losing time. We need to leave and get her out of there. We can ask questions later."

"Jaz, send me the New Atlantis' blueprints to my phone and all the data you have about the base and its defenses."

Daniel's phone rang.

"It's your father, Mr. Wolfe," Jaz announced.

"Wait," Jenna ordered before he could pick up. "You shouldn't tell him anything about our findings. We still don't know who took her and why. You say that your dad was aware of the location of your base. He didn't seem happy about your marriage. Jade was concerned about him. It seems that he was digging about her past, and I don't like this coincidence."

*She is right.* Daniel couldn't trust anyone.

Signaling Jenna to stay quiet, he tapped the LCD display to answer. "Yes, Dad, did you find anything about what happened to Jade?"

"Hello, Daniel. There aren't any matches to the drawings of the perpetrators. The plane hasn't been found. We are analyzing the videos, and we might have a suspect that's been outside your home taking pictures. Since there were so many paparazzi and reporters, we aren't sure if he's the perpetrator or another reporter. I've called to tell you that we are following a lead with one of your employees. He has received a huge sum of money recently, and he may have sold personal information about you and your wife."

"Okay. Call me when you know something else," Daniel told him, staring at Jenna's narrowed eyes. She trusted no one by the looks of it.

"How are you feeling?" Dominic asked before he could hang up.

"I'm nervous and stressed. I'll be better when we find Jade."

"You have gathered a team. Do you have somewhere you want to send them? Do you have a lead?"

"No, it's a precaution for when we have a lead."

"Okay, I'll talk to you soon." Dominic hung up.

"I think he was too curious for my liking," Jenna mumbled.

"I'm not going to accuse my father based on suppositions. I'll get to New Atlantis and apprehend the kidnappers. Only then will we find out who is behind all this."

"If she is there and she's alive," Jenna added.

Getting up, Daniel gritted his teeth and balled his hands. "Don't even think for a second that Jade's not alive. I can't even consider that possibility."

"They haven't asked for a ransom."

"They want to..." He didn't know what they wanted. In their best interest, Jade had better be alive, or they wouldn't see the light of day. "Jaz, what type of defenses does the underwater compound have?"

"Electric defenses against sharks and that's about it," the computer answered.

It was a peaceful compound. It wasn't armed. They handled viruses and diseases. *Why would scientists want to kidnap my wife?*

"Pull all the employees' files and tell me who oversees that facility. Who is the leading scientist?"

"Alexander Powell. He has worked for Oroborus

for almost thirty years now. He's the leading researcher for the cure for the Luna Argentus' disease."

"God, he's hot," Jenna said when she saw his picture on the screen. "He can't be more than twenty-five. Is he a vampire? He doesn't look like one. He's not that pale."

Daniel indulged her curiosity. "No, he's not a vampire. He's something else. We are going to visit Mr. Powell."

"Are you insane? If you go there, and he's behind all this, he will run away with Jade, or worse."

"I'm not going to announce my visit. It's my compound. I don't need their authorization to enter my own building. Jaz will override their passwords, mess with their sonar, and we'll arrive without them detecting anything."

Smirking, Jenna nodded and balled her right hand. "I like your idea. Then I'll kick some ass to get Jade back."

"We are going to locate, infiltrate, and secure the facilities. If Jade is there, we will find her and the people responsible for her kidnapping."

Jenna's expression changed from excitement to concern. "What if we find opposition and it's not a nerds' lab, but a place that's heavily secured?"

"Then we will kick some ass. I'll take a heavily armed and trained vampire squad with me. I'm not playing around. If Jade is there, I'll find her. Whoever grabbed her is in serious trouble."

"And Stevie?"

"Sakura will take him to safety. I'll find them a safe place to hide while we discover what is going on. I'll make arrangements to investigate my dad. I don't think he's behind this, but better safe than sorry."

"I like you," Jenna said. "I didn't like you before. If you are so keen on keeping Jade and her brother safe, I'll make an effort to accept you into our family."

"Thanks, I guess." Daniel rubbed the back of his neck. "Are you ready?"

"I'm more than ready." She put her hand behind her back and took out a gun and a knife from under her leather coat.

Daniel arched an eyebrow and sank his hands in his pockets. "What are you planning to do with that?"

"Protect myself and save Jade. Don't worry, I know how to use them."

Removing his hands from his pants, he smirked as the hope of finding his wife soothed his pain. "Fine. Let me call my men on a secure line, and I'll make arrangements for our underwater excursion."

# CHAPTER THIRTY-ONE: REMINISCENCE OF CHILDHOOD

**JADE WOKE UP DIZZY AND** nauseated. Her body was sore and her limbs felt heavy. She grumbled while opening her eyes. As she focused on where she was, all the emotional pain crushed her heart once again.

In her dreams, she was with Daniel, and she was happy. In reality, she was trapped in a secret facility, underwater, with a man saying the most ludicrous things about her husband, her father, and her sweet, innocent brother. To her despair, that man was seated on a couch, staring at the oceanic subaquatic view with a tray of food next to him on a small coffee table.

"Hello, have you slept okay?" Alexander asked with a smile.

"How long was I asleep for?" Jade's voice was hoarse. She was in no mood to correspond to his joyful mood. It was creepy to have such a cheerful kidnapper.

"You were tired, so I let you sleep. I thought you may be hungry," Alexander said, getting up from the couch.

Jade grabbed a pillow and hugged it to her chest. It wouldn't help her against that man but, at least, she felt more secure.

"You don't need to fear me. You are the daughter of one of my best friends. I would never hurt you."

"You can say whatever you want, but I don't

have to believe you."

"I can prove it to you. Now, please eat. I've brought you some bread and fruit. I didn't know if you liked tea or milk, therefore, I brought both."

"Tea will do just fine."

"As I was saying, I'm going to prove to you that I knew your parents. You may not remember me because you were a child, but you've spent quite some time on my lap, playing and asking me questions about my work with your dad."

"You are right. I don't remember you."

"I even went to your birthday parties."

Squinting, Jade added, "I've never seen you in my family's photos."

"Yes. I know that some were lost when you had to run away. That's why I brought this," he said, showing Jade a small chip in a plastic box.

Jade frowned at it. "What is it?"

"Proof. I'll get the screen ready for us. Feel free to serve yourself with some food. You need to keep your strength."

Jade nodded and dragged her tired body to the couch next to her food. Sitting down, she analyzed what was edible. She was starving; she had barely eaten at the wedding. Eventually, she picked up the cup and poured some tea. Then she placed cheese inside two slices of bread and nibbled on it. It tasted good, so she kept eating.

"All set," Alexander stated, picking up the remote control for the screen on the opposite side of the couches.

Alexander sat on a different couch and pressed start. Jade kept eating small bites of her bread, following Alexander's every move. Even if he had kidnapped her, he didn't seem like a threat. He was calm and his eyes were kind. Weird attitude for a kidnapper, without a doubt.

"That's your dad on your first birthday," Alexander said, pointing at the screen while smiling.

Jade stopped chewing. Her attention was on the figure of her dad, grinning at her mom with a small child in their arms. It was her when she was a baby. Tears rushed to her eyes. It had been quite some time since she had let herself watch her parents' homemade videos. It was too much for her heart to take. She missed them terribly.

Stevie still asked a lot of questions about their parents. Jade didn't stop her brother from seeing the pictures and watching the videos, she just didn't normally push Stevie to watch them more often. It hurt her. She often cried herself to sleep and would still cry when seeing them in the kept memories of their lives inside digital recordings.

"That's me recording. I'll appear in a second," Alexander explained. "Your dad wanted me to be your godfather. He eventually asked someone else because I had to go back home to take care of family business. But you were adorable. Do you see how much they loved you?"

"You didn't need to tell me that. I know they loved me," Jade said grumpily.

Pointing at the screen, Alexander said, "There I am. I had longer hair. It was the new hippie generation decade. I dressed informally." Jade frowned at his words while he kept rambling. "I was young and naive. I thought I could save the world." Alexander's voice sounded a lot gloomier this time.

Jade asked no questions and made no statements. However, it was true, Alexander was in the video, looking exactly how he looked now, but with longer hair. He didn't get old and seemed to be Jade's age. Werewolves were an intriguing race.

While pondering about her situation and her kidnapper, Jade listened to her dad talk to Alexander. He liked him. They laughed and bickered with each other like good old friends.

She witnessed Alexander playing with her younger self, taking her in his arms and talking to her in a baby voice. He liked children. It was clear in his eyes. Her dad noticed it, too. Alexander was telling her dad that he would want a lot of kids once he found his soul-mate. Jade wouldn't be able to give kids to Daniel. It saddened her.

"Do you believe me now, Jade?" Alexander asked, fast-forwarding the video.

Her eyes were on the screen as time passed by, and she grew up in the videos. She walked and talked, clinging to Alexander's neck when he picked her up, and he let her do whatever she wanted. She liked him and called him Alex. Alexander was a family friend. It was impossible to fake that.

Tears streamed down Jade's face. She wished that she could jump into the videos and spend more time with her parents. She wanted to hug and kiss them again and tell them how much she loved them.

"If we both agree that you don't wish me any harm, and you understand that my husband loves me and wishes no harm to my baby brother, will you let me call Daniel?" Jade wiped away her tears and focused on Alexander.

He turned his head to face her. "It wasn't my intention to kill your husband..." His eyes changed to a darker shade as his face became solemn.

Jade's heart clenched in her chest as she snapped at him, "Daniel isn't dead. He can't be dead. He's a vampire. Vampires aren't easily killed. It wouldn't be fair if he died. I wouldn't forgive you if something bad happened to him."

Alexander leaned forward and entwined his fingers as his expression remained calm. "I may consider letting you talk to Daniel. But you need to give me your word that you will do everything you can to make Daniel send Stevie to a safe place. Somewhere where I can go get him, and we can understand how to help your brother."

"Alexander, I wouldn't trust you with my brother's life. You have told me that other people are after him. That he's the solution to vampires' vulnerability to light. Why should I trust that you don't have other intentions? You were my father's friend, but you weren't part of his life when he needed a friend the most."

Alexander raked his fingers through his hair. "I wasn't in the country. After going to my family's lands, I started my own research. I had to leave to gather exotic plants. I was unreachable. When I came back, I couldn't find you or your brother anywhere." He reclined in his seat. "You need to trust that my intentions are good. I have the proof that your dad trusted me. I have the video he sent to me, talking about what he had done, about his research. He told me all about Stevie and the secret that lies in his genetic code."

"I want to talk to Daniel. He must be worried sick. I'm worried sick. I miss my husband. I want to talk to him." Tears prickled her eyes. "I need to know that he's okay."

"Okay."

Jade frowned. "Really?"

Alexander nodded. "I'll let you call him, but you can't tell him where you are. First, we need to understand if Daniel is playing you or not."

"We are soul-mates. Daniel loves me. I love him. He knows nothing about what Dad did to my brother!" Jade yelled as shivers ran down her arms.

"Okay!" Alexander waved his hands in a soothing movement. "If you are so sure about him and are willing to put your brother's life at risk, I'll trust your judgment."

Jade folded her arms. "You do?"

"It's your brother and your life. If you claim that you don't need to be saved, I won't keep you here against your will."

Sucking in air, she leaned forward. "Can I call Daniel now?"

"Once you watch your father's video where he explains what he did to Stevie, you can."

Jade held her breath and stared at him with mixed emotions. She only needed to watch a video.

"Okay." She needed to endure a bit more to talk to Daniel.

Alexander got up, gave her the remote, and walked away. "Just press start. I'll be back with the phone."

DANIEL WAS IN HIS PRIVATE plane when his phone rang. Looking at the display, he squinted at the anonymous number. It could be the kidnapper, therefore, before he picked up, he ordered Jaz to trace the call.

"Yes, this is Daniel Wolfe speaking. Who is at the other end of this call?"

"Daniel." Jade's voice trembled.

Daniel sat straight in his seat at the sound of her voice. "Jade, Jade! Honey, where are you? Are you okay? Are they treating you well? Did they hurt you?" Daniel's questions came out rushed and breathless. The sound of his pounding heart echoed in his ears.

"Daniel, is that really you?"

"Yes, it's me. Are you okay, honey?"

"I'm okay," she assured him. Her voice cracked with her next words, "I'm so glad that you are alive. I was so scared!"

"I'm okay, too. Don't cry, Jade. Everything will be all right. Just tell me what they want to return you to me."

“They don’t want money.”

“Then what?”

Jenna sat beside him, motioning for him to turn on the speaker, so she could hear the call. Daniel signaled for her to be still and not to open her mouth. They were a few minutes away from Jade’s last known location. If his wife was in the underwater facilities, he was moments away from saving her and imprisoning her kidnappers.

“Is Stevie okay? Where is he? Is he there? Can I talk to him?”

“I’m in my office,” Daniel lied. “But Stevie is safe. He’s with Sakura. Tell me what they want.”

“Daniel...” Jade’s voice was cut momentarily when the plane shook and submerged.

“Jade,” Daniel called, looking at the windows and seeing the water surrounding the plane.

“I’m okay, Daniel. I’m fine. They didn’t hurt me. We need to talk. Alexander wants to talk to you in a video conference.”

“Who?”

“My kidnapper. Well, Alexander thought he was saving me... It’s complicated. But you need to trust me. I’m okay, and you need to get Stevie to somewhere safe.”

“Jade, are they forcing you to say this?”

“No, Daniel, please listen to me. Alexander took me because he thought that I was in danger. We need to talk in a video conference. We will explain everything to you.”

"I want you to tell me where you are. I'll go there, and we can talk face to face," Daniel asserted as he looked at Jenna who was frowning at the conversation.

"Did she bump her head? Isn't it a bit early to have Stockholm syndrome for her kidnapper?" Jenna questioned.

Daniel shrugged.

"Is Jenna there with you?" Jade asked. "You two need to trust me on this. I'm okay and Alexander..."

Daniel interrupted her, "They tried to kill me, Jade. I was dormant for three hours because of their wooden bullets close to my heart. They kidnapped you. Now you are telling me that your kidnapper and you want to talk to me? Is everybody crazy?"

"I know it sounds crazy. But we can explain. Aren't you glad that I'm okay?"

"Of course, I am! If Alexander, *your kidnapper*, wants to talk to me, I'll talk to him. Just give me five minutes."

"Five minutes? Alexander, he needs five minutes," Jade said to the person Daniel assumed was next to her.

Meanwhile, Daniel pointed at his watch to question Jenna the amount of time he needed to stall while they reached the underwater compound.

"Almost there," Jenna mumbled, staring at the screen in front of her seat.

"Five minutes, Jade. I'll go to my conference room where we can talk."

"Okay. I'll call you in five minutes... Daniel, I love you. You have no idea how worried I was."

His voice came out husky and emotional. "I love you, too. Don't worry, everything will be fine."

"We'll be together soon enough." Jade hung up.

"What's the status?" Daniel asked Jenna. He was impatient but less worried since he now knew that Jade was alive.

"Just a second," Jenna replied while Jaz showed her the blueprints.

She talked with the computer, analyzing which entrance they should use and following the red dots on the screen.

Looking at Daniel, she informed, "I'm counting thirty people inside the compound. We'll enter through the dark area on the screen. Jaz is activating life support in the unused cubes. Our team won't be detected by anyone until it's too late."

Daniel reclined in his seat and folded his arms. "Good."

Jenna added, "I'm seeing two dots in the residential area. Another five in the dining area. The rest seem to be concentrated in the labs. There is someone going to the residential area. However, it doesn't seem to have any guards patrolling it. They must assume that they are safe and no one knows their location."

"What if Jade isn't there because they found her tracker and all this is just a diversion?"

"You should trust me more. I'm pretty good at

what I do. At this point, I don't think anyone found the tracker. Soon enough, we'll save Jade. Then you can both go on your honeymoon to watch the Aurora Borealis and bond."

"Jade's phone call intrigued me. I was trying to find out if there was some hidden message in her words. Despite sounding emotional, she didn't seem scared. I hope they are treating her right."

"It was strange," Jenna agreed. The plane shook again. "We are docking and we'll have the doors unlocked in two minutes. Jaz is overriding the passwords and restoring the pressure to human settings."

Daniel turned around in his rotating chair. "Tell the rescuing team to get ready. We need to move fast and subjugate the enemy," he ordered to his Special Ops commander.

The big man, dressed in black camouflage clothes, moved to give orders to his commando troopers in the other compartment of the plane.

Daniel got up and fixed his clothes. He was wearing black pants and a cotton sweatshirt. Grabbing a gun, he checked the tranquilizing bullets and put it behind his back.

"Okay, Jaz will give me the enemy's coordinates," Jenna said, putting a small communicator in her ear. "You will follow my lead."

"I think I can take care of myself. You should worry about yourself," Daniel said. "My men can handle this. Just stay behind them and let them do their job."

Jenna narrowed her eyes and got up from her

seat. "You said that I could lead the team. Now shut up and give them the order to obey me."

Daniel faced her gaze. Jade's friend was bossy, and he was in no mood to argue with her. Yet she was bright and seemed to know what she was doing. He could let her have some fun and command his team while he could break formation and search for Jade in the residential area of the compound.

"Fine, but if you harm yourself and Jade kills me, it's all your fault."

"That didn't make any sense," Jenna complained as she tied her hair in a bun. "Just relax and let me handle this."

Daniel shrugged and touched the intercom in his ear. "You heard the lady, men. Follow her lead and don't kill anyone. I don't need the bad publicity."

JENNA ROLLED HER EYES, checked her gun, and put her gloves on.

The plane shivered and made a loud noise as if it was an old submarine complaining about the pressure outside. Jenna's ears were popping with the pressure changes.

"It's time to party." Jenna smiled and rushed to be the first to get out of the plane and enter the underwater cubicle.

The moment the plane opened its door, the

lights turned on inside the white corridor.

“Creepy,” Jenna whispered, motioning for the men behind her to follow. “It’s clear. Let’s move. Three men teams. Daniel, stay behind me. Aim for their neck and the ones that aren’t put to sleep need to be restrained. Don’t harm Jade. You all saw her picture. I don’t want anyone wrongly shooting her.”

“Yes, ma’am,” the commander said.

Dropping her arm, Jenna hurried down the corridor, following the computer instructions with Daniel and the commandos on her tail.

# CHAPTER THIRTY-TWO: INVASION

**JADE WATCHED ALEXANDER** pacing up and down her bedroom like a caged animal. Daniel had asked for five minutes. His five minutes were up, and Jade couldn't understand why he wasn't answering his phone. She was losing patience, too. A thousand and one theories were running through her mind about why her husband wasn't replying to her call.

"I don't think he wants to negotiate," Alexander said, breaking the silence and coming near Jade. "I don't know what game he is playing or why he doesn't pick up the phone. We must assume that he doesn't want to negotiate with me, and your life isn't that important to him."

"That can't be true. Something might have happened to him," Jade protested, feeling her heart bleed because of Alexander's words. Daniel's love was the only certainty she had in her life. After so many years alone, trusting few people and keeping a safe distance from a love relationship, losing that would shatter her soul.

Alexander stood before her and placed his hands on her shoulders. "Don't worry, Jade. I won't hurt you. I promised your dad that I would take care of you and your brother. I won't let them hurt the boy."

Jade waved him away and walked to the screen where she pressed the redial button.

Alexander sucked in a breath. "We can try calling him later."

Jade moved back and bumped into Alexander's

chest. Before she could apologize, a young man entered her bedroom.

"We are under attack," the man said with urgency. "They are coming this way. We need to leave, Alpha."

"Who's attacking us?" Alexander asked, glancing at the guy and fisting his hands. His posture changed from worried to alert. Jade noticed his eyes become darker. There was a dangerous vibe coming from him, something primeval.

"The reports were unclear. They are overriding our computers and progressing deeper into the compound. We need to go to the emergency pods and get away from here before they get to you and her."

"How the hell did they find us?" Alexander asked.

The guy raked his fingers through his hair with a worried expression. "We don't know, but we need to leave."

"Jade, let's move out of here," Alexander ordered, grabbing her arm and urging her to follow him.

"I don't want to go. They are here to save me," she protested as she pushed his hands away and tried to get free.

"Jade, please. We need to move. We don't know who's coming."

Jade gulped as she endured Alexander's glowing eyes.

"Come." Alexander offered his hand. "Someone

might have sent those people to kill you. Don't fight me, or I'll have to carry you over my shoulder."

Jade dragged her feet, rejecting his hand and exiting the bedroom. "Daniel wouldn't hurt me."

"It may not be Daniel. Move faster," Alexander ordered, quickening his pace. Far away, the sound of guns was heard. "They are using guns. Sam, tell the men to retreat and run to the emergency pods. We are leaving this place. Tell Sabrina to start the submarine."

"She went to fight the intruders," Sam clarified.

"I told her to stay in the lab," Alexander growled.

"She's too stubborn," Sam complained. "She ordered me to warn you, and she took some men to delay their arrival here and facilitate your escape."

"Just let me talk to them. If it's Daniel, I can talk to him and explain what's going on. He won't hurt you or your men," Jade appealed. "Please, let me talk to Daniel."

"I understand that you love him and think he's better than what I want you to believe. But we called him to explain things and come to an understanding. He chose to ignore our call and is probably killing my men, as we speak, to get to you."

"Because he loves me and thinks I'm in danger."

"We are not dangerous and violent people unless we are provoked. We will retaliate and if he gets hurt or killed..."

"We are running," she pointed out. "I don't see you facing Daniel. I see you running away."

"They are gaining on us," Sam said, stopping and sniffing the air. "Vampires."

"They must be using the computer to track us down. We need to stop running and face them," Alexander said, stopping and looking at the doors. They were already in the laboratory aisle and around them were rooms filled with plants and other machines used to run experiments.

Jade was going to speak again but thought better of it when she saw Alex glaring at her. She glanced back and folded her arms.

WITH HIS HEIGHTENED HEARING, Alexander listened carefully to the noises that were around them: punches, guns with silencers being shot—which was not that inaudible to him—more kicking and punches. His attention was drawn to an alluring scent. He focused on that, finding it peculiar.

Jade made a movement to escape him, but he grabbed her by the waist before she could run down the corridor to meet the vampires that were attacking the compound. The silly girl believed that her vampire lover was coming to save her. But Alexander was not that sure and wasn't willing to put her life at risk.

"Sam, take Jade with you and keep her safe."

"And you, Alpha, what are you going to do?" Sam asked, grabbing Jade by her arm.

"I'm going to get Sabrina. Wait fifteen minutes for us in the submarine. If we don't arrive by then, I command you to leave and take the girl to her home."

"And then? How are you going to get away from here?"

"You need to save your future alpha and keep the girl safe. You are my beta. I trust you."

"Alexander, don't be stubborn. Let me talk to Daniel," Jade said, struggling to get free from Sam. Her voice reached a higher pitch, revealing her distress. "Please, let me talk to Daniel."

"Take her away," Alexander ordered.

His beta obeyed and, without looking back, forced Jade to follow him to another part of the underground compound.

IN ANOTHER CORRIDOR, Jenna and the rescuing squad fought the few stray attackers that crossed their way. It hadn't been too difficult so far. The werewolves were wearing white scrubs and seemed more like scientists than fighters.

The soldiers kept shooting tranquilizers at the shifters. The ones who avoided the darts were knocked out cold. Jenna wasn't finding a lot of resistance or skilled warriors.

*I hope Daniel is wrong and this is not a decoy.*

Sighing, Jenna proceeded. After another turn of the corridor, the two advanced troopers were attacked and knocked out by an acrobatic jumping werewolf girl with two big guys covering her back.

Grabbing the vampires' guns, the enemy shot at the team. Jenna only had the time to dodge the flying darts. Before she could do anything else, the girl leaped on the wall and came at significant speed to attack Daniel. Jenna secured Daniel behind her back as she turned around to face the girl who had just landed in front of her.

Looking around, Jenna made a quick assessment of her surroundings. Five soldiers were knocked out cold and the remaining members were shooting at the two werewolves while Daniel was safe between her and his men.

Jenna focused on the enemy as the girl's dark hair fell into place around her pretty face. With big brown eyes, red lips, and a smug smile, the girl looked like an exotic and deadly beauty. Jenna knew she had to beat her to keep moving and find her best friend.

The girl threw a jab and a left hook. Jenna moved left and right and kicked the side of the girl's knee. The girl jumped back, avoiding the blow.

"You move too fast for a human," the girl muttered.

With her lips curled into a smile, Jenna said, "I guess my secret is out. I'm not just human."

Daniel asked from behind Jenna, "Can you handle her alone? I need to keep moving,"

Jenna glimpsed at him and noticed that the other werewolves had been left unconscious. The girl was the only threat left.

Waving her hand in dismissal, she assured, "I can handle her."

"Good. As much as I would love to watch a girl fight, I need to get to Jade."

"Just leave already," Jenna muttered.

"Don't take too long." Daniel signaled for his two remaining men to follow him down the corridor.

"You aren't going anywhere," the girl said, making another move to attack Jenna.

Jenna was fast enough to evade the first punch but was unable to prevent the second one hitting her cheek. Before the werewolf could land a punch on Jenna's stomach, she grabbed the girl's wrist, only to receive a knee to her stomach. It was enough to make Jenna let go and step back to assess the situation. The girl was faster than Jenna anticipated. She had to stop fooling around and take their fight seriously. The girl wasn't soft like the other werewolves she had encountered so far. She had been trained and was set on winning that fight.

"I didn't know that werewolf packs let girls become fighters," Jenna teased.

"Our pack isn't like a normal pack," the girl clarified.

"I'm Jenna, by the way," she said, moving back when the girl tried to punch her again.

"I couldn't care less," the girl hissed, coordinating her steps with her punches.

Jenna kept ducking and holding up her fists.

"You are quite fast for a human girl."

"You werewolves think you're better than the rest, don't you?"

It was a rhetorical question. Jenna didn't like werewolves. They were cocky and judgmental of the other races. They didn't like to mix their race either. She had more than a plausible excuse to despise werewolves. Hence, she wasn't going to let a werewolf beat her and prevent her from saving her best friend.

"We," the girl said with the same sarcastic tone, "don't think anything. I'm just here to stop you from hurting my alpha."

"Your alpha?" Jenna mocked. "Your possessive, narrow-minded, and probably womanizing alpha is going to regret the day he decided to kidnap my best friend," she muttered, grabbing the girl's fists in her hands and pushing her back into the wall.

The girl grimaced in pain. She only had time to tilt her head to the right before Jenna's fist left an imprint on the wall.

"It's kind of rubbery," Jenna complained, staring at the wall that had absorbed her hit.

The girl pulled Jenna back and a sequence of punches and kicks started between them. Jenna backed up and moved forward to throw punches and find an opening for a takedown or a powerful kick.

JADE WAS TRYING TO delay her captor, making it hard for him to get her to supposed safety. But he was much stronger and was set in obeying his alpha's orders.

"You are hurting me," Jade complained. Sam was bruising her shoulders while pulling her.

"Stop trying to run away then. I have no intentions of hurting you, but I won't let you run away. You will follow me, and we'll wait for Alexander in the submarine."

Jade growled.

"Do you want me to carry you over my shoulder?"

As loud as she could, Jade screamed, "Daniel."

The guy's hand covered her mouth. She shook her head, so he would release it. It had no effect. She bit him and screamed again.

Sam spoke in a lower tone. "Are you trying to get us killed?"

Jade stepped on his foot and struggled for release. The guy was a rock, too strong for her, and she eventually started to cry.

"For crying out loud, missy, I'm not trying to hurt you. You need to stop fighting me," Sam said, turning her around to face him. "Look at me. I'm just obeying my alpha's orders. Please, don't fight me."

"I want my husband," she sobbed.

"He's an evil vampire."

"He is not," Jade protested.

"Jade," a male voice screamed her name.

Jade's head snapped back, recognizing Daniel's voice.

"Daniel! Da—"

Sam's hand covered Jade's mouth a second time.

"They are closer. Sabrina must have failed," Sam muttered, pulling Jade into one of the laboratories where scientific machines were working with test tubes. "Stay here and don't scream. I need to go..." He pushed Jade into a corner. Raking his fingers through his hair, he sighed. "I need to help my alpha."

Jade's breathing was heavy, and she felt her face burning. Her eyes were stinging from the tears, but she tried to control the sobbing. Using the back of her hands to wipe away her tears, she looked around as she tried to figure out what she was going to do.

Her captor was clearly stronger. For once, she wished she wasn't a fragile human girl.

"I need to help Alex," Sam mumbled with a blank stare. "But he said not to. I need to get you to safety and then get the boy."

Jade leaned against the wall and folded her arms. "Alexander isn't being logical about this. He could trade me for the safety of his men. You could do that instead of him. Trade me, and Daniel will let you leave."

Jade hoped that fear would make Sam want to fight for his life and let her go to Daniel.

"I'm not a fool. Vampires don't keep their word. I know what you are trying to do, and I'm not going to fall for it. I get that you are in love with the guy. Nevertheless, you shouldn't trust a vampire so willingly."

"I don't trust them. I trust Daniel."

"Why?"

"He's my mate."

Sam's face became pale. His lower lip trembled when he spoke again. "Wasn't it a lie? You are really soul-mates?"

Unfolding her arms, Jade assured, "We love each other. I'm his beloved!"

Jade's eyes moved to the exit with the sound of her name being called. Daniel's voice was echoing along the corridors. "Jade!"

"He's here for me. Please let me go," Jade begged, feeling her heart beat so fast, she thought it was going to come out of her mouth. She wanted to see him, touch him, and hold him. The pain of not being able to run to him was excruciating.

"Don't you have a mate? Don't you love her?" she asked Sam, wanting him to relate to her pain.

He shook his head. "Not yet, but I want to find mine." His voice was a whisper and his eyes seemed sad and lonely.

Jade felt sorry for him. "You won't find her if you keep me away from Daniel."

"STAY THERE," SAM ORDERED. His emotions took over, and he couldn't leave his alpha alone.

Opening the door, he listened to the sound of

punches and bodies being thrown against the wall of the compound. They assured him that the walls were resistant. Yet he became afraid that they may crack and the water would come in. It was a silly fear, but he wasn't ecstatic to be underwater with nowhere to escape in case of a disaster.

At the end of the corridor, he saw Alexander fighting some armed men in black camouflage clothes. His alpha was a skilled fighter, but Sam couldn't help running to assist in the fight. The two of them had better chances in taking the girl out of there, even if Sam knew that she wanted to return to her vampire lover.

# CHAPTER THIRTY-THREE: NO ESCAPE

**DANIEL COULD SWEAR THAT** he had heard Jade calling him. His mind might be playing tricks. Screaming her name was a way to cope with the pain that threatened to shred his heart.

His other team had reported that they had seen the alpha. He was heading their way. Despite trying to reach them, the comms were down.

Daniel and his two men headed down the corridor. His eyes were on his phone, following the red dot that would lead him to his beloved.

Every time he opened a door to another division, or entered a new empty corridor, he knew he was closer to finding her. So far, all he found was scared scientists.

"Jade!" he shouted. Even if she couldn't reply, he wanted her to know that he was coming for her.

He paused and listened. All he heard was fighting. There was a guttural sound of animals at the end of the corridor. Not far from where the red dot placed Jade.

Daniel rushed and turned right. He suddenly stopped, seeing his other team unconscious. Two big werewolves had snapped their heads and were looking at him.

The beasts smelled powerful and had put out of commission five of his best vampire men. Daniel's guards began shooting darts on sight, but the werewolves were faster. They picked up velocity and ran at them with black eyes and feral speed, escaping the darts unharmed.

"Take the other one. I'll take Alexander," Daniel ordered his men, showing his fangs as his eyes darkened.

If the werewolves wanted a fight, he was going to give them one.

ALEXANDER LOCKED ARMS with Daniel. Their hands locked on each other's forearms and their eyes showed a clear demonstration of power. Neither Alexander nor Daniel moved. They seemed to be too caught up in measuring strengths and going nowhere with the staring contest.

Alexander growled, and Daniel growled back. When one took a step back, the other followed. It was a pointless strength showdown. They matched in power. Therefore, both started to growl in frustration.

The vampire made the first move. He turned his wrists around, so he could twist Alexander's arms, leaving his chest open to take a low blow.

But Alexander wasn't stupid. Daniel must be trying to drop him to the ground. He let go of the vampire's hands and stepped back, evading Daniel's quick punches that were aimed at Alexander's face.

The werewolf ducked and leaned back several times, dodging every blow that the vampire threw at him. He was fast and was studying Daniel's movements and strength. Vampires were deadly and devious. Alexander needed to use Daniel's frustration and rage towards him to knock the vampire out. The vampire wasn't thinking straight. Alexander knew he was furious because he had lost his beloved. He could use that in his favor.

"Where is Jade?" Daniel asked between gritted teeth.

Alexander stopped Daniel's strong punch with his opened hand. He backed away maintaining his distance.

The vampire growled and twisted his fist inside his hand, pulling down Alex's arm and counterattacking with his left hand, which Alexander blocked with his arm.

"Fight like a man," Daniel ordered him.

"We aren't men," Alexander said nonchalantly. "And you just became outnumbered," he stated, looking at Sam, who had broken a vampire's neck and put to sleep another one with the vampire's gun. "You've invaded my compound and attacked my men when I called you to make a deal."

"This is my compound, and I don't deal with people who harm what's mine. Where is Jade?" Daniel said, stepping back and looking at both werewolves with dark eyes and menacing face.

Alexander's stern expression suddenly changed. His nose moved, sniffing the air.

Daniel's voice interrupted his unexpected distraction. "Where is my wife? Give her to me, and I might consider letting you live."

"We aren't afraid of your empty threats, vampire," Sam said.

"I'll show you how empty they are," Daniel barked. He balled his hands and moved in front of Alexander's beta.

A door opened behind them, and Jade ran with a heavy object in her hand that she crushed against Sam's head.

"Leave him alone," she shouted.

"Ouch!" Sam complained, cradling his head and closing his eyes.

It didn't knock him out as Jade expected.

"What the hell do you think you are doing?" the wolf asked, turning around to face his attacker. "I told you to stay put."

"Jade... Jade!" Daniel's voice changed from surprise to shock.

Alexander opened his eyes in disbelief. "Sam, calm down!"

Looking at Jade's mate, Alexander saw his expression change. Sam only had time to remove the object from the girl's hand before Daniel grabbed her by her waist and pulled her away from the werewolf.

"You touch her, you die," Daniel growled as he protected Jade with his own body and glared at Sam.

Once again, Alex's vision blurred and his senses were drawn to the entrance of the corridor. There was a pull in his chest that made the air escape his lungs and burn his nostrils. For a few moments, it became hard to breathe until all he could do was close his eyes and almost kneel. His head kept spinning. He secured his hand against the wall as his eyes focused on the figure that was coming their way.

The sound of Sam's worried voice reached his ears, but he couldn't concentrate on anything but the young blonde who was heading their way. She seemed to be dragging Sabrina's body.

Alex heard a growl, a powerful and angry sound. Snapping his head, he saw Sam drooling as he bared his teeth and his fingers turned into claws. His beta was in attack mode after seeing his sister unconscious and being pulled.

Before Alexander could order him to stop, Sam was running to the blonde beauty with deadly intentions.

The alpha's heart stopped beating. He felt the deadliest pain shattering his soul only to revive his heart with a burst of adrenaline. Anger flooded his veins.

"Sam, stop!" He used his alpha voice on his pack member in a futile attempt to reach him. It was in shock that he witnessed as his beta rushed to tear the blonde goddess apart.

He had waited for her for so long and now it was too late! His best friend was going to murder her.

STOPPING AT THE ENTRANCE of the new corridor, Jenna let go of the werewolf's arm and watched how a big and growling guy ran in her direction. He didn't look pleased to see her. Maybe he was the hot brunette's mate. The girl wasn't easy to knock out. It had been fun, though. She was just dragging her, so she could ask Daniel to take the girl to the infirmary. It had been foolish of her to attack Jenna. Although, with a bit more training, the girl could become a worthy fighter. Of course, first, she would need to leave her pack and stop depending on a chauvinistic alpha.

Jenna had no idea why she was worried about the girl who tried to kill her when there was a big scary guy coming her way. His eyes were changing and his face was becoming dangerously feral. He moved fast, but for Jenna, it was like he was running in slow motion. She had time to study his intentions and glimpse the hot guy at the end of the corridor who was watching her. Behind him, Jade and Daniel were sheltered in each other's arms against the wall. She almost rolled her eyes at the scene. Those two should stop cuddling in public. Daniel should deal with the hot guy, Alexander, before reaching for Jade. The guy was hotter in person than in his picture. He was also, without a shred of doubt, the alpha of that pack.

SAM RAN TO TACKLE THE BLONDE against the wall, wanting to crush her and then snap her neck. He would do much worse if she wasn't a girl. And if Sabrina was dead, he was going to rip that evil bitch apart for hurting his little sister.

The woman ducked when he reached her. She used her arms to grab him around his waist and, before he understood what was happening to him, Sam flew over her shoulder and landed with his body turned around against the wall. His head faced the ground and his feet the ceiling. Dizziness took him over and his body slammed against the floor.

The blonde straightened up and gazed at him from above.

He growled at her. He should have understood that she had fighting skills, or she wouldn't be able to beat his sister.

"Did I hurt your mate?" she asked as she tilted her head and smirked at him.

Sam gritted his teeth, embarrassed by being so easily handled by a young woman. He picked himself up, brushed off his clothes, and observed the stunning blonde from head to toes. She was freaking hot for a vampire. She didn't smell like one. Was he just beat by a human? Alexander would tease him for life!

"Sister," Sam explained.

"She's alive. She was a worthy opponent. You should be proud of her. Did you teach her to defend herself?"

Sam tilted his head to the right, confused by the questions. Was she trying to be nice to him or distract him?

"I don't like it when people hurt my sister," he declared, moving closer to grab her. He was reluctant in hitting a female, especially now that he knew his sister was okay. Any other wolf wouldn't be so concerned. But he didn't like to hurt women. He was just going to restrain her and stop her from helping the vampire.

"Hey, I don't like hugs from strangers," the female complained, ducking away from his arms. "Be a nice wolf and let me talk to your alpha."

Before the woman could say another word, Sam's body was slammed into the wall.

Alex growled menacingly at his beta. "Don't ever do that again." His gritted teeth and glowing eyes made Sam lose his breath.

"Alpha," Sam gasped, assessing what was going on. His alpha had flown to him, bunching the front of his shirt to lift him from the ground and make him look into his dark eyes.

"Mate," Alexander growled, his breathing becoming heavy.

Sam's face became pale in understanding. "Mate?"

"Oh, you are both mates. That's cute." The girl clapped her hands.

Sam looked at her, puzzled, as she checked out Alexander's butt and grinned.

"A bit of a shame, though," she added.

DUE TO THE TWO WEREWOLVES acting strangely, Jenna momentarily forgot her purpose.

Regaining her focus, she turned to face Daniel and Jade. She could hear the background noise of their whispers. Daniel should be helping her deal with the two werewolf lovers instead of trying to calm Jade and ask her a million questions. *Lovers! Cute but nerve-racking.*

From the corner of her eye, she noticed the movement behind her. A hand was reaching out to her. Before he attacked her, she grabbed his hand, turned the guy's arm around, flipped her leg over his arm, and made him do a backflip and land heavily on the ground.

The alpha had tried to catch her off-guard, and she almost kicked herself for it. She straightened up, facing Sam and waiting for him to attack her. He didn't move. Instead, he laughed out loud and held his stomach as if he had just witnessed the funniest thing.

The guy kept laughing as he slurred, "You have just been beaten by a girl. That's a moment to remember. Too bad I can't record this."

Turning around and putting her hands on her waist, Jenna asked, "What the hell is so funny about this?"

Alexander pulled her down and grabbed her arms, making her land on top of him.

She cussed for being so damn rookie about her actions. She fell straight into his arms, having his ripped torso to cushion her fall.

His hand brushed the hair away from her face. "You are not a vampire."

"Really? I didn't know that," she said

sarcastically, trying to ignore the weird vibe that was coming from him, the amazing scent, and how damn hot he looked.

It was hard because she was fighting against him, and he looked even hotter when he was confused. She could drown in his eyes if she wasn't careful. But she didn't hook up with werewolves for a good reason. Besides, the guy had kidnapped her best friend. His gorgeous chocolate eyes weren't enough to make her give in to the attraction. Plus, they were fighting. Weren't they?

"Let me go, creep," she ordered, using her hands to get up and get away from the unwelcome closeness.

"Allow me," the other wolf said, offering his hand.

Reluctantly, she accepted his help. Straightening up, she fixed her clothes and narrowed her eyes at them. "Did the vampires drug you two with a different sleeping potion?" Her eyes followed Alexander's movements since his eyes were fixated on her figure. Those two were acting weird. They must be high on something. "Do I have something on my face?"

The alpha shook his head and no words left his mouth.

The other wolf looked at his alpha and added, "I still don't like her. She hurt Sabrina."

As if he reminded himself of his sister, his head snapped to the place where Sabrina was lying unconscious. He walked to her and made sure she was okay. Leaving Jenna and Alexander face to face.

Before Alexander could say anything else, the sound of a flying dart was heard, and Jenna's eyes were drawn to the projectile that pierced the back of his shoulder.

Daniel had grabbed a gun and had shot the alpha.

Somehow, the alpha didn't fall unconscious. He took out the dart and growled at the vampire.

Jenna cussed mentally the moment she saw his eye-color change. Werewolves changing eye-color wasn't a good sign. Before she could further gather her thoughts, Alexander jumped on Daniel, and they started to punch each other.

"Alexander, stop. Please, stop," Jade requested, moving to try and break their fight. "Please, stop, both of you. We need to talk."

"Don't." Jenna ran to stop Jade from getting between them.

Jade could be killed by any one of them. She was human and fragile. A single punch could kill her. Jenna grabbed her friend and took her far away from the fight, entering the door of a lab.

"You need to do something. Don't let Daniel hurt Alexander."

Jenna sighed with exasperation. "Are you crazy? That dude kidnapped you."

"Please, make them stop."

"Damn it, Jade!" Jenna growled because her friend had real tears in her eyes. She was upset with what was going on. But those two were big boys, they could handle themselves, and Jenna was rooting for Daniel to swing some punches toward that werewolf.

“Make them stop,” Jade begged.

“Just stay here.”

Jade nodded and cleaned her eyes with the back of her hands.

Walking away, Jenna entered the corridor and backed away instantly because the guys were punching and grabbing each other. How was she supposed to break them up and reason with them?

She cleared her throat and screamed out loud. “Stop!”

Nothing happened. They were still pulling at each other’s shirts, throwing punches, and growling. She decided to cut in the middle and push them apart. Before she did, Alexander’s arms dropped to her waist, swirled her around, and protected her from Daniel’s rage.

“What the hell do you think you are doing?” he asked, drowning his head on the hollow of her neck and talking in her ear.

Jenna immediately felt her legs trembling. Her skin shivered with tiny particles of electricity that ignited the butterflies in her stomach.

Daniel stopped the attack. “What the hell, Jenna? Go take care of Jade. Let me deal with this guy!”

“Jade wants you to stop,” she managed to say while trying to pull Alexander’s hands off her waist and leave his tight hug. “Dude, let me go. You’re creeping me out. If you don't remove your hands, I'll make you." She shot a frustrated glare at her captor.

He chuckled, increasing her frustration.

She snapped, seeing red because she didn't appreciate him making fun of her for being a girl.

*Does he think that I can't beat the crap out of him? The nerve of this cocky and annoying Alpha!*

Meanwhile, Jade hadn't listened, and Jenna heard her calling and peeked out from outside the lab.

Jenna pushed Alexander away as Daniel turned around and sped to stand in front of Jade.

"Why are you crying?" Daniel asked.

Jenna sighed in frustration. Jade was begging him to talk to the Alpha, again. She was also frustrated because the Alpha seemed to be under the impression that he could put his hands on Jenna without her permission and sniff her as if she was a flower or food.

"Dude, let me go," Jenna ordered.

She leveled her knee up to hit his crotch, but the Alpha moved back just in time. She didn't lose any time and threw him a punch that he caught with his hand. Jenna's back leaned against the wall, and he held both of her hands above her head.

"You need to stop trying to hurt me," he whispered with his face close enough for her to feel his warm breath.

"And you need to stop..." She lost her breath, trying to get free and push him back. "What the hell!"

Alexander said huskily, "Stop fighting me."

"Stop grabbing me!"

He grinned. "You are amazing, aren't you?"

His face hovered over hers, and she swallowed.

*Is he attacking me or trying to kiss me? Is it normal to find his voice sexy and for me to lose the will to fight him? Is it normal to flush with the closeness?*

Jenna was sure that wasn't normal. That werewolf was out of his mind.

"Let me go, you creep. What the hell is wrong with you? Just let me go!"

"I need you to understand something," he said, holding her hands in his left hand and lowering his right hand to raise her face to look at him.

She faced him with narrowed eyes and deadly intentions.

He grinned. "Mate," he said gruffly, lowering his head to smell her. "Oh, you are so much better than I'd hoped for."

"What?" she gasped, trying harder to get free. She was sure she hadn't heard him right. It couldn't be.

She struggled, trying to free her arms.

Alexander seemed to sense her panic. He lowered her hands, putting his arms around hers, so she couldn't escape.

"You're my mate. Do you know what that is?"

“Very funny. Now let me go before I hit you in the nuts.” She tried to pull away without success.

“I’m not trying to hurt you,” he explained, loosening the embrace and freeing her hands. “Look at me.”

Jenna breathed out. Something inside of her was burning, ready to explode, and the floor seemed to turn under her feet. She wanted to get away from him, but the guy was heavy and was lowering his mouth to hers.

Putting her hand on his face, she pushed him away. “Don’t even think about that, mutt.”

# CHAPTER THIRTY-FOUR: OUTBURST

**"ALEXANDER, COULD YOU PLEASE LET HER GO?** You are scaring her," Jade requested, witnessing the madness that was happening and not sure if she should be happy or worried about Alexander's claim.

"I'm sorry. I didn't want to scare you," Alexander apologized to Jenna, letting her go and stepping back.

Jenna looked at him through squinted eyes.

"Jenna, please don't do anything stupid," Jade pleaded, not liking the way she was staring at Alexander.

"I can explain myself to you." Alexander waved his hands in front of him in an attempt to calm her down. "I'm sorry if I hurt and scared you."

"Did you hear what he said?" Jenna asked Jade, who nodded. She ignored Alexander's pleading eyes. "Did he just call me 'mate'?"

Jade nodded again.

Jenna's face turned pale and her eyes became big and troubled. "No..."

"I can explain," Alexander said. "Are you okay? You look mad. Why aren't you happy?"

"No, no, no," Jenna repeated over and over again.

Jade could tell Jenna was panicking.

Jenna yelled, “No! That can’t be true.”

Alexander moved closer as if trying to calm her down.

Wrong move.

Jenna grabbed his head and snapped his neck.

“Fuck no. No way. No, no.” She kept cussing after Alexander’s body fell on the floor.

Jade bumped into Daniel’s arms as she lost her breath.

“Did she just kill him?” Jade asked. Her heart stopped beating. “Did she kill him?”

Jade panicked.

Daniel grabbed her before she could reach for the werewolf.

“Yes and no. It’s temporary. He will come to life again,” Daniel assured, massaging her back. “But what’s wrong with her?”

“Jenna...” Jade called.

Daniel rubbed his forehead. “I know that finding out that the werewolf who kidnapped you is her mate might not be good news, but still... She overdid it. It’s not as if her world fell apart. Snapping her mate’s head... That’s not cool at all.”

Jenna entered the lab, followed by Jade and Daniel. They regretted that move because a table flew into the air and bounced against the wall.

Daniel grabbed Jade and pulled her outside. Then he shut the door, leaving Jenna to fume and destroy things like a mini-Hulk.

"I guess she doesn't like werewolves," Daniel said as he rubbed his wife's shoulders.

Jade watched Jenna's crazy response to the event in shock. She was smashing things.

"No. She hates them," Jade confirmed, peeking into the room through the glass-door. "Her werewolf dad raped her mom after rejecting her because she was a human. Jenna is also keen on not having anyone bossing her around. She hates chauvinistic behavior, and the packs have hierarchies that are old-fashioned. Plus...most of them don't mate outside of their packs and loathe hybrids like her."

"She must have known that she had a high probability of finding her mate among werewolves," Daniel said.

"I can't say. She always had a crazy obsession with vampires. I knew she hated werewolves, but...still. Alexander seems like a nice guy."

"Should I be worried about your infatuation with him?" Daniel asked, scowling at the door.

Jade turned to look at him. "We have a lot that we need to talk about. Alexander has a plausible explanation for why he took me."

"For now, I'm just worried about the expensive things that Jenna is breaking. We'll talk about the wolf after Jenna calms down and stop smashing things."

"It's not safe to enter a room when she's acting like this," Jade warned.

"I'm fully aware of that."

"Sir, what do we do with the wolf?"

Jade looked at the team of armed men that were watching over Sam who had the unconscious girl in his arms.

Daniel turned around. “Take the girl to the infirmary.”

“I’m coming with her!” Sam yelled before they could remove the girl from his arms.

“I don’t want you killing any more of my men,” Daniel warned him.

“No one killed anyone. They are all unconscious. We aren’t barbarians.”

“Sam won’t harm anyone. Just let him take care of his sister,” Jade said.

Daniel looked at her. “Darling, I’m getting uncomfortable with your affection for your kidnappers.”

“What is going to happen to my alpha? Are you going to kill him? Is the blonde girl insane?” Sam asked.

“No one will harm Alexander,” Jade said promptly.

Daniel scowled at her.

“I’ll be extremely upset if you harm him,” she added.

“Put him in a holding cell. I want to talk to him when he wakes up.” Daniel ordered after sighing deeply. “I’ll deal with this matter once I have a serious conversation with my wife. Apparently, she’s a bit…confused.”

“I’m not confused. We need to talk about

Alexander." Jade folded her arms and narrowed her eyes at him.

"We will. Take him out of here. And you, big guy, take your female to the infirmary but don't try anything stupid."

Sam growled in reply and turned away to take his sister to see the doctor. Daniel's men grabbed Alexander and took him away. The only other living soul left with them was Jenna who was using test tubes as painting material against the wall.

"TELL ME THE TRUTH, did he hurt you?" Daniel asked, turning to hold Jade in his arms and leaning closer to stare into her eyes. He had missed her and the last thing he wanted was to let her go. He was afraid that she would fade away like a dream. "I was worried sick!"

"I'm fine. I wasn't hurt." She cupped his face. "I've missed you. I've worried so much! I didn't believe that you were dead, but the thought of it was horrifying."

"Did you really think that I would die before our honeymoon?" he joked, trying to cheer her up. "I love you, baby. I'm so happy I've found you."

Touching her lips, he kissed her.

When he was forgetting the time and the place, a door slammed open. Jenna got out of the room, still burning up with rage. She glared at them, startling the couple.

"Are you good?" Daniel asked Jenna.

"No, I'm not good," Jenna barked, fisting her hands and looking at the corridor. "Do you know how many times I've prayed not to be a werewolf's mate? Do you know how much I hate werewolves?"

"Come on, Jenna. He seemed happy to find out that you were his mate," Jade said, touching her shoulder. "He seems nice."

"He kidnapped you!" Jenna snapped at her.

Jade kept trying to calm down her best friend and urge Jenna to stop acting like a hurricane in a confined space.

"Yeah, that's true. But he didn't treat me badly, and he tried to explain to me why he kidnapped me. He thought I was in danger."

Jenna kept shouting. "I don't care. I don't do werewolves. There is a reason why I would rather have a vampire for a soul-mate than a wolf. Vampires don't judge. They don't kill their mate if they happen to be human."

"Not every pack does that, Jenna," Daniel said. "I understand your reasons, but you need to calm yourself and give him a chance."

"Like I gave Daniel a chance," Jade added.

"I'll kill him now before I get attached to that thing," Jenna said, pushing Jade's hand away. "Don't try to convince me. You have your wife back, I have my friend. Let's kill them and go home. Pretend that this never happened."

"Jenna..." Jade was going to say something else, but Jenna walked away and ignored her.

"Call me when it's time to go," Jenna said, waving goodbye. "I'll be on the plane."

Turning around, Jade's eyes reflected her fear. "Don't kill him. You aren't going to kill him, right?"

"Of course not. I'm not a murderer. They will be brought to justice for what they did."

"You can't do that either. You need to listen to me first. It concerns Stevie, and we need to keep him safe. You need to get him out of your house and take him somewhere else," Jade urged him.

"He's safe. Sakura is with him."

"Are you sure?"

Daniel stroked the back of her neck, entangling his fingers on the softness of her hair. "Yes. Nothing will happen to Stevie. Relax, honey."

"I'm so happy that you are here," Jade said, hugging him.

"Let's go somewhere private, so we can talk about what is happening."

"I have my own room. We can go there, and I can show you something important." She grabbed his hand and led the way.

# EPILOGUE

**DANIEL HAD BEEN QUIET** since he watched the video that Jade's father had left for Alexander. Not in a million years could he imagine that something like that would happen. He couldn't believe how bizarre the whole situation was. Finally, he understood why Jade was so keen in defending the werewolf.

Things weren't as black and white as he had thought. There was a lot at stake, and Daniel had to do everything in his power to help Jade and her brother—especially to help Stevie. He loved that little kid as if he was his own. He was Jade's most precious thing, and Daniel loved Jade with all his heart and soul. They were a family now.

"So, let me see if I got this straight," Daniel began. "Your dad combined Alexander's DNA with some random vampire's and implanted an embryo inside your mother's womb. Nine months later, Stevie was born."

"Yes, you've summed it up perfectly." Jade's eyes were shining brightly. She had cried during the entire message. Sobbing against his chest, she added, "I'm going to lose Stevie. Alexander wants him. He wants to raise him as his son. He says that Stevie is meant to be the new alpha of his pack when he comes of age."

Stroking her hair, Daniel muttered, "What? That's insane. Alexander can't steal Stevie from you."

"He can claim Stevie as his son. A DNA test will prove that they are related."

"It can't be that easy. If your father combined the DNA of both species, Stevie has two fathers."

"My dad doesn't say where he got the vampire's DNA from. And Stevie is the first vampire-werewolf hybrid. His DNA may hold the key to cure vampires or make them invulnerable to sunlight."

"Stevie is extremely precious," Daniel agreed.

Jade raised her face to look at him. "Please tell me that you didn't know anything about this."

"Of course I didn't. I had no idea. I love you. I chose you because you are my beloved. I wasn't interested in using your brother." Daniel held her face between his hands. "I understand Stevie's importance. Hell, I'm excited about the idea of curing myself or, at least, being able to face the sun again. But what's more precious to me is you and your happiness. I won't let that werewolf steal your baby brother from us. We are a family. Alexander has no right to want Stevie. As far as I'm concerned, he might be the one interested in using Stevie's blood to profit from it."

"He seems to have good intentions, and he was Dad's best friend."

"So, what do you want to do?" Daniel inquired. "It's your brother."

"I should let Stevie...have a father. He never got to know Mom or Dad. I don't expect him to understand how he can have another Dad. I'm not going to tell him that his existence is due to a crazy experiment Dad did. My dad. He planned to give Stevie to Octavius in return of leaving me alone."

"It's messed up, but your dad was desperate."

“I don't know how to feel about his actions. I'm torn,” she confessed, nibbling on her lip. “But he also said that he wasn't able to give Stevie up once he was born. We ran away. Dad loved Stevie. I know that. All he did was for love, even if it was morally incorrect.”

“Something is bothering me. Who told Alexander where to find you and when was the best time to kidnap you?”

“I don't know. He claims that he saw me on TV, but I don't know how he was able to know about our trip, so he could kidnap me.”

“Only a hand full of people knew where and when we were going. Someone helped Alexander, and I want to know who that was.”

Jade said, “Maybe it was someone who knew about Stevie and wanted Alexander to study my brother’s DNA. If someone can do it, it's him. He has worked alongside Dad, and he's a brilliant scientist.”

“There's a lot that still needs explaining, but I'm tired. I've been looking for you like a madman. I haven't fed since they removed the bullets from my chest.”

“You look pale.” Jade held on to his shirt.

“I'm much better now that I've found you. Everything is fine.”

“I thought that I would never see you again. I was so scared!” Jade reminded herself of what she had endured.

“You look so sexy when you look at me like

that," he mumbled, smirking.

"Like what?"

"Like you've missed me and you love me."

"I've missed you and I do love you. I'm just..." She didn't finish her sentence because Daniel brushed his lips against hers.

He spoke close to her mouth. "I thought I would die if I wasn't going to see you again. If I couldn't touch you. I wanted to destroy half the world because I had lost you. I don't want to feel that ever again. So please, try not to get kidnapped or feel empathy for the ones who kidnap you."

"It wasn't a normal kidnapping," she reasoned. "And we need to talk to Jenna. What happened was insane. Alexander is a sweetheart. I—"

Daniel put a finger against her lips. "Let's forget Alexander for a bit. I've missed you, I've saved you, and we are alone, in an underwater bedroom with a view of the ocean. I think we should find a good use for this bed and this scenario. What do you think?"

Jade chuckled only to smash her lips against his, kissing him deeply.

"What about Stevie?" she asked seconds later. "I'm feeling guilty for spending time alone with you. I don't want to neglect my brother's safety."

"I'll keep him safe. We'll talk to Alexander and strike a deal to please both parties. If Alexander is so keen in claiming parenthood, if he really wants to protect the kid, then we should have him on our side. What do you think?"

"I think you are perfect," she said. "I didn't want

us to argue about it because I don't want you to harm Alexander or accuse him of kidnapping. I want Stevie to meet him. I want Alexander to help Stevie figure out what will happen to him. Will Stevie survive? His health is so fragile that it's hard for me to believe that he'll be one of the strongest creatures when he gets older... If he can get older. Alexander is afraid that his body may reject one DNA and fight the rest like a disease. I don't want my brother to die. He is more than an experiment to me."

"I know, Jade. I know." Daniel rubbed her arms. Kissing her forehead, he added, "We'll figure this out. I'm rich, Alexander is a scientist, and I have a lot more scientists on my payroll. Stevie will get the best treatment and medicine. You aren't alone anymore. You have me, and I have you two to care about. Okay?"

"Okay," she whispered as her body relaxed. "You are the best husband in the world."

"I know," he said cockily.

Jade giggled. "I'm not even going to get mad at your lack of modesty," she stated, caressing his face. "But we still have another problem."

"Yes, we have to consummate our marriage before it's annulled," he teased.

"Not that, silly." She chuckled but then lost her smile.

"What's bothering you?"

"I had the sexiest lingerie for our wedding night."

"Don't be sad," he said sweetly. "You'll have

plenty of other opportunities to wear it. But, in my opinion, you are sexy in anything you wear or don't wear." He smiled mischievously, kissing her lips.

"We have another problem."

"What is our other problem?"

Breathing out, Jade reminded him, "Alexander is Jenna's mate."

"Yes, apparently."

"What are we going to do about it?"

"Nothing. Jenna made it clear that she would rather kill him than accept him as her mate."

"She was overreacting. A mate is something special, unique, amazing. I should know because I have the best of mates."

"Are you trying to manipulate me into doing something you want?" Daniel asked with a raised eyebrow.

Jade looked at him with big, begging eyes. "You could talk to her. You know, explain to her the importance of a mate."

"Honey, I don't want to be used like a throwing ball against the wall," Daniel said. "She's scary!"

Jade laughed. Shaking her head, she added, "She's just scared."

"Alexander has serious hard work ahead of him. I kind of feel sorry for him. Mates can be ruthless and evil when they aren't willing to give in to the attraction."

"Are you talking from experience?"

"Oh, definitely." He smirked, slowly biting her lower lip. "You look extremely sexy when you get mad at me, but you are sexier when you act all sweet and in love with me."

JADE HELD HIS STARE, touched by his sweetness. They had come a long way since the first day they met. She hardly remembered being mad at him. She couldn't do anything but assault him with kisses. He was the kindest and wittiest man she could have asked for. Though, he was a bit of an arrogant jerk in the beginning.

"I want Jenna to be as happy as I am. That's why we need her to understand that Alexander is a nice person, and she doesn't need to be afraid."

"I don't know about that, Jade. We don't actually know Alexander."

"I do."

"Honey, I'm starting to feel jealous."

"Why?"

"You like him a bit too much for someone who's ready to steal your brother from you."

Jade shrugged. "I know that he's a good person, that's all."

"A good werewolf, you mean."

"Whatever he is, Alexander seemed pleased to find his mate. He looked at Jenna like I always wanted a guy to look at her. They need to be together."

"Are you going to be a matchmaker now?" Daniel questioned.

"If I have to," she stated.

Daniel smiled.

"What?"

"I love when you look so sure about something. In any case, baby, the fact that Jenna is Alexander's mate is something providential."

"How come?"

"Alexander wants Stevie, so his pack has a successor, a future alpha. Well, he found his mate now. He can make plenty of baby werewolves to be the next alpha in his pack. Plus, he will be distracted with his mate so maybe he will be more reasonable about sharing Stevie's custody."

"Oh, you are right," Jade agreed. "And Jenna loves Stevie. She won't let him do anything to harm him. Oh my God! If Jenna accepts Alexander, she will be Stevie's stepmother."

"Oh, yes, we will be a big happy family," Daniel teased, apparently amused by the new family ties. Meanwhile, he was leaving small kisses on her cheeks and lips, rubbing her shoulders, and making Jade relax and forget about her problems.

"It's not funny, it's strange," Jade lectured him, slowly giving in to his actions.

"Yes," he agreed between kisses.

He caressed her back and leaned closer to kiss her face. Yet she was preoccupied, with her own thoughts.

“Let's not think about that right now. Let's enjoy the quiet and the time we can be alone.”

“What do you mean?” she asked, focusing her eyes on him.

He smirked, teasingly.

“Oh, you want to consummate our marriage?”

Daniel chuckled. “You are adorable. You have no idea how much I lust for you all the time. I’m addicted to you. Yes, you can say that, Mrs. Wolfe. We need to think about a solution to fix that right away.”

“I have no idea how we can fix that.”

Daniel trailed small kisses on her cheeks and neck, tickling her. “Don't worry, I have plenty of ideas.”

“Wouldn't it be wiser to wait until we get home?”

“Aren't we leaving for our honeymoon?” he inquired, slowly descending his hands down her back and holding on to her hips.

He pulled her closer to him, making her cheeks turn red, and her eyes close in passion. His hands, his lips, and playful words were enough to make her forget about her problems and give in to desire.

Jade hungered for him. Her husband was sexy beyond words. Even if there was nothing wrong about lusting for him, she would still feel shy about it. They were in love. Giving in to the yearning and obeying her body’s needs shouldn’t be that hard. Daniel loved her. She shouldn’t be feeling guilty for spending time with her husband. After all, she had missed him and couldn't imagine her life if he had died.

Sighing, she was able to voice her thoughts. "We need to postpone it for a couple of days. At least, until I get to see my brother and can introduce him to Alexander."

She giggled when his lips landed on her neckline. Concentrating was a challenge since he was teasing her, and her body was being assaulted by a wave of heat and goose bumps.

"We'll do whatever you want. But, for now, relax. You are tense, and we should rest for a bit."

"Rest," she whispered, amused by his choice of words. "Yes, we can rest and try something different." Her body relaxed as she enjoyed his kisses and hands on her body.

"Like what?" he asked, raising his head to kiss her mouth.

She cupped his face, stopping the kiss. "You said you haven't fed. You can...feed on me if you want."

"I'm not that hungry, and we've talked about this. You said that you weren't ready. I don't want to scare you."

"I won't be scared. The other night, when we were making love, it felt good when you put your fangs on my neck," she said, showing her neck for him to kiss. "I know you want to taste me. I trust you, and I want you to feel pleasure, too."

"I already feel a lot of pleasure when we make love. Or do you think that I don't?"

“I always think that I should do a lot more to please you.”

“Don't be silly, baby. You are a complete turn on in bed and outside of it. I don't need to bite you to feel more pleasure,” he assured, trailing kisses down her shirt and grabbing her legs. “You are perfect.”

“And if I want you to bite me when we are making love?” she asked, grabbing hold of the comforter when his teeth ripped the button of her shirt, showing her cleavage. Her breasts shuddered in anticipation, and she gasped for air.

“Then, I'll bite you,” he whispered huskily, pulling out her shirt from inside her pants. Brazing her skin with his right hand, he moved it to cup her breast.

She exhaled and shivered when his lips touched her belly button and kept kissing up her stomach until they fell between her breasts.

“You are gorgeous. This place is gorgeous. I should have thought of this for our honeymoon.”

“Do you want me to pretend to be a mermaid?” she asked with her eyes closed. “You can be my sailor. The one I've saved from the sinking ship.”

“I can be whatever you want,” he mumbled against her ear, softly biting on her earlobe. “But, you being a mermaid sounds extremely sexy.” He kissed her neck while trailing his fingers down her shoulders to open the rest of the buttons of her shirt.

Jade giggled. She had missed his touch and presence. They were back together, and nothing could keep them apart. She was once again in his arms, feeling safe and loved. Whatever curve ball life would throw at them next, they would handle it together. For now, the pending problems could wait a bit longer while they consummated their marriage.

**END OF BOOK ONE**

**Sign up for news and updates on my books, by tapping HERE.**

**Read the extended summary of the next book in the series, *His Mate.***

***Be Notified when it's out by tapping HERE.***

# HIS MATE—EXTENDED SUMMARY

## She didn't want an Alpha, but Destiny had other plans...

At first sight, **Jenna** may look like the typical cute blonde girl with amazing curves and a manipulative smile. Yet what many don't know is that she's an active member of the Paranormal Victims Society and a deadly fighter who was trained in several martial arts. She's also a hybrid with a fascination for vampires and resentment for werewolves.

Saving her best friend, Jade, from the kidnappers, puts Jenna face to face with her soulmate—a werewolf Alpha. Panicking, Jenna does the only thing that comes to mind—she tries to kill him.

**Alexander** believes he's protecting the daughter of a dear friend from vampires. In fact, he stole the beloved of a powerful vampire who will stop at nothing to get her back. After being mateless for decades, he wasn't expecting to find his soulmate amidst a battle, or that she would despise what he was.

Trapped in an underwater research facility, the sexy Alpha has a few days to convince his elusive mate that they are meant to be and that he's the last person she should fear.

Subscribe to be Notified!

## MORE ABOUT THE AUTHOR

Anna Santos is a Bestselling Author in Paranormal Romance.

Anna always keeps her readers on their toes with her adrenaline-fueled adventures, suspense-filled cliffhangers, and romantic scenes.

When she isn't writing, Anna is considering plot twists for her next novel or delving into the world of her favorite authors. She loves superheroes, and she's a geek at heart. She grew up watching *Star Wars* and plotting a way to become a Ninja. She has a fascination for Chinese Kung Fu movies and cherry blossom flowers.

She also enjoys writing poetry, watching a good movie, and spending time with her husband and family.

Meanwhile, there's more to come, and if you'd like to know about it, you can join her at:

http://www.annasantosauthor.com

https://www.facebook.com/AnnaSantosAuthor

https://twitter.com/AnneSaint90

https://instagram.com/annasantosauthor

**You can sign-up for her newsletter here:**

https://app.mailerlite.com/webforms/landing/w4r0o1

Made in United States
Troutdale, OR
04/25/2024